"Only a truly skilled novelist can achieve an exquisitely delicate balance of heart-squeezing empathy interspersed with just the right touch of humor. Cynthia Ruchti is that caliber of writer, and *Facing the Dawn* is that kind of book."

Becky Melby, author of *Candles in the Rain*

"In *Facing the Dawn*, author Cynthia Ruchti confronts painful issues such as the loss of a spouse and other deep griefs, but undergirds the story with her trademark perspective of hope. As her fictional characters asked honest questions we all wrestle with, Ruchti's realistic writing kept me turning the pages—and she never settled for pat answers or clichés. *Facing the Dawn* isn't an easy read—but it is a compelling must-read."

Beth K. Vogt, award-winning author
of the Thatcher Sisters series

"*Facing the Dawn* is a beautiful story about how hope and friendship can provide redemptive opportunities for second chances. When we tenaciously love others during their toughest of times, that kind of friendship leads the hurting and broken from darkness to light. Cynthia Ruchti's newest novel is another golden gift hemmed in hope."

Janet Holm McHenry, author of 24 books,
including the bestselling *PrayerWalk*
and *The Complete Guide to the Prayers of Jesus*

"Fair warning: this book takes the reader on a perilous journey from overwhelming circumstances, through devastating grief and breakdown, and into transformation and peace. Also warning: life may take us on a similar path. That is why I'm thankful that Cynthia Ruchti has offered her new novel, *Facing the Dawn*, as a treatise on how God and friendships are essential in discovering soul strength amidst the harsh realities of life. If you start this book, be sure to finish it; if you find yourself in the midst of crisis, be sure to keep hanging on to God's promises and truth."

Lucinda Seacrest McDowell, award-winning author
Soul Strong and *Life-Giving Choices*

"Cynthia Ruchti took me on a beautifully healing emotional and spiritual journey through grief that shines a bright light on God's love and faithfulness, with an additional colorful spotlight on the power of graciously relentless friends. Tears and smiles for miles in this one."

Rhonda Rhea, TV personality, award-winning
humor columnist, and author

facing
the
dawn

CYNTHIA
RUCHTI

Revell

a division of Baker Publishing Group
Grand Rapids, Michigan

© 2021 by Cynthia Ruchti

Published by Revell
a division of Baker Publishing Group
PO Box 6287, Grand Rapids, MI 49516-6287
www.revellbooks.com

Printed in the United States of America

Library of Congress Cataloging-in-Publication Data
Names: Ruchti, Cynthia, 1952– author.
Title: Facing the dawn / Cynthia Ruchti.
Description: Grand Rapids, Michigan : Revell, a division of Baker Publishing
    Group, [2021]
Identifiers: LCCN 2020042279 | ISBN 9780800737290 (paperback) | ISBN
    9780800739690 (casebound)
Classification: LCC PS3618.U3255 F33 2021 | DDC 813/.6—dc23
LC record available at https://lccn.loc.gov/2020042279

Published in association with Books & Such Literary, www.booksandsuch.com.

21 22 23 24 25 26 27   7 6 5 4 3 2 1

To those whose life's journey
leads them on a detour
through grief,
which is all of us.

And to the women in my life
who've become
forever-no-matter-what friends.

one

He held the paper—the indictment against her—six inches from his face, which made him look like a blank sheet with bushy hair. "Mara Jacobs?" he asked, his voice the texture of a coconut husk. "You know what your name means, don't you?"

"I know."

"Hobby of mine. Anthroponomastics."

Mara shifted in the armless chair, her hands safely tucked under her thighs where they had no hope of fidgeting. Nothing could fidget under the weight of her—

"And," he added without yet making eye contact, "etymology, of course."

"Of course." The principal's office. At her age.

He lowered the sheet of paper, but his face was just as blank. "In antiquity, the meaning of the name Mara was 'bitter.' And in modern America, the meaning of Mara is . . . 'bitter.'" His smile needed a crutch or cane.

"Thanks for pointing that out, Principal Slacker."

"Schlachter. North German. Occupational name for a . . ."

Mara folded her hands in her lap, convinced her daughter's sass may have had origins in her side of the family after all.

"Yes? I find this all fascinating," Mara said. Truthfully, she found nothing fascinating these days. He didn't need to know that.

Principal Schlachter—less than a year into his job and already balding in spots—curled two corners of the paper. "Occupational name for a slaughterer of animals." He smoothed the curls and asked, "What do they call you for short? Mar?"

Mara resisted the urge to make a spitball out of her gum. He was trying to make small talk. He just wasn't very good at it. "My mom told people Dad wanted to name me Budgie."

Still no measurable expression.

"Or Chunkadunk. Said he wanted something unique." But that's not something her dad would have done.

So much for small talk.

"Well, Ms. Jacobs, the reason I asked you here is to discuss school treats."

A warm rush started at her scalp and exited through her toenails. School treats? It could have been so much worse. Expulsion of one of her kids. Pick a kid. Any kid. Chelsea caught making out behind the bleachers again. Smoking behind the bleachers again. Pregnant behind the bleachers again.

Library fines to rival the national debt.

Dylan three credits shy of graduating in May. Which meant he wouldn't move out. Ever.

No. The issue was school treats. That, she could handle. "What about them, Mr. Schelacher?"

"Schlachter. We'd like you not to send any."

"Excuse me?"

"Some of the other parents feel it would be best if you . . . used your gifts . . . in some other way."

Mara mentally apologized to every child she'd ever chided for badmouthing the principals of the world. She would have been one, maybe—a principal—if calculus hadn't kicked her sophomore derriere, made her rethink teaching as a life goal, and redirected her toward other pursuits. Graphic design seemed like a fair trade. Now she was twenty years post-college graduation and it had been eighteen years since she'd designed anything more rewarding than a fundraising poster or two.

"Ms. Jacobs?"

"It's Mrs., technically." She couldn't fault the community for assuming she was a single parent. Her husband Liam had last been home . . . when? And what was the anthrosomethingology of the name Liam?

"My apologies."

Mara's spine stiffened. "Are you saying I'm banned from sending treats to school?"

Mr. Schlachter tapped the "we have an issue" paper on his desk. A normal person would tap it twice for emphasis. He tapped at least six times. "Not banned, per se."

"Then what? Per se?"

"Actually, our lawyers advised—"

"You took my Rice Krispie treats to a team of lawyers?"

"Your treats weren't gluten-free."

"And . . . ?"

"You frosted them."

"Yes."

"With chocolate."

"Yum."

"And sprinkled them with—"

"Crushed peanuts. But I also labeled them with their ingredients and brought fresh fruit for those allergic to peanuts or gluten."

"Yes, but . . ."

Mara loosened her grip on her last nerve. "Please go on."

"The fruit. Mixed fruit."

"I prefer the term 'integrated.' Fruit is good for kids. They don't eat enough fruit. And when fruit looks fun, there's a greater chance they'll—"

"Spend time in the emergency room." The principle/

principal player in the room leaned back in his plush office chair and crossed his arms.

Mara leaned forward. "I'm sorry, did you say emergency room? Did I miss an apple seed or something?"

"No need to grow hostile, Ms. Jacobs." He picked up a pen and wrote something on the paper.

Why was she arguing? Being banned from school snacks was not a death sentence. It would remove one normally uncomfortable, last-minute, stress-producing task from her to-do tome. She'd long abandoned the term to-do *list*. "Please, Mr. Schlachter, tell me what happened. How could skewers of fresh fruit be a—" Skewers. Ah. "This was for sixth graders, not preschoolers."

A growling sigh from the other side of the desk told her the point she tried to make was duller than a fruit skewer.

"When sword fights erupt in the classroom, Ms. Jacobs, the age of the child makes little difference."

"Couldn't the teacher have slid the fruit off the skewers ahead of time if she was concerned?"

"Oh, if that were the only issue," Mr. Schlachter replied, eyeing his smartphone as if as eager as she was to end the conversation. "There's the matter of the pineapple."

"Pineapple?"

"It's clearly on the updated list of potential food allergies."

"What list?"

He clasped his hands together and plopped them on his desk, a move uniquely suited to the sour look on his face. "The list your Jeremy took home last week, as did all the students."

"Last week."

"Yes."

"And Jeremy's birthday was two weeks earlier. I was only a week late with his birthday treat, so that was still a week before the message came home to parents."

"Let's just cut to the bottom line, shall we?"

Oh, could we? Yes, let's shall. Mara chose silence rather than the responses roiling through her brain. She couldn't afford any more time praying for forgiveness today. She already owed the Lord an explanation for her attitude toward Liam after he'd called last night.

Drilled another well, did ya? Made a village dance around you as if worshiping The One Who Makes Water? And yes, that's what I meant. So happy for them, Liam, and for you. Another humanitarian award in the works, I'm sure. Now, can we talk for a minute about our hot water heater? There's a puddle under it that—Losing the connection? Talk to you next week, then, Absent One.

Yes. She and God Almighty had a few things to talk about. A is for Attitude.

"The bottom line as I see it, Mr. Schlepper, is that I've been asked not to send treats for my sixth grader's birthday next year, at which time he will be a seventh grader and no longer allowed to bring birthday treats anyway."

"Well, yes."

"So this conversation really wasn't necessary, was it?"

"There's this year's Halloween, Winter Holiday, Spring Fest . . ."

Mara picked her slouch purse from the floor and stood. "Do you need me to sign anything?"

"That won't be necessary. Thank you for understanding, Ms. Jacobs."

"It's *Mrs.* Jacobs. Technically."

⁓

But I don't understand. Not any of it.

Mara snapped the metal tongue of her seat belt into the buckle. The car seemed to murmur, "Go ahead. Try to start me. I dare you."

It had taken three attempts when she'd left work an hour

earlier to attend to her "consultation" with the principal. Poi-
soning kids with pineapple. Who knew that was even possible?
She'd heard of the traditional peanut, gluten, strawberry allergies. Pineapple too now? How much harder could she have tried
to accommodate everyone's needs, short of making Jeremy's
birthday treats out of water.

Ugh. That word.

She pressed her fingertips against her eyeballs. The orbs
felt like grapes under her eyelids. Can someone be allergic to
grapes?

It took a few moments for the world to come back into focus.
Or as focused as it could these days. Would it leave a mark
if she laid her forehead on the steering wheel for the rest of
the afternoon? Probably. How would she explain that to her
coworkers when she walked back into the cheese factory? Bat-
tered wife? Impossible. Her husband was too far away to leave
visible marks.

With almost eight thousand miles between them, Liam could
do little more than bruise her heart muscle.

Guilt snaked its way through her veins. How could she entertain a thought like that about a man who'd sacrificed everything
to rehydrate a desperately thirsty continent? Once-parched villages lauded him and the mission—Deep Wells, Inc.—as their
saviors. A steady supply of clean water was changing their landscape, their health, their daily routines, their ability for them and
their children to survive. That man—her Liam—coaxed water
from dust with his Deep Wells innovations.

And as his devoted wife, her response was to withhold her
applause and instead gripe that he wasn't beside her to help bear
the load of their three needy children, to help fend off the glares
of a fruit-phobic school principal?

Despite her protests, her forehead fell against the steering
wheel with a bone-rattling clunk.

She could hear her grandmother's voice in her ears. "Now

don't you go and take up drinkin' over this, Mara. Ain't worth the trouble." The woman had lived in the middle of Wisconsin her entire life. Where would she have picked up any kind of accent other than elongating the *o* in Wisconsin? Grandma Lou was something, all right. Mara wouldn't have dreamed of correcting her grandmother's grammar, even if the voice was only in her head.

What if she'd retaken calculus? She could have done that. Maybe aced it the next time through. Not that she had much cause to use calculus skills raising babies, or now, selling cheese curds to tourists to help cover mounting bills that all the water in Africa couldn't cover.

Liam's salary from Deep Wells, Inc., wasn't unreasonable. But the older the kids got, and the more Dylan's brushes with the law cost them, the less distance his paycheck covered. Making up for gaps had been her theme song for a long time.

The tap-tap-tap on her driver's side window jolted her upright. Through the tempered glass, Mara heard a muffled, "You okay, ma'am?"

She turned the ignition to *Accessory* and powered down the window. Safety patrol. No way. She'd been outed as a whiner by an elderly gentleman in a neon yellow vest with a fiberboard stop sign tucked in his armpit.

"Fine. I'm fine. Just, you know, praying."

"Oh," the man said, eyes wide, leaning back a little. "Carry on then."

"I . . . I will. Thanks."

He backed away with a "God bless you," as if that's how you say "Have a nice day" to someone who's caught praying right there in the school parking lot.

She muttered an amen to make it official and turned the key. Started on the first try. Mara was not going to flirt with the idea that fake prayer had anything to do with it.

If the safety patrol volunteers were on duty already, that

meant the school day was almost over. She glanced at the dashboard clock. If she hurried, she could scoot back to work, make up the hour or more she'd been gone, and still clock out and get to the house before the home visit from Dylan's new PO.

Post Office. Power On. Power Off. So many other decent uses of those two letters in combination. Since when had Mara started abbreviating Probation Officer? A random memory flitted through her mind. Her mother pulling out the big guns of intimidation. "Wait until your father gets home, young lady!" It hadn't taken much more than that to get Mara to back off from the edge of whatever minor mischief she'd pulled. Daddy hadn't been harsh. He'd been her safe place. Disappointing him was out of the question.

Even the "wait until your father gets home" parenting tool had been stolen from Mara's arsenal. What kid would take seriously a threat that couldn't be realized for another year of Liam's four-year contract with Deep Wells?

She nodded to the safety patrol as she pulled out of school property and headed toward the cheese factory, where she might just overdose on dairy samples while waiting for her shift to end.

—

"Mara, do you have a minute?"

She tucked the tiny dill Havarti sample into her cheek and turned toward her supervisor. "Sure, Chuck. What do you need?"

"My office?"

His office was separated from the sales area of the factory by a solid door but a very large picture window. If she was in trouble for whatever—taking off work, devouring more than the allotted employee limit for cheese samples—any of her coworkers skilled at reading lips would know about it. *Oh no. A layoff. Not now. No. Please, Lord . . .*

Huh. An actual prayer. Score one for rekindling her faith.

"Mara, I know you've been working long hours."

"I don't mind." Well, she did, but what kind of idiot would admit that with a possible layoff in her future, perhaps her immediate future?

"But we have a problem." Chuck sat in his Costco office chair and indicated she should sit in one of the two folding chairs. She'd have her back to the window. Lip-readers would know her "problem" but not be able to detect her response. The atmosphere held a hint of principal's office shame. Principal's office déjà vu all over again.

"How can I help?" she heard herself asking. Grandma Lou smacked her in the back of her head from heaven on high. *That question gonna get you spent before your days are done, Mara. Mark my words.* She'd been telling Mara that since grade school, when she'd volunteered for every single extra credit opportunity and answered yes to any other student's need for a peer tutor.

Somehow, she'd given birth to three children without an epidural—"I don't need it"—and with not one overachiever among them.

"Mara?"

Ah, Chuck. He expected her attention and she'd failed him. She leaned forward to make up for it, feigning extreme interest in his dilemma, which she hoped wasn't her. His face was a study in neutrality. Great. Time for Twenty Questions? "How large is this problem? I'd ask if it was bigger than a bread box, but nobody keeps a bread box anymore, do they?"

Not even a small chuckle. Chuck-le.

"Some of us are going to have to pull double shifts until after the Harvest Fest crowd thins out." He too leaned forward.

Nice try, Chuck. You can't possibly include me in your "us" statement. Your sense of humor is worse than mine.

"And by 'us,' I mean any able-bodied—"

"No." Where did that come from? Such a foreign word.

Maybe it was the indentation in her forehead—so frown-like, she imagined—that gave her the flash of courage. "No, I can't add one more—"

Chuck leaned back in his far more comfortable chair than hers. "Not really giving options," he said.

He couldn't fire her. He needed her cheese-selling abilities now more than ever. Right? He couldn't . . . wouldn't . . .

Two truths about Wisconsin were undeniable. Cheese and heating bills. Mara might need to turn down the thermostat through the winter if she didn't have cheese to demo, package, and arrange in refrigerated cases by variety, with cheese's resultant paycheck.

"Chuck, I know we've been short-handed, but I have kids who are—"

"Demented. I know."

"I was going to say 'needy.' But whatever." Appointment with Dylan's PO fast approacheth. *Delinquent* seemed so much softer a word than *demented*. What gave him the right to—

The overhead light, if not fluorescent, just as annoying, dimmed. Not enough to worry about a power outage. Just enough to throw shadows on the scene.

"Everyone has their own legitimate reason not to be happy about double shifts or overtime, Mara. A father in hospice."

"That would be Danielle," she said.

"Last weeks of her pregnancy."

"Sheila."

"Surgery to amputate three toes."

"Larry." Oh man. Mara intended to make a pan of lasagna for all three of the people he'd mentioned to help ease their loads. And maybe Rice Krispie treats. "You can't expect Larry to work overtime."

"No, of course not."

"Are you saying I'm the least stressed of all your employees? That's a little scary, isn't it?"

"I know you can handle it. And it's only temporary."

Liam's exact words before he'd boarded the plane for Uganda.

In that indescribable, frostbite numbness that burns like fire, she'd staggered forward, rehearsing all the biblical reasons to "stand by her man."

two

The house Liam and Mara called their own had suffered from the lack of his presence. Sad and tired-looking, Mara thought. They'd always intended to tackle the needed home improvements one at a time until they were done. Something always stood in the way. Lack of time or money. Lack of Liam.

Mara had learned a few household repair tricks even before they became her responsibility alone. But once someone reaches the point marked "Overwhelmed," even basic upkeep bows to the kids' needs, and every loose hinge or carpet stain threatens to unhinge a person like Mara, the responsible one. The one who spent a lifetime convincing people she could manage fine.

Now this. More hours at work.

"Chelsea, I'm going to need you to step it up a notch or twenty for the next several weeks."

Her daughter's facial expression would have made her a perfect model for horror movie advertising, except for the trendy fuchsia in her beautiful hair. "Mom, no!"

The word came so easily to Mara's eighteen-year-old, adult in age but not in behavior. She must get that from her dad's side of the gene pool. *Father, forgive me, for I have sinned by mentally resenting the girl's absentee dad. What's my penance? Never mind. I think I'm already living it.*

"I have no choice but to pick up extra hours at work for a while." Saying it aloud made it sit even heavier in her stomach.

"This is a critical moment in my social life, Mom."

"Oh. Is it?"

"Yes. You wouldn't understand. Why do I even try?" She slammed her backpack on the kitchen island as if offended by its presence. Both the backpack and the granite. Or granite-like material.

"Chelsea, Jeremy is too young to be left alone every night after school."

"What about Dylan? He's already on house arrest. So he has to be here."

Under curfew was not the same thing as house arrest. Not exactly. "Dylan shouldn't be left alone either."

"Nice one, Mom. As a nineteen-year-old, I'm sure he'll be happy to hear you feel that way."

Mara stretched her neck until the knot under her shoulder blade popped. Was there such a thing as respite care for parents? And if so, where did she sign up? "I have a feeling Dylan already knows. I wish there were another way, but you don't have any more choice in this than I did when my boss delivered his decree. Besides, the family could use the extra money right now."

"Can I help it you couldn't get a job that paid better?" Chelsea extracted a can of diet cola from the fridge and slid her thumb under the tab.

"Hey. That's the last one."

The tab clicked. "Your point?"

Whatever Mara expected out of this stage of life, this wasn't it. She'd never been a tidy cottage with a white picket fence kind of dreamer. But this wasn't even a galvanized chicken wire fence dream.

"Extra money, huh? *Then* can we finally get a dog? People have dogs, Mom. It's a thing. And it could be my emotional support animal."

"You need a service animal?"

"For my fatherlessness anxieties."

"You're not fatherless, Chelsea." She pressed two fingers to her temples. *Ocular migraines are a "thing" too.*

"Sure feels like it."

Great. Dramatist that she was, the girl was pulling the misty-eyed card. It would not get to Mara this time. Not this time.

Maybe one small hug. If her daughter would let her get that close.

⁓

The probation officer came with a Mini-Me. Albeit an equally tall Mini-Me. A "peer" counselor not much older than Dylan, by the looks of him. Mara figured this was as close as their family would get to having company over. *There's a sad testimonial for you.*

"Would either of you like coffee?" It seemed only appropriate to ask.

"No thanks," Brad the Body Builder answered for both of them. "Logan and I won't be here long."

The day was taking a sudden turn for the better.

"I have to say, Mrs. Jacobs, it's refreshing that you didn't try to create a Pinterest-worthy façade for this home visit."

The Body Builder knew what made something Pinterest-worthy and knew the word *façade*? Wait a minute. What did he mean by that comment?

"Many people clean the house and hang pictures of their loving, not at all dysfunctional family just before a home visit. I guess they try to give a false sense of normalcy. But I wouldn't be here—we wouldn't be here—if everything were normal."

Proper grammar too? Mind blown. But to be fair, she had vacuumed. And dusted not that long ago. Several times this year, in fact. And she'd flipped the faded patio cushions to the non-faded side.

"Dylan's here?" Brad asked, glancing around the non-Pinterest-worthy living room as if Mara's son might be playing a delinquent's version of hide-and-seek behind the couch. From her perch on Grandma Lou's reupholstered wing chair that would make a great reading chair for a person with time to read, Mara caught a glimpse of the Dylan in question vaulting over the neighbor's lovely redwood fence and hurtling across the backyard toward the house. She prayed the probation officer didn't have mom eyes in the back of his head.

Before she could answer the "Dylan's here?" question, he was. There. Breathing hard, but with a well-practiced look of indifference on his face.

"Hey. Officer Bob. You must be Bob, Jr." He wiped his right hand on his jeans and extended it toward the visitors.

Half polite/half snarky. Her firstborn. The child who'd made her a mom.

Brad stood and introduced Logan Coppernall.

"Peer counselor?"

The look on Dylan's face made Mara's heart twist. Was it possible he felt something? It had all the earmarks of embarrassment. In the last few years, Dylan had perfected the art of intimidating peers. He always stayed a sliver shy of bullying, but let others know he was the alpha male in any pack. This could get interesting. How would he cope with a male near his age but with a level—however small—of authority?

"So, like an AA sponsor?" Her son wiped his palm again after the handshakes. Somewhere in the animal kingdom, that must be a subtle sign of aggression.

Dylan, come on. You're the one in the hotseat here. Could

*you at least pretend to be kind for a few minutes? Like you
were before—*

She had to stop that, stop marking time B.L.L. and A.L.L.—
before Liam left, after Liam left. It's not as if he *left* them in the
strictest sense of the word. They were merely collateral damage in his dream to quench the thirst of strangers in a foreign
land.

When had she started thinking of her husband as gone rather
than on temporary assignment?

Brad was in the middle of something. She attempted to focus
on his no doubt informative explanation of the role of peer
counselors in cases like Dylan's.

"The alternative to having a peer counselor is double the
community service hours or double the jail time, Dylan. You
pick." Brad could play The Dispassionate One well too.

How could Mara not admire that?

"As if I ever have a choice in this. And before you say anything, Mom, yes, I realize how ironic that sounds to my live-in
parental figure."

Logan turned to face Mara, eyebrows raised. "You're single
parenting, Mrs. Jacobs?"

She caught the tenderness in the young man's voice. Dylan
would somehow find a way to mess with that compassionate
spirit before the week was over. Dylan, who'd once been the
child she could count on to care if she'd had a hard day.

"Bob, dude," Dylan interjected, "you need to prep your in-
terns better, man."

"Dylan!" Mara took a breath to keep herself from taking
verbal aim. "And his name is Brad. I'm sorry, Brad. I didn't
catch your last name."

"Logan isn't an intern, Dylan," Officer Brad said, his voice
more even-tempered than Mara's. "And I expect you to treat
him, treat both of us, with respect. It matters . . . *dude*."

"You must have heard of my dad, Sir Logan," Dylan said,

shoulders back. "He's, like, Man of the Year or something." His gaze fell to and lingered on the tips of his scuffed biker boots. "He's been to the UN two or three times. Right, Mother?"

"Three."

"See there?" Dylan leaned his back against the wall. "Humanitarian hero. Loved by all." He crossed his arms as if daring anyone to argue . . . or wishing they would.

"Can we see your room, Dylan?"

It was part of the home visit protocol Mara had failed to remember. What lurked behind that always-closed door to Dylan's bedroom? And what mom hopes for month-old pizza and an avalanche of smelly socks over other incriminating options?

"There's nothing hidden that won't be revealed."

Not the Bible verse I needed, Lord, just so you know.

⁓

Passing the probation officer's inspection seemed like a pop-the-champagne-cork moment, if champagne wouldn't have violated Dylan's probation. To celebrate, Mara and the kids decided on takeout pizza rather than the frozen version they'd leaned on too heavily.

She should cook more often.

She should do a lot of things.

She should stop "shoulding" herself. Social media told her so. And the Bible. The Bible told her so, she was pretty sure. It had been a while since she'd looked.

"Jeremy." Mara gestured to the corner of her mouth, hoping beyond hope that her youngest might take the hint and use his Pizza Palace recycled paper napkin. Nope. Sleeve, as usual.

"Have you no manners at all?" Chelsea piped up, her affected British accent more a tribute to her flair for the dramatic than true concern for her baby brother.

Mara stared at her so-close-to-gothic-but-not-quite daughter.

"Your words might carry a little more impact if your feet weren't propped on the table, Chels."

"I'm asking my *friends* to call me Chelz—with a *z*—now." She slid one foot off the table and left the other where it had been pre-conversation. "But you can too, if you want."

Mara sighed. "Both feet, please." It didn't surprise her that as Mom, she fit a whole different category than "friends." As it should be. The stab wound was no more than a pinprick.

Chelz replanted her floor foot on the table.

Yep, that Jacobs family. A class act. And she was the revered matriarch with a husband missing in action.

"All this," she said, surveying her Midwestern, lower-middle-class kingdom, "and the love of a good man."

"Dad?" Dylan's comment was muffled by a wedge of pizza he'd folded New York style. Where'd he learned that habit?

Wait. She'd said the "good man" part out loud? "Who . . . did you think I meant?" *Wading in murky waters, Mara. You're the real live adult here. Someone has to get their act together. Tag. You're it.* "Hey, troops. Remember how much fun we used to have playing board games?"

"No," Jeremy said.

"You weren't born yet," Dylan added.

Chelsea slid both feet to the floor. "And Dad was here."

Dylan folded another slice of pizza, took a bite, then said, "He's the fun one."

Stab. Stab. Stab. "And that makes me what? The unfun parent?"

"It makes you the responsible one, Mom," Jeremy said, hugging her from behind. Baby of the family. God bless him.

"Your father is responsible." *I can show you a whole continent that thinks he's—*"Whose phone has that wicked song as the ringtone? Answer your phone, then get it changed, okay?"

Dylan slipped his phone from his jeans pocket and tapped *Accept.* He moved down the hall extra-casually, as if the call was no big deal, nothing for a parent to be concerned about. Which was what worried her.

Trouble somehow felt safer to Dylan. Trouble fit like his favorite torn jeans. Love itches, he said. Despising himself felt normal. *That part, I get, Dylan. Just so you know.*

Forgiveness pinches, he said. Freedom is supposed to be a butterfly, isn't it? But Dylan seemed to look at it as a cocoon, as mummy-wrapping. At nineteen and still in high school, when he should have longed for freedom and forgiveness, he gravitated toward the ankle bracelets and necklace of regrets and poor decisions from his past. Self-destructive.

I get that too, Dylan.

He'd accepted the call? They were in the middle of a family moment, minutes away from having fun with their—*oh, the horror*—mother. "Chels? Chelz? Jeremy? A board game?"

Chelsea tilted her head to the side, eyes wide and mouth a thin line of nothingness—her way of analyzing her mother's sanity. Mara expected nothing less.

"Jeremy?"

"I have homework, Mom. Sorry."

"Homework?"

"It was"—he squirmed out of his chair and headed for his room—"kinda due last week. Tomorrow's the last second chance Mr. Posley will give me, so I kinda have to get it done."

The final second chance? Does that make it the third or fourth chance? *Overachieving, people. It's a thing. Try it sometime, would you?* Could she order a bumper sticker online? "Proud parent of a D student."

Depended on the cost. She'd need to buy three stickers.

Or one special one in honor of Dylan: "Honk if you love posting bail."

Or for her: #dontneedanyhelp, #fail.

How long had she and Liam debated the difficulty they'd have paying for college for their kids? It started when they were still toddlers. Not being able to save for college came with the territory. She couldn't fault Liam for choosing jobs that paid less than he was worth but made him feel good about himself and the impact he was making. And how magnanimous of him to always have the needs of others at heart. What a guy.

Sincerely.

A good man. Who sometimes forgot that he was married and had children who were—No. She couldn't use the *N* word. *Needy*. Whispers of the word pointed their accusatory fingers at her pillow too many nights, jostling her awake. No. She was competent and capable and . . . adequate.

That was how her mother-in-law had described her—publicly. Adequate. *If my daddy were still alive, Mom Jacobs, and if cancer hadn't already whupped you within an inch of your life before he died, he would have taken issue with your words. My defender.*

Daddy, I miss you. It's so gray here.

She should pile her kids in the car and visit her daddy's gravesite. And her mother-in-law's. Check on the artificial flowers, since Liam wasn't here to do it. But that meant Mara would have to leave the house, which she didn't want to do.

And she wouldn't if she didn't have to, except for this mandatory overtime cheese crisis.

Or would she get a reprieve? If the Harvest Festival crowd butted up against the Thanksgiving and Christmas cheese rush, she might not be expected to accomplish anything else until after the New Year.

She'd need another bumper sticker: "Didn't Even Final in the Daughter-in-Law of the Year Contest."

Impossible to final if you don't enter.

One good thing about bumper stickers is that they'd help cover the unexplained dings in the car's back fender that suddenly appeared after Dylan returned from a friend's garage band gig. Dylan had "no idea" where the dings came from. "You know parking lots," he'd said.

The room had cleared now. She was alone. Again. It was okay. She didn't have the energy to move playing pieces around a game board anyway. Or keep score.

She should stop keeping score.

three

With bright sunlight streaming through the family room patio doors exposing the need, Mara ran her sock, still on her foot, over the dust accumulation on the lower shelf of the nicked coffee table. Her children had cut their first teeth on the squatty table's wooden lip. They'd first stood there, not noticing their ineptitude for standing because their attention was captured by some toy or forbidden object on the surface. They'd toddled their first toddles holding on to that raised edge, eventually making their way around the entire rectangle solo. Without her help.

When had they lost their ability to maneuver without her assistance?

Or had she stepped in too often to rescue, as some of her church "friends" suggested? They didn't know. They didn't live with *her* kids. They didn't cope with her concerns. How could they know that single parenting doesn't just apply to the unmarried?

Chelsea needed Mara to schedule yet another attempt to secure her driver's license. What was this? Her fifth try? And yes, if Mara had time to take her on the road to practice more often, they might have been done with trips to the DMV long ago.

Or if Liam were there.

"Let her set up her own appointment for her driving test," parenting experts might advise.

In Mara's mind, where it was safe to be snarky, she countered with, "But then it'll never get done. Literally. She'll still be living at home, asking me to give her a ride to crochet camp when she's a senior citizen."

Dylan . . . What *didn't* Dylan need from her? His house arrest /curfew arrested more of Mara's activities than his, not that she had many. But she was responsible for his compliance with the rules of his probation. No pressure. All she had to do was ensure her wild child stayed relatively domesticated—to put it in cat terms—until he left home or graduated, which she'd begun to hope would happen simultaneously.

Knowing Jeremy, he'd already forgiven Mara for having to devote so much attention to his older brother and sister lately. The needy ones. She owed her twelve-year-old a trip. He'd probably say all he wanted was her time. *Sorry, kiddo. That's in even shorter supply than money right now. Hang in there, though. Your father will be home in a year.*

A year. Twelve more months of her kids being left in the care of the parent who didn't have all the answers. The unheroic one.

Mara glanced at the clock on the wall—a wedding gift—and calculated its typical "loses two minutes every day" pattern. Time to leave for work. It's not that she thought so highly of cheese curds, smoked Gouda, and the company's specialty cheddar shaped like the state of Wisconsin, but the call to the DMV would have to wait another day. Or six.

She tore off her dust mitt socks and tossed them on the laundry mountain. *Pile* of laundry didn't begin to describe it. Then she slid into her work shoes. And slid back out. What was that? She shook her shoe over the wastebasket. A handful of sunflower seeds? In the shell?

Great. The mice were back. They must sense the approaching winter. Did it occur to them that hiding their stash in a woman's shoe was not the safest way to prepare their storehouse for the future? Time to set up the trapline again. If she couldn't rid the house of their seasonal guests, she could at least discourage a few.

But not now. Duty called. Making sure both shoes were vacant—free of food and any other undesirables—she set them on the patio and opted for sandals instead. Maybe she'd wear sandals all winter to prevent toe surprises like this morning's.

She'd likely get written up at work for inappropriate footwear. And frankly didn't care.

So that's where Dylan got his rebellious streak.

When she stubbed the toe of her sandal on the threshold into the garage, she faulted only herself. She knew better. That thing had been wonky for months. Enlightened twenty-first-century woman that she was, she'd grabbed a Phillips head screwdriver—right after she tried using a butter knife—and made a valiant effort to tighten it. But it wouldn't hold. She could hear Liam's voice from eight time zones away telling her the screw hole underneath was probably stripped. Big help.

Duct tape, by the way, is not the answer to everything. Nor is Super Glue.

She'd spray-painted the threshold construction-cone orange as a warning until she could afford to have a professional, or any willing body, take a look at it. But you know warnings. When they become habit, no one notices them anymore. A person would think bright orange might be the one exception, but no.

Maybe she could lure the mice to stuff enough sunflower seeds into the hole that the screw would finally hold. Good plan. A tick or two shy of full sanity. *Mara, get a grip.* Grip and gripe—so close to each other in the dictionary.

She filed her now ragged toenail on the rough cement of the crack in the garage floor where the frost had heaved it the year before, then climbed in the car. *Cheese won't sell itself.* Her daily allowance of samples would have to do for lunch. She had no time to pull together something nutritious.

Only partially true. It hadn't occurred to her she'd need to pack a lunch. "In my defense," she said to the deaf air as she turned the key in the ignition, "I've only been working there for three years. So . . ."

———

They say reading for as little as six minutes can reduce your stress level by 68 percent. Mara pondered if that applied to rereading a ten-second parking ticket message thirty-six times during her lunch break. Parking ticket in the *employee* parking lot. Full somehow, despite all the employees who couldn't work so she had to pull double shifts. The math didn't jive.

In her estimation, the Employee of the Month sign on the spot where she'd parked as a last resort wasn't that far from accurate. Management may not have recognized her contribution. But if the real Employee of the Month was late for work, wasn't the spot up for grabs? Technically?

She read the note again. Thirty-seven times now. The wording hadn't changed. She'd understood every syllable the first time through but couldn't resist the sick magnetism of the inky note. Signed by her boss. Letting her off "easy" with a mere reprimand. This time.

She backed her car out of the spot and spent the rest of her midday break searching for a non-existent slot. As the *second* last resort of her day, she parked in the customer lot, marched up to the retail counter inside, and purchased a package of string cheese and hickory-smoked beef jerky to make it official. She did, indeed, qualify as a customer.

Which significantly dropped her earnings for the day.

She tossed the parking violation notice in the ladies' restroom garbage so she wouldn't be tempted to read it again. What might happen if her stress level dropped by any more than 68 percent? Coma? Well on her way to that.

———

"What day is it?"

It hadn't occurred to Mara until she heard her beloved husband's voice that his corny way of starting each international phone conversation might not be his attempt at humor. Perhaps it was a thinly disguised test of her cognitive abilities. As in, "Do you know your name? What year is this? Who's the president of the United States?"

"It's Wednesday where you are, Liam. Tuesday here." Though they'd had an occasional video call over the years, today's was audio only. She'd have to imagine the softness in his eyes that had won her heart.

"I still have a hard time getting used to that," he said. "After all these years. By the time I do finally acclimate to the thought that we're living in two different days sometimes, I'll be home," he said, a detectable good news/bad news tone in his voice.

Why was she having difficulty imagining that day—his walking through the door and back into their lives? His reclaiming his chair in the family room, his sink in the master bath, his role in the kids' lives, his warmth in their bed . . .

She should move from the bedroom out to his chair in the darkened family room for the rest of the phone call. But that would require more energy than she had.

"Great day yesterday, Mara," he said, his voice almost tangibly begging her interest.

She'd done that to him, squelched his excitement while pretending she could handle the home front without his help.

"And an even better one coming up today, we hope," he added.

"Oh?"

"After sunrise, we're going upriver to another village that has

32

water quality issues. They've been resistant to our intervention until now. But they've seen what Deep Wells has done here, not only with wells but educating the children and teaching life skills and agriculture techniques to the parents. Other villages are starting to ask questions. So we'll venture up there and see if we can make a connection. This is what I live for."

"I know." *I know you do.* "Tell me about your day, Mara. Parking violation? How rude! Don't they know how hard you're working? I miss you, Mara. It's hard to be away from you and the kids. But I'll make it up to you when—"

"Are you still there, Mara?"

"Still here." *Right here.*

"It's not a great connection this morning. Could be the cloud cover. Look, I don't have much time before we head out to the river. Just thought I'd check in. Kids doing okay?"

Nice of you to ask. She dialed back the snarky retorts. "Had an interesting conversation with Dylan's probation officer this week. And a sweet young man, Logan, has been assigned to him as some kind of peer counselor. But I'm concerned about Chelz too."

"What?"

"Yeah, that. She wants to be called Chelz. With a z. Whatever."

"I didn't catch that last bit."

"Chelz! With a z." Did she think shouting would help him hear better when two continents, an ocean, and years of neglect separated them?

"Listen, I have to get moving. Lots of needs here. Especially among these adorable children. Oh, Mara, I wish you could see these kids. Wish you'd been able to come here to visit."

"Our own children are cute and needy too."

"I only caught every other word of that. Really bad connection."

"Liam, we need to talk."

"Gotta go, Mara. You're breaking up."

Click.

I certainly am.

—

Jeremy tapped on her bedroom door. She recognized the distinctly polite sound as opposed to Dylan's side-of-his-fist pounding or Chelsea's knock-less "Moooooom!"

"Come on in, buddy."

"Was that Dad on the phone?"

Mara noted the disappointment her youngest couldn't mask. "Yes, honey. Bad connection." Oh, so bad.

"He didn't want to talk to me?"

Didn't mention you, except to use the word "kids." Like a lump of kids. "I'm sure he would have. But you know how hard it is to talk when the connection's breaking up."

"He didn't say anything about my letter, did he?" Jeremy ran his hand along the edge of Mara's four-foot-long Ikea dresser, then looked at his palm and wiped the dust on his jeans.

"What letter?"

He drew what looked like a complex mountain switchback road in the remaining layer on the dresser top. "It doesn't matter. Maybe he didn't get it yet."

Jeremy. The thoughtful one.

The one who practiced hoops in the driveway in the dark. She'd asked him why. "I have to practice by moonlight, Mom, to get better enough to play in the daylight." He'd also been the one to put his arm around her on her darkest days and tell her, "Mom, maybe you need to practice some things in the dark so it comes more naturally in the sunlight."

He'd had no idea what he'd said. Or how much she didn't want to admit he was right.

Jeremy had written an actual letter to his father? "It does take a while for mail to reach him. It'll go through the Deep Wells offices first. Then I think they periodically deliver their onsite workers' mail in bulk." The tendons or whatever body parts held her heart in place collapsed a little.

"How many stamps did you have to put on that envelope, Jeremy?" And why didn't she know? Because in all the years her husband had been stationed overseas, she'd relied solely on phone calls, emails, and texts for communication, when the terrain or poor connections didn't block reception.

"My teacher mailed it for me. She said I didn't owe her anything even though mine was to another country. We all wrote letters to someone . . ."

The sentence didn't sound finished yet. Mara waited.

"To someone important to us." His finger stopped writing in the sand. Dust. He looked up, his eyes glassy, eyebrows creeping up his forehead. "I would have written it to you, Mom, but I see you every day."

"I'm not offended, buddy. I think it's sweet that you wrote to your dad." *I think it's unforgiveable that I didn't. But good for you, son.*

He chewed on the inside of his cheek and let his gaze land on the floor. "I guess."

Preteen boys and the word *sweet*. And never the twain shall meet. Except for her Jeremy. She wouldn't laugh aloud about his ultra-humble "guess" that his writing to his dad was a thoughtful thing to do, but come on. Sweet was the only word that covered it.

"Aren't you supposed to be sleeping, young man? It's late."

"I heard you talking."

Not for long. "Come here." He was the one who didn't resist her hugs. She squeezed him tight and whispered, "Next time I talk to your dad, I'll be sure to ask. And you can get on the phone then too."

His arms were limp at his sides, but he didn't pull away.

She breathed in the wonder of closeness with one of her

children. Jeremy's growth spurt startled her. When had that happened? Boy body odor. The hug abruptly over, she watched him turn to go. "Hey, buddy? Leave time in the morning for a shower before school, okay?"

"Why? I don't have any clean clothes. I'll still smell like this. And I can't turn my sweatshirt inside out to get more wear out of it. I already did that once."

Mara followed him out the bedroom door. "I'll throw in a load now." *And stay up until the washer dings for the transfer.* "Look for them in the dryer in the morning, okay?"

"Okay."

"And after school? You and I have a date for me to teach you how to do laundry."

"Mooooom!"

Normalcy. There's something to be said for first world problems.

four

How is it that a text message *ding* at six in the morning would seem more offensive than an alarm clock? Mara intended to ignore it. She was groggy but not stupid. It could wait. She flipped her pillow to the fresh side and repositioned her stiff shoulders.

But it dinged again. At three in the morning, she would have answered. Chelsea needing a ride home from a party she shouldn't have attended. Dylan needing a ride home from the police station. But 6:00 a.m. wasn't an emergency hour. Just way too early.

She rolled over, appalled that it took so much effort. Mid-October in Wisconsin meant that the heavier quilt was back on her bed. But she didn't need to be in good physical shape to maneuver her body into a different position under a quilt, did she? Standing on concrete at work. That was the culprit. No wonder she was achy.

The text dings could mean something good, she supposed. A message from her boss telling her she didn't have to work today after all. In which case, she'd crawl deeper under the covers and keep one ear open to make sure her kids got themselves off to school on time. Or . . . she could rise early and bake them crustless mini quiches and blueberry scones like she used to on special occasions.

But it was Wednesday. And she'd been up too late making sure the mountain of laundry was two loads smaller than it had been the night before. Blueberry scones would take too long anyway. Probably wiser of her to sleep in and sleep off the laundry hangover.

Could be good news, though. For once.

She reached for her phone. A text from one of Chelsea's teachers. How weird that both her older children were in the same graduating class, thanks to their births eleven months apart and the stretch of time Dylan had spent in rehab necessitating another go-round at his senior year.

Not that Mara could be completely sure either would graduate in the spring. Dylan was a definite maybe. Chelsea was so much smarter than she acted, as evidenced by the text message warning that Chelsea had failed to turn in an assignment—an open-book test—that anyone with access to the internet could have aced. The teacher was concerned that Chelsea's teetering grades could topple if she got a zero on that test, and the teacher thought Mara would want to know.

Nope. Didn't want to know.

Yes. Yes, she did.

Was 6:00 a.m. too early to confront a surly eighteen-year-old with clean clothes waiting for her but probably not *the* outfit she wanted to wear that day? Probably too early.

~

"Mom. You made breakfast? Why?" Dylan must have smelled the bacon.

Jeremy had already eaten his fill and was stuffing his backpack with whatever a preteen keeps in their backpack. Chelsea shuffled into the kitchen behind Dylan, tugging the neckline of her scoop-necked shirt higher.

Aww. She does care about what I think.

"Breakfast? Because I love you. And, you know, nutrition and stuff." Mara slid a blueberry lemon pancake onto the stack and set it on the island next to the paper plates, due to the perpetually broken dishwasher, and the forks. "Oh, I heated maple syrup. Just a sec."

She retrieved warm syrup from the microwave and positioned the small ceramic pitcher near the stack of goodness.

Chelsea raised a stop-sign hand. "I don't need or have time for breakfast, Mom. Count me out. Nice gesture, though."

"Chelsea, sit. We need to talk."

"Mom, school."

"I'll drive you today. You won't be late."

Dylan filled his plate. "Can I get a ride too?"

"Me too?" Jeremy asked, shrugging into the straps of his backpack.

"No. Use your feet to get you there. It's not far. Build those calf muscles. Chelsea and I have something to discuss."

"Packing my breakfast to go," Dylan said, stuffing his pancake into a large plastic cup, slathering the contents with maple syrup, and inserting two strips of bacon like chopsticks. "Do we have any plastic forks?"

Mara pointed to the drawer that held unused takeout utensils.

"Come on, shrimp guts," he said to Jeremy. "We don't need to be around for any female drama. I'll be your bodyguard today."

Bodyguard?

Chelsea rolled her eyes. "Mom, I'm off of carbs this week."

"Eat bacon then, Chelsea. It's keto or something."

"It's pork."

"Your point?"

Chelsea sighed and plopped onto a stool with the ocean of an island between them. "What is it now?" she asked.

"Your grades."

"Oh, them." Chelsea pushed the stool out as if she intended to end the conversation there.

"Chelsea. Chelz. Your Creative Writing teacher texted me today."

"Put technology in the hands of old people and—"

"This isn't funny. Why didn't you hand in your latest test?" Open book. *Honestly, child.*

"We don't hand in assignments anymore, Mom. We submit them. Electronically?"

"Why didn't you?"

Chelsea picked at the meatier pieces of bacon in front of her. "Because it was worthless."

"Not to your grade point average."

"You may have noticed I am not college material." She held her arms out as if her mother ought to find that obvious by looking at her.

"You are too." Sometimes a parent is called upon to express a hopeful attitude not necessarily aligned with reality.

"We could argue that until next week, Mom. I have friends waiting for me. Can we go now?"

A person is supposed to count to ten slowly before responding. Did counting to a hundred really fast have the same effect? "Tell me why you thought the assignment wasn't worth your time."

Chelsea sighed one of her signature sighs again. "Did you know that a bunch of crows is called a *murder* of crows?"

Mara pressed two fingers to her temple to keep it from throbbing. "As a matter of fact, I did."

"And that a group of hippopotamuses is called a bloat?"

"No. That one I did not know." Liam might. He might have actually seen a bloat of them. "Is there a reason—"

Chelsea planted her palms on the faux-granite surface of the island. "Mom. Seriously? When would I ever need to know this stuff? Anybody can look it up with one click. Why do I need

40

to know, as in *be tested* on it? Especially if I'm just looking it up in that ancient booklet she gave us? Complete waste of my pencil, as if anyone uses pencils." Her lips barely moved, and she wasn't practicing for a ventriloquism act. She looked that disinterested, that removed from the subject.

"Creative Writing, Chelsea. Creative. We learn things because we don't know when we might need them or how we might one day apply them imaginatively."

"A shrewdness of apes," she said, monotone, eyelids half-mast.

Another one Liam might know.

Only Daughter held her phone toward her mother. "I won't need this information. Ever. And if I do, I will look it up."

Mara snatched the phone. "Not if you can't graduate, which will mean you can't get a job that will earn you enough money to pay for your own phone, which as of right now is where life stands for you until you turn in—pardon me—submit that test."

"You can't be serious." Chelsea reached for her phone.

"Complete the assignment and you can have it back." Not how Mara hoped this conversation would go.

"This is about as unfair as . . ."

"As what?"

"As Daddy leaving us with *you*!"

Mara pocketed the phone, shoved the uneaten pancakes into a zipped plastic bag and into the freezer, and grabbed her keys. "I'll meet you in the car."

"Mom, I didn't mean it that way."

Oh, but you did.

—

Mara had tried too hard to convince Liam she could handle his pursuing his dream. She'd soft-pedaled the truth about how much she could and could not bear, about their financial status, about her ability to solo-navigate the hurricane winds of parenting. Her pride wasn't doing her any favors. She should have been more open with him from the beginning, shouldn't have been so insistent that she could manage. Had it made him feel unnecessary? That was never her intent.

But she wouldn't be a dream-killer. She'd watched her mom destroy her dad's dreams. Pick at them, trivialize them, until he'd packed them away somewhere and stopped talking about anything other than current reality. By the time her mom left the two of them, his dreams were buried so deep, they never resurfaced.

Besides, Mara had earned her status as capable, competent, adequate. She couldn't afford to lose the one thing going for her.

It would have been inhuman and un-American if she'd stomped her foot and insisted Liam come home. Or that he not go. Four years. Four critical years in the lives of their kids. Mara had insisted they could make it work.

Maybe they could have, if she'd been more honest with him, and honest with herself. Liam had talked about leaving it all to come home after Dylan's last misdemeanor arrest. Mara shivered. She'd been the one to talk him out of it, had said it would have weighed on Dylan's shoulders long into adulthood if he'd crippled his dad's dreams.

Mara held her silent phone in one hand—*starkly* silent now—and turned her dulled attention to the view through the windshield of her parked car.

Her mind raced through what she knew for sure. A scold of jays. A streak of tigers. A charm of finches. A cauldron of bats. A knot of toads.

That one made no sense.

But Mara knew them all. Quiver of cobras. Bloom of jellyfish. Risk of lobsters.

Also made no sense. *Richness* of lobsters. That would be far more logical than the real answer—richness of martens. Really? Probably a throwback to fur trade days.

Mara had found the assignment intriguing, fascinating as a high school senior, not at all worthless. And yes, she should remind Chelsea, it was *too* useful later in life. During college, Mara had won dinner out at an Italian restaurant answering a radio show trivia question about moles. For the record, a labor of moles was easier to remember than an obstinacy of buffalo.

Or an unkindness of ravens.

Four ravens strutted around the squirrel carcass in her view — a single squirrel, not a scurry of them — on the cheese factory's grassy patch dotted with picnic tables. Picnic tables. As if cheese purchasers couldn't wait to get home to open their packages, or planned their picnic to the smallest detail . . . except cheese. *Forgot the cheese. No worries. We'll eat on the cheese factory lawn.*

From her perfectly legal parking spot at the lawn's edge, she watched ravens pick at the carcass, tears pooling in her eyes but not yet spilling. "You earned the title Unkindness. Earned it, birds." The tears spilled now. She wasn't sure she had a tissue in her purse. Wasn't sure if she could will her arms to reach for it.

"Somewhere, that squirrel's wife is in mourning, and you care not. Go ahead. Fill your stomachs. But know you've gutted someone else's."

The phone blurred when she looked at it again, but she couldn't set it aside. She pressed it against her chest. It felt warm. Sun-scorched. As much as she wanted to believe she hadn't understood the message clearly, she had. Every word.

Liam wasn't coming home.

An unkind river had swallowed him whole.

Details sketchy at this point, the voice had said. Unsure if the capsize was due to angry, angry hippos (*A bloat, or alternately a thunder*, she thought reflexively), if the motorized canoe had hit a submerged rock, if it had to do with the sudden rare downpour, or if rebel forces in the area had suspected Liam the Water Hero and the two villagers with him of encroaching on their territory.

She couldn't even remember who had called. The name. Someone from Deep Wells, Inc.

Mara watched the unkindness of ravens and felt pieces of her flesh tear away as the squirrel grew proportionately smaller. If the cheese factory maintenance team knew this scene was happening on their lawn . . . If her boss knew she was in the parking lot but not coming in . . .

If Liam knew what he'd just done to her . . .

Her heart had sunk a few minutes earlier when she saw "Deep Wells" on the caller ID. And not because she'd had a premonition. She'd thought the company was calling to announce her husband had been nominated for the Nobel Peace Prize and she'd have to find an evening gown at Goodwill for the ceremony.

Her intuition had failed her.

An unkindness of Maras. She'd resented the phone call before she even knew what it was about.

Could she call in sick from the parking lot? Grief leave, or whatever? *Lord, you've taken everything from me. Couldn't you have left me my mind? I need it now more than ever.*

She had to let the kids know. How does a mom announce a thing like this to her kids? She could take a photo of the scene in front of her, point to it, and say, "That. That just happened."

A raven tugged hard and dislodged the deceased squirrel's strawberry-shaped heart. Flew away with it in the tip of its greedy beak. Mara opened the car door and emptied her stomach on the parking lot asphalt.

⁓

The clutch of Jacobs children had been successfully extricated from the comfortless cement block walls of the school complex and moved to the just as comfortless interior of their home. None of the three reacted as she'd expected.

Dylan and Chelsea wouldn't leave her. They planted them-

selves on either side of her, heads on her shoulders, hands engulf-
ing hers. She had no answers for any of their questions, so they
stopped asking a minute into their minutes-old grief.

Jeremy stood across the family room, near the sliding door
to the patio. Looking out. He probably wasn't aware she could
see his reflection in the glass and knew his still form belied the
tears coursing down his cheeks.

"Jeremy, come join us. There's room here on the sectional."

"You didn't have to pull us out of school." His voice resonated as emotionless as she'd ever heard it.

"Jeremy!" Chelsea said it before Mara could.

"Well, it was embarrassing getting called out of class."

Mara leaned forward, but Dylan stopped her. "I'll get this,
Mom."

She watched as her eldest crossed the room to talk to her
youngest.

"Dude, what's with the lip? That's kind of my department."
Dylan bent over his brother, an arm across Jeremy's back. Their
conversation moved too low to overhear.

"Do you want some tea, Mom?" Chelsea swiped at her nose
with a well-used tissue.

"Oh, honey." *I don't want anything except to have your
father back, warts and all.* "That would be very kind of you."

"Okay. How do you make tea?"

Mara sighed. "We'll do it together. Anything for you two?"
The boys shook their heads no.

She hadn't taken the time to teach Chelsea how to boil water
and pour it over a tea bag, much less how to make a proper
cup of tea, which Mara hadn't enjoyed since . . . Since that one
time with Ashlee when the two friends crossed paths briefly
in Galena and met at the teahouse. Ten years ago. Ashlee was
widowed two years later. Mara had cried with her on the phone.
But she didn't know what to do with a friend who was widowed
so young. Ashlee's ever-faithful Christmas cards—which Mara

had given up responding to for lack of time—kept coming. With one signature rather than two. Widowed.

Her forever friend knew this gut-wrench.

Mara had been widowed.

Liam wasn't just dead. Mara was a widow. Her children were fatherless, practically orphans. And all hope of figuring things out, of finding a better rhythm for their marriage, of bridging the distance between them, was gone forever.

Which cut deeper? That he was gone? Or that hope was gone?

"Mom, the water's boiling. Now what?"

Great question, Chelsea.

five

*T*he arrival of dawn has less impact on those who lie awake all night. *Dawn, huh? No point even pretending to sleep anymore, then.*

It wasn't like in the movies. Mara didn't slowly slide her hand across the bed to where Liam would have been if he hadn't died the day before. No need. His pillow hadn't been warm for years. She could have been using the whole bed, she now realized. But for three years, she stayed on her side. Is that what hope does? Until it's stripped away by ravenous ravens of grief?

Liam died on two different days. It was Wednesday in the Dairy State—*which Wisconsinites insist is* not *California*, she whispered into the hollow room of her mind—when he died on Thursday. And now it was Thursday, but he died yesterday. How ironic that his attempt at humor was now part of his death story.

Drowned.

Died sounded better. How sad was that?

He died because he drew muddy river water into his lungs. Water. The whole reason he'd gone to Africa. He'd been consumed with taking water to the parched. Cause of death? Water. *Liam, my red-headed, fair-skinned, sun-blistered beloved. Who else but you would die from your life's pursuit?*

Maybe all good people did, eventually. Spent themselves for others. Suffered heart attacks on the basketball court or playing golf or took a bullet in the line of duty or succumbed to a virus because they'd put themselves in harm's way.

Died of hypothermia while trying to keep a stranded hiker warm.

Gave their scuba oxygen supply to one whose tank had run out.

Starved to death because they chose to feed their children instead of themselves.

Speaking of children . . .

"Come on in, Jeremy." Mara had slept in her clothes, so there was no real need for her to have pulled her covers to her chin as the bedroom door creaked open.

"It's me. Dylan."

Without the fist-pound? "How are you doing, hon?"

He shrugged. The simple action broke her heart. "Did you sleep?" he asked.

"No. You?"

"Honestly, Mom, if I weren't on house arrest, I probably would have found some—"

"Dylan, don't go there."

He clasped his hands behind his head. "I didn't."

"I mean, in your thoughts."

She should talk. She'd spent the entire night entertaining bizarre ideas no sane woman would invite. Would she need to sell the house? How dare Liam leave her with the dishwasher still broken? Can a hippo overturn a canoe? This was all her fault. She should have stopped him from pursuing his dream. No, that was ridiculous.

Were these disjointed, outrageous mental meanderings part of the fallout of fresh grief, its nuclear mushroom cloud? If she'd known, she would have been more sympathetic to other people who lost someone suddenly.

"Mom, you have to make it stop."

"Make what stop?" Her cell phone dinged.

"That." He pointed at her phone.

"I'll mute it."

"No, I mean social media. You have to stop them from talking about Dad. It's crazy-making."

She'd turned off all notifications except private messages from friends and extended family. What more could she—He was shaking now.

"Show me what you mean, Dylan." She propped herself up in bed, all the pillows crammed behind her back. Even Liam's.

Her oldest son sat on the edge she'd left for him and swiped his phone open. "Look at this. They've made Dad a thing. He's trending. Mom, he's trending! Like a national disaster or a foiled terrorist plot. It's *our* disaster, not theirs."

I'm losing my mind. I'm stuck on Dylan's use of the word foiled *and can't focus my eyes to see his screen.* She blinked. A little better.

"Look at this one." Dylan enlarged a list of comments. "Uncle Harold is miffed because he hadn't heard about Dad yet. I don't blame him. How can stuff like this spread so fast before the family even knows?"

"He's only your honorary uncle, one of your dad's college roommates. But your point is well taken." Another name to add to the list of people she needed to call.

"The whole world knows by now. It's big news. And I—" Dylan stood and paced, hands fluttering. "It's like they knew him better or cared more about him than we do. Did."

She'd seen him agitated before. That wasn't new. But the emotional anguish was, and it pierced her. "Has Chelsea seen this?"

"You have her phone."

"Oh. Right."

"But I showed her mine. So, yeah, she's aware of the media frenzy. Can't you somehow ask them to stop it?"

Of all the impossible requests . . .

Mara slipped on her mom mask that she hoped hid all that swirled behind it. "It's bound to let up in a day or two. Or a week. When a humanitarian dies—" Garbage. Every comfort she could conjure felt like garbage spilling out of her mouth.

"He wasn't a humanitarian to us." Dylan's face scrunched.

You don't have to work so hard to keep from crying, son.

"Not to us," he said.

Tell me about it.

"He was our human. Our dad guy. Dad."

Mara threw back the suffocating covers and crawled out of bed.

"Don't hug me, Mom. Don't. I think I'll crack wide open." He tossed his phone into the corner and turned toward the door. He hadn't taken a full step before he pivoted to retrieve his phone with a resigned grunt.

Not even twenty-four hours yet and the numb period she fully expected—counted on—had already worn off.

Mara knelt in the same corner, planted her palms as high on the adjoining wailing walls as she could reach, and stayed that way until the current of tears abdicated to her leg cramps and the insistence of her bladder.

⁓

I'm the mom who was called to the principal's office for non-compliant birthday treats, the non-hero married to the now-deceased hero. Why would you want to interview me?

She hadn't said it aloud, but the answer crossed her mind as a logical option when the calls kept coming. She'd probably made things worse by turning down the local news stations, some philanthropic news source she'd never heard of, *World* magazine, and CNN. Or was it CBN? Didn't matter. They'd call back.

Jeremy was holed up in his room. Dylan sat in a patio chair in the backyard, texting friends as fast as his thumbs could fly. Chelsea made tea, by herself, and kept Mara well-supplied. She also appointed herself tissue distribution manager, grabbing a new box from the pantry as needed.

It was too soon to think about funeral arrangements.

How does one go about getting a water-logged body back from a foreign country? Where was Liam now? In a . . . a cold storage room at the Deep Wells, Inc., field headquarters? Did Uganda have Americanized funeral homes? He wouldn't be shipped in a flag-draped casket on a military plane. Would his body be flown home on a regular passenger plane? Would they make her go get him? What an unkindness of ravens! How much would that cost?

She bit the tip of her tongue hard for thinking about finances at a time like this. But she had to, didn't she? Maybe Deep Wells had travel contingencies for catastrophic events like this. A special two-for-one flight discount? But one of them wasn't going to need a package of too-salty almonds and a plastic glass of ginger ale.

She'd have to pick up the phone one of the next times Deep Wells tried to call.

Did she need to make an appointment with herself to have time to think about how much she missed him? How much she would miss the future they hoped they'd have together?

"Here's another," Chelsea said into the strange emptiness of the family room. She'd been happy to get her phone back, despite the flood of social media. Mara had been more than happy to return it and let her daughter field some of the onslaught. "'Water Bringer Perishes in Ugandan River. Details Muddy.' Mom, that's just plain tacky."

"An unkindness of ravens."

"What?"

"Mumbling. Never mind. Yes, tacky."

"Two thousand views and forty shares already. Hundreds of crying emojis. One laughing, but I think that was just a mistake. Or the person thought it was a joke headline."

Chelsea's words both floated over Mara and drove themselves deep into the raw wound. Her husband was gone and the world thought it had a corner on mourning. Maybe Mara had no right to disagree. Her love for Liam was unarguable. But so was her—She hesitated to let her mind rest on the word. *Resentment.*

It didn't matter if she cried now. Anyone watching would assume it was because she missed her husband. Which she did. Starting three years ago.

"'Do the best you can until you know better. Then when you know better, do better.'"

"Were you talking to me?" Chelsea glanced up from her prodigal phone.

"Maya Angelou." Mara couldn't peel her eyes from the phone screen.

"Maya Angelou was talking to me?"

"No. To me," Mara said.

"Who's she?"

"Another shoutout to learning things you don't think you'll ever need to know."

"Mom, you're mumbling again."

Dylan shot through the house, headed toward the front door. The doorbell rang a mere second before he reached it.

Logan? And how did Dylan know . . . Ah. They'd texted.

"Mrs. Jacobs. Chelsea. I'm so sorry for your loss." The young man only a few years older than Dylan stood in her foyer with an insulated casserole carrier and a pie.

"Food! Come on in." Dylan ushered him in to the open

plan kitchen/living room no one told Mara would mean that all kitchen noises drifted into the family room and vice versa.

"I'm not going to stay," Logan said. "My dad and I thought you might not want to cook today."

Today or ever. But yes, especially today. "Thanks so much, Logan. Thank your dad for us too, please." *Just a dad, huh? No mom in the picture?* Mara unzipped the casserole keeper and extracted what looked like enough lasagna for the rest of the month. Smelled like her favorite Italian restaurant. How curious that any of her senses registered. But she definitely smelled oregano, basil, and garlic. Felt the strange texture of the insulated keeper. Could almost taste the butter in the homemade pie crust. "You made all this?"

"Yes, ma'am. Dad made the pie. He's got instincts." Logan nodded as if agreeing with himself. "You can keep the containers. They're disposable."

Disposable.

So is life, apparently.

———

It somehow seemed rude not to at least peek at the social media posts. To read how the world described her husband. The answer didn't surprise her.

Selfless. Devoted. Innovative (complete with a photo of Liam kneeling beside a young boy who had created a home-made irrigation system Liam later mechanized and helped market to others on the boy's behalf). The image caught her by the throat. Liam with his signature khaki sunscreen hat and impish smile.

She had no trouble remembering what he looked like. But that smile in the photo. It revealed he'd been in his element in that image. Doing what he loved and for all the right reasons. But when Mara and Liam talked, almost all their communication had been rooted in a laundry list of household breakdowns, financial woes, or parenting dilemmas. She'd needed his support but, thinking she was doing him a favor and protecting her own image, had couched their conversations in a feigned lack of their need for him. In the process, she'd stifled his ability to smile in any role but what was evident in the image.

No. Not always. They'd laughed together at some of the stories he told. She'd listened when he reported victories or significant accomplishments. She'd cheered him on. At least in the beginning. Before the weight of it all and her overconfidence that she could "handle it" bent her in two.

Mara scrolled through a few more posts. One news source reported that they had been "unable" to reach the family for comment. How long could Mara put off answering their "Tell us how you felt when you heard your amazing husband died?" questions.

"Well, genius," she imagined herself answering, "I felt like my lungs had been ripped out, twisted in a knot, and stuffed back into my chest. I felt like I'd eaten a bag of cement followed by a chaser of Ugandan river water that swelled the dust until it hardened in every cell. And, by the way, you don't know everything about Liam Jacobs. What you saw wasn't the whole story. How do you think I felt?"

But she wouldn't say it. She'd come up with something tamer than that, something printable, shareable, quotable. Something she could live with seeing in print and spread on social media.

Just not today.

Dylan microwaved a generous hunk of lasagna. Chelsea dug into the blueberry pie. Where was Jeremy? Oh yeah. His room. Still in his room.

Time to pull out the big guns. She skirted around her two oldest and extracted a tin from a shelf beside the stove. The expensive tea Ashlee sent her for her birthday, even though they'd decided years ago not to exchange gifts. Mara read the label: "A bracing blend of ginger and lemongrass with a touch of cayenne."

Bracing. *Good choice, Ashlee. How did you know I'd need bracing?*

six

"C an't get your body back? Click here for the supplement many are calling miraculous."

So much for losing herself in mindless TV. She clicked it off with what some might call an excess of irritation. No supplement was going to bring Liam's body back. Three weeks and no one knew where it was? How was that possible? Deep Wells claimed they didn't have it. The local government in the region said they didn't have it either. *Come on, people. How do you lose a body dragged from a river?* It's not like someone stuck it in the back of a closet and forgot about it.

Mara's stomach rebelled against the mental image. Her husband deserved more respect than that. From her too. It wasn't a laughing—or sarcasm—matter. Her deceased husband's body had gone missing. The funeral was on hold while the pulse of grief went on and on and on, tha-thump, tha-thump.

And now Deep Wells was dodging *her* phone calls.

She'd googled "How do you get a body home from overseas when he or she dies unexpectedly on foreign soil and he's an American citizen but has been living in the country for three years?" And, not unexpectedly, multiple sites popped up with partial answers. She probably could have googled "Liam Jacobs" and gotten the answer even more quickly.

"When a US citizen dies abroad," she read, "US consular officers assist families in making arrangements with local authorities for preparation and disposition of the remains."

Disposition. Disposal. There had to be a kinder word than
that. Did they even try the thesaurus?

"Options available to a family depend upon local law and
practice in the foreign country. US and foreign law require the
following documents before remains can be sent from one country to another: Consular mortuary certificate, affidavit of local
funeral director, and transit permit."

She'd bookmarked the page and referred to it often the past
three weeks. Consular mortuary certificate. Affidavit. "Yes, he's
most sincerely dead." And transit permit. Like, what? A bus
token?

"Additional documents may be required depending on the
circumstances of the death. The consular officer will ensure that
all required documents accompany the remains to the United
States." Only in this case, the three documents were a long time
comin'. Deep Wells, Inc., blamed everyone but themselves. The
consulate had all the social media info but none of the official
anythings. "We're working diligently to obtain . . ."

It wasn't unexpected that "the circumstances of the death"
complicated matters. But the delay made Mara feel as if she were
going in to have orthodontal appliances tightened every single
day. Her teeth hurt. Like fury.

Odd as it sounded, in the middle of the tragicomedy, she drew
a measure of comfort from Liam's having been gone for years.
Before he left, they'd changed their financial info so she'd be
able to deposit, withdraw, or sign legal papers with her signature alone while he was out of the country. She wasn't dealing
with the trauma many widows face when the death of a spouse
freezes assets until those all-important death certificates appear.

But her ability to withdraw now approached its limit, not

for legal reasons but because the well—so to speak—was about to run dry.

She couldn't face cheese. The cheese factory had given her a month of family leave, although because she was an overworked part-time employee without benefits, it merely meant they'd leave her alone for a month. Why couldn't she enjoy her work there like other employees did? All in all, her boss was a good, fair person, except when stressed. Customers came in happy and left happier. What made it soul-draining for her?

If she'd needed more than a part-time job to keep them afloat, and if she'd figured out another job that would leave her relatively free to keep up with her quest for volunteer-of-the-year at church and still leave time for creating award-winning—or principal office visit—school treats . . .

All she'd wanted was a paycheck. She hadn't dared to look in her field of college study. The time and energy she needed to maneuver through her kids' crises dictated that a pursuit in graphic design would have to wait. It was all up to her to manage.

Couldn't face cheese anymore. She had less than a week to secure other work if she found something and had no interest in filling out applications or showing up for an interview. *God, if you're real . . . Okay, I know you're real, but that's how these prayers start. If you're real, please, please, please find me a job doing something that doesn't involve cheese before next Monday. Something that doesn't involve cheese or water.*

Couldn't face water the same way either. Who would have thought she'd have to pull out her Lamaze breathing to turn on the shower for fear of drowning? On the positive side, she'd trained herself to hold her breath for the entire shampoo process. That might come in handy someday.

Yet another bizarre thought gripped her.

They didn't swim.

In one of their first conversations after Liam called home

58

on his earliest assignment in Uganda, he commented on how curious it was that with all the rivers that crisscrossed the area he'd been in, most Ugandans did not swim or even wade into water. What was behind that? Fear of what lurked beneath the surface—a legitimate fear? Creatures with teeth or microscopic dangers? Superstition?

Liam had been invited to witness a baptismal service in the Nile. For many of the Ugandans baptized that day, it was the first time they'd ever had their head under water, the first time they'd purposefully stepped into a river.

No wonder the capsized canoe was a death sentence. No one but Liam knew how to swim. What happened? Two of the many questions that swirled around her: What happened? And what now?

She could guess what happened. He would have known the villagers in the canoe with him couldn't swim. So he would have tried to save them. Likely died trying. Because that's who he was.

Can a person literally suffocate from guilt? Mara would volunteer for the case study if there was one. She'd call the CDC or the AMA or whatever the department was that deals with psychological anomalies just as soon as she found that elusive life insurance policy info that had picked the worst possible time to play hide-and-seek. Who imagines they'll need it in their early forties?

Or a refrigerator and freezer full of casseroles and twelve different home cooks' versions of lasagna sent by well-meaning friends and neighbors?

Jeremy was home from school again today. Stomachache. She couldn't prove he didn't have one, and the school hadn't objected when she called in for him again, although they did suggest the on-campus counselor might be an option for him.

Mara checked in on her youngest. His room smelled like a showerless preteen, but he said he didn't need anything. *Yes, you do, buddy. The problem is I don't know what it is, other than the one thing I can't give you. I can't give your father back. I can't even let you lay your sweet hand on his casket and say your pent-up goodbyes.*

She closed his bedroom door as quietly as possible and created her mental list. First, the insurance policy, then another round of calls to Deep Wells. Then she'd throw the comforter from Jeremy's bed into the washer and replace it temporarily with the spare one she kept for company. Wow, it had been ages since it had been used.

She'd pawed through the important papers in Liam's long unoccupied office space in the basement days earlier but now second-guessed her powers of grief-fogged observation and tried again. Didn't lost objects often appear in a spot that had already been searched?

The basement had never been a magazine-worthy "lower level." Today, it smelled especially musty. The area rug under Liam's desk squished when she walked on it.

She abandoned her paperwork search to investigate the source of the water. The sump pump hadn't drained the leakage from recent rains. Smelled like the motor had burned out. A sump pump wasn't supposed to smell like burnt wire, rubber, plastic. She disabled the breaker dedicated to the sump pump as a precautionary measure, though by all accounts, the unit was dead.

A lot of that going around.

Purchase new sump pump. Noted.

She couldn't do anything about it now, so she squished her way back to Liam's desk and the file folder drawers. Neatly labeled old-school file folders, the army green kind. Home appliance warranties. Procedure manuals for items they no longer owned. Tax records. Medical invoices. A folder marked "Someday" that she couldn't bring herself to peruse. Car insurance.

Homeowners insurance. Where would he have put the folder for his life insurance policy?

If she'd tugged any harder, the whole desk might have toppled onto her, but the bottom drawer finally opened its mouth. Nothing remarkable. Unlike the orderliness of the top drawer, this looked like a mishmash of nonessentials. She dug through what appeared to be junk mail she would have thrown away without reservation. Maybe he'd swept the surface of his desk and shoved it all in here so he could leave everything neat and tidy when he disappeared for what they then thought was only four years.

She glanced at the ads and tossed anything already expired. "Liam, why would you have saved this catalog of educational excursions? You were already booked for one. And forgive me for resenting such a small thing. And the rest of the things."

Jeremy wasn't the only one who could benefit from a counselor. They probably all needed one. She'd have to tap into the life insurance money to pay for counseling. That seemed wrong. And impossible if she couldn't find the policy information.

A white business-sized envelope caught her eye. Several sheets of paper were held together by the envelope flap. Less obtrusive than a paper clip, she supposed. The policy update.

Unsigned. Unsealed. Undelivered.

No, no, no. This couldn't be. A copy. It had to be an unsigned copy of the fully completed version he'd sent in. Right? But if so, why had he saved the envelope addressed to the life insurance company? The one that said "No postage necessary if mailed in the United States."

Liam, what have you done? Or not done?

Panic tinged with anger crept up her throat. Hero or not, this was unacceptable. Thoughtless. Cruel. *What were you thinking? You were probably thinking we'd never actually need it. You were wrong.*

True to her guilt-magnet nature, Mara redirected her anger to herself. She hadn't followed up to make sure everything was in order. And that it had been mailed. She hadn't conducted a thorough enough search earlier. Now she was instantly three weeks behind in figuring out how much financial trouble they were in.

Her pulse made her eyes bulge. That couldn't be healthy. She pulled herself up the stairs by the rail, hand over hand, an Everest she wasn't conditioned to climb. Tepid tea waited for her in the kitchen. She'd better drink it. They couldn't afford to waste so much as a tea bag ever again.

Not in the way she'd wasted the last three years of international conversations without once thinking to ask if Liam had taken care of the life insurance policy. If she never forgave herself for that, it would be too soon. And yes, she knew that made no sense. Nothing did.

The doorbell rang. She'd conditioned herself not to answer it. Questions and/or sympathy always waited on the other side. Mara watched on her phone screen through their door cam app as two women from church stood waiting. They whispered to each other, indistinguishable but likely, "Do you think anyone's home? What should we do? Leave it here? Probably. Then we'll text and let them know food's on the front porch. Good idea."

She waited three full minutes after they walked away before retrieving their gifts. Muffins. Cupcakes. And another pan of lasagna. Carbs solve everything, including grief, apparently. Oh, wait. A veggie salad. Could she bribe one of the kids to write thank-you notes for her? Could she hope she'd someday feel up to writing them herself?

Nah. Highly unlikely.

Her church had been more than kind despite her notable absence. They'd absolved her from all obligations she'd accidentally or intentionally signed up for, telling her to reconnect with them when she was ready to serve again. If it weren't for the death-of-a-loved-one part, the break would have felt like a refreshing sabbatical.

"God, I know I can't afford to take a sabbatical from you, because that would kind of be like an anti-sabbatical. But you do understand if I don't have it in me to sit beside people who all want to put their arms around me, and that I'm doing all I can to squeeze out 'Jesus, help!' from time to time. No offense, but I can't read your Word right now. It's . . . it's not you. It's me."

Stop praying, Mara. This is not helping your situation.

She grabbed her Bible from the end table in the family room and held it for a minute. Inside were life words. Maybe that's why it was hard to read right now, with death center stage. She laid the book reverently on the island and contemplated how much courage it would take to open it, much less read it. What's the expiration date on courage? How long can love afford to be exposed to shame before it spoils?

Get over yourself, Mara.

That was her own voice, not God's. Right?

She drew a breath and exhaled slowly. Opened to a spot about two-thirds of the way through. She'd grab a nibble of comfort and then come back later for a serious read. Her eyes landed on Matthew 27:58. "He approached Pilate and asked for Jesus's body. Then Pilate ordered that it be released."

Mara rearranged her mental itinerary. First on the agenda, ask again, politely—if absolutely necessary—for Liam's body. She needed to find someone at Deep Wells, Inc., named Pilate.

Oh, look. A sympathy card tucked among the muffins she hadn't intended to eat.

seven

From her traditional spot at the kitchen island, Mara swiped her phone and clicked the app to see who was at the door this time. Interesting. A man in a Deep Wells, Inc., blue athletic jacket and matching logoed ball cap. She couldn't see far down the street in either direction, but he hadn't come in a hearse, not that the company would have assigned one of their team members to personally deliver Liam's casket to their house.

Would they? No. Of course not.

Autumn's glory faded a little every day. Few bright colors on the trees. More leaves now brown and crispy lying on the ground or skating across the sidewalk at the least stirring of a chilled breeze. A pile of them had collected at the front door threshold like forgotten mail. Several of them blew inside when she opened the door. They chattered across the tiled entry floor. *Ticka-ticka-tick.* She'd deal with the unwanted guests later.

"Mrs. Jacobs? I'm Levi Williams from—"

"Mara. Kind of guessed where you're from." She nodded toward his cap, which he quickly removed. "Come on in."

"Is this a bad time?" He wiped his feet on the welcome mat.

The snarky in her wanted to challenge him to name a moment that hadn't been a bad time since she'd first heard Liam was gone. Instead, she said, "I didn't expect Deep Wells to send someone to the house. That wasn't necessary. All I need is information."

Levi sat where she suggested, on one of the stools by the island.

"Would you like a cup of coffee or tea?"

He stared at the almost-granite for a moment. "Coffee, if you have it."

She handed him a basket of K-Cup pods and let him choose his flavor. Zanzibar dark roast. How far was Zanzibar from Uganda? She fought off the compulsion to look it up. Zanzibar was on an island, wasn't it? Did it matter? Did anything really matter anymore?

While coffee-colored water dribbled into the chunky mug she'd shoved into place under the single-serving spout side of the coffeemaker, she turned to face him again and noticed for the first time that he carried a leatherette zippered folio. With, of course, the Deep Wells, Inc., logo.

"You have an answer for me? You've located my husband's body?"

Mara guessed the man was in his early sixties. A touch of gray at his temples. The company had sent their wisdom guy. But he wasn't talking. And his Adam's apple was moving up and down.

"I don't remember having spoken with you on the phone, Mr. Williams, but if I did, I should probably apologize right up front for my attit—"

"We've not spoken directly. But I've been aware of the situation. I considered Liam a dear friend."

"Oh. I'm sorry for your loss." On record now as the dumbest thing she could have chosen to say.

"I asked to be the one to bring you this news. Well, more than one piece of news."

Mara handed him the coffee mug and a coaster. Again, as if it mattered. "Good news/bad news?"

He laid his cap on the stool next to his. "I don't know how

to answer that. I suppose it depends on your perspective. None of this is easy, I'm sure. Deep Wells is, as you know, not a religiously affiliated organization, but several of us on the team have been praying for you and your children."

"Thank you." He was stalling. Not a good sign.

"We now know where your husband is."

"So, not outside in a curbside delivery hearse?" He did not know her well enough yet for her to pull out the sarcasm coping mechanism. *Mara, act like a grown-up.*

"No. He is . . . technically . . . still in Uganda."

"That word—*technically*. It means . . ."

"Mrs. Jacobs, it's been a long, long trail of red tape and misdirection and uncertainty. The early information we'd received was not correct. Or complete. We now know that your husband did not drown when the canoe capsized."

Where he is. He's still alive? "Tell me he's still alive."

"No. I'm so sorry."

"But you have his body?"

"Again, not exactly."

"What, exactly?" It took all Mara had in her to fake patience with this obviously gentle and deeply moved man.

"The way we now understand it is that he was still alive, barely, when he was pulled from the river. The villagers were mourning two of their own who did drown in the accident, but they sent someone to another location, a little larger village, in search of a vehicle that could transport your husband to a hospital."

"How long did that take?"

"The young man apparently ran all the way, but it took hours. Then the return trip with a driver and a . . . a truck."

I should thank that young man. "And they got him to the hospital?"

"Mrs. Jacobs, your husband, from what we've gathered, was by that time quite ill. High fever. His lungs were full."

She hadn't meant to let the whimper escape.

"He was loaded into the back of the truck. The young man sat back there with him, apparently. They headed for the nearest medical facility, which was almost half a day away, despite the fact that no one from the village held out hope he would survive the journey. From what we can surmise, the driver appeared to have made several attempts to skirt around the wildfires that were raging at the time, but . . ."

"Who told you that?" Throbbing temples. A swooshing sound in her ears. Vision moving in and out of blurry.

He stood and offered her his stool. Against her instincts, she accepted.

"The charred remains of the truck, and the three men, were discovered just recently by a village search team led by the young man's father. They had expected his son to return after seeing Liam—or his body—safely to the hospital."

Mara rehearsed the words she'd heard, her mind struggling to make sense of them.

Liam had sent digital images of the larger, modern-looking cities. The spectacular countryside. Beauty and lushness contrasted with the desperation of small villages fighting hard to grow enough food. Raising cattle or goats to sell, sometimes only one to a family. He'd captured images of villagers walking for hours one way to draw water for the day, water that was as likely to kill them as it was to quench thirst. And images of the bright blue Deep Wells units he'd been involved in installing.

Oh, Liam, by the way, our sump pump is broken.

Deep Wells, Inc., knew where Liam had been serving. They made periodic contact, didn't they? How was it that this much time had passed before they'd been able to discover "the whole story"? Whose fault was that?

The odor of burnt wires, rubber, plastic was joined by another burnt smell.

"Maybe it wasn't Liam. Maybe the truck he was in . . . got

lost or . . . Could they . . . could anyone positively identify him? This makes no sense."

"That's been one of the complications we've been dealing with. All three bodies were burned, almost beyond recognition. When they were found, the villagers had no means of transporting the remains safely to—"

"Safely? He was dead! What was going to happen to him at that point that would be worse than death?"

Levi put his hand on her arm but removed it when she flinched. "I understand you're frustrated. We have been too. Mrs. Jacobs, all three bodies were essentially cremated by the wildfire's intense heat."

She pressed both hands to her mouth, then full palms over her face.

"Even though it wasn't by human hands, cremation has been taboo in most of Africa for centuries, perhaps millennia. The villagers were naturally unsure what course of action to take, under the circumstances. Their customs and burial practices are distinct, village to village, in fact. But very important to them."

His neck had grown red and blotchy. She almost felt sorry for him.

"They took a portion of his ashes back to the village, out of respect for your husband. The hot winds have blown much of the rest away. We were able to retrieve enough bone fragments"—he seemed to choke on the word—"to positively identify them as Liam's. Which will enable us to move forward with the government forms and . . ."

"He drowned. But not all the way. And must have contracted something from the water. And died on the way to the hospital in a rogue wildfire? Do you understand why this would make a better movie than an accident report, Mr. Williams?" Her tears flowed hot and heavy by that time.

"Mara, how would you like us to handle this from here?"

"What do you mean?"

"We have the rest of the bone fragments we were able to retrieve. The villagers have apparently preserved or buried some of his ashes."

"Are you asking if I want them back?" *How incredulous!* "Bits of my husband? No."

Her husband had become part of the dust of Uganda. The villagers thought he belonged to them. Maybe in a deeper way than she'd realized before, he did.

What does a woman do with that? She loved a man who loved her but who gave himself to save others. And the "others" thought he was theirs.

When even she couldn't stand the empty void in the conversation, she answered, "No. We don't need his ashes."

"I can't imagine the difficulty of that decision."

"I can't imagine your volunteering for an assignment like this." She drew a steadying breath. "Thank you for letting me know."

Levi Williams hadn't touched his coffee. He did now. Another stall tactic?

"I considered him a friend. And a brother in Christ."

Mara's gaze landed on the kitchen faucet and stayed there. The drips she couldn't seem to conquer pinged on the stainless steel of the sink, eerily in sync with her tears.

Liam's body would have turned to dust eventually anyway. All bodies do. If she focused on that reality . . .

"About the death certificate," he said.

"The what? Oh. Death certificate."

"We were able to reach a government official who will help us expedite that process for you using DNA recovered from the bone fragments. We're working now to get Liam's few belongings returned to the states. To you. I apologize for needing to share details like this."

"Please don't apologize." The man had lost a friend, after all.

He centered his mug on the coaster. "Additionally, under the circumstances, because Deep Wells works within a self-funded insurance cooperative, we've been able to procure partial payment of Liam's life insurance policy."

"I don't understand." Her vision was clearing, but apparently not her hearing.

"Our employees qualify for a pretty significant life insurance benefit from the first day they're with us, Mara. Liam probably had another policy in effect as well. But our plan is designed to provide well for family members, especially in cases of death while in the field, in the line of duty."

"We're covered?" It couldn't be healthy that her heart missed a series of beats.

He reached into the padfolio. "This is the first check. The hope is that it will tide you over until we have all final papers in hand. If you need help locating a trusted financial advisor to help you with investing, we can assist with that as well."

"We're covered." How long would it take for the words to sink in?

"Liam is taking care of you and the kids even now, Mara."

~

Mara couldn't look at the check. Not yet. Even after Mr. Williams left, she refused to open the envelope. She did not want to profit from her husband's demise. Or was it truer that she didn't *deserve* to profit from his demise?

All the silent sighs she'd sent winging their way across the space between her and Liam converged in a toxic, cosmic swirl of what-kind-of-woman-are-you? Others saw his humanitarian side, his sacrifices on behalf of others. She'd lost sight of all that in the mire of trying to survive without him near. Was it that? Or was it her incompetence?

Would it have been as hard if the kids hadn't suffered? Made lousy choices? Needed their father's presence so much? Would it have been as hard if she'd been able to manage it all better? If she'd been more skilled at the single parent thing?

She could blame her mother for naming her Mara. That could work to divert a little of the guilt.

Sooner or later, she'd have to open the envelope. When the kids got home from school, she'd need to be prepared for a "Ramen for everyone!" and "Don't throw away that perfectly good used plastic bag!" speech.

Or she needed the words to let them know they could breathe again, their mom could take her time looking for another job, and if any of them pulled their grades up, they might be able to go to community college.

She used the tip of a butter knife to loosen the flap. Read the number on the check, then the words to confirm. Far more significant than she could have imagined.

"Oh, Liam. Bless you."

No more generic paper plates. They could afford the brand name.

Now all she needed were the words to explain to her children the harsh realities of the ashes-to-ashes, dust-to-dust principle.

~

"Where is that little twerp?" Dylan stormed into the house, vaulted his ragged-on-purpose backpack in the general direction of the couch, and pounded down the hall.

Not the way Mara intended their family meeting to start, but fairly typical of the Jacobs Family Saga of late. "You mean Jeremy?"

"What other little twerp is there?" he answered, slamming Jeremy's bedroom door shut again. "He took something from me, and I need it back."

"What did he take? Cupcake?"

"No, he didn't take my—Oh. Thanks. I'll have one later. I have to find him. He is in so much trouble."

Mara took a sip of freshly brewed tea. New tea bag and every-thing. "He should be home soon. Probably talking to friends."

"He doesn't have any friends, Mom. You're sure he didn't come home already?"

No friends? Was that an offhanded, angry brother comment or something that should concern Mara?

"Yes, Dylan. I'm sure. I've been here all day. We need to have a chat, all four of us. So if you can cool your jets a little, it would help—"

Dylan swung around to face her. "Mom. You don't under-stand. He *took* something from me. And I need it *back*, if you know what I mean."

Dylan did not wear the facial expression of a big brother who wanted his Snickers returned uneaten. Or his love note to whomever. Or his math test. He couldn't mean—

"No. No, that's not possible." *Dear God, no.*

"It had to be him. I caught him messing around in my bag yesterday. He said he was looking for a pen. Like an airhead, I believed him."

"Dylan, no. No, you're wrong. Jeremy would never—"

Her oldest clouded up. His lips were firm, but his eyes be-trayed his emotions. "I bet you thought that of me once too. That I would never—We have to stop him, Mom."

"Stop him from what? Throwing it away? You know how much he cares about you. Maybe this is his compassion show-ing up, his own version of an intervention. Maybe that's it."

"Using." Dylan collapsed against the wall. "Have to stop him. He's just a kid."

eight

The rocking chair made a gentle, not unpleasant creaking sound similar to the chair she'd used to quiet all three infants she'd birthed. With the lights low, Mara rocked in a steady rhythm, not wanting to upset anything.

"You were my easiest baby to comfort, Jeremy." *Creak, creak, creak*. "I held you just like this, tight against my heartbeat. I knew you could feel the vibrations of my voice as I sang to you. Prayed over you. Can you feel them now?"

"Mom?"

"Shhh. Hush now. Just rest, son. Rest. Such a brave boy. You know how much I love you, don't you?"

"Mom, please."

She ignored the insistent voice behind her. "Oh, Jeremy. You always find a way to make me smile. You're so thoughtful. Such a tender heart. Look at that. Your hair still curls in front of your ears. I hated the first time we had to cut those curls. Glad you're letting it grow longer now. I wonder how many moms say that to their boys. Not many, I imagine."

Mara refused to acknowledge the hand on her shoulder. She would have brushed it aside, but she needed both arms to cradle her boy.

"Mom, they—"

"Did I ever tell you that your father and I always wanted a third child, Jeremy, although neither of us could explain why? A boy and a girl already should have seemed enough. Did you know human brains are wired to prefer even numbers? That's what neuroscience says, anyway. Come to think of it, Jeremy, I think you're the one who told me that. Your dad and I disagreed with the science. We thought five Jacobses sounded like a complete family. But we had to wait so long for you. You do know, don't you, that I forgave you years ago for erasing my whiteboard of second career brainstorming ideas when you wanted to play tic-tac-toe. Don't give it another thought."

"Mrs. Jacobs?"

"We waited so very long for you. You should have seen your father's face when I showed him the pregnancy test. He could hardly believe it. I think we both held our breath those first four or five months until we felt you kicking. It's okay if you kick now, Jeremy. It would mean a lot if you'd kick. Such a . . . beautiful . . . sign . . . of . . . life."

"Mom, listen to me. You can't hold him anymore."

"Chelsea, keep your voice low. You'll wake him."

"He's not going to wake up. No matter how long you hold him. He's been gone for hours."

"He's sleeping. And for good reason. He has to . . . rest so all those . . . toxins . . . leave his body."

If she couldn't stop her voice from quavering, they'd win. The nurses and doctors. The psychologist who thought his degree made him an expert in things like this. Chelsea. Dylan standing outside the room. Dylan knew better than to get near her. If she could stay calm and didn't make a fuss, they wouldn't take Jeremy away from her. They'd said they'd give her time with him.

This was not enough time. Not nearly enough.

Chelsea needed her, though. The poor girl. Her face was bloated and blotchy. How long had she been crying? She needed her mom. She needed someone to tell her everything was going to be okay.

"Jeremy, son. I don't know what's wrong, but your sister's a mess. I think I have to let you go so I can help her deal with whatever it is. You understand, don't you?" She kissed his forehead. Cold. Dry. Hard, like cement. As cold as the cement patio on which Chelsea had found him.

The weight of her youngest son lifted off her chest as if she'd been trapped in the wreckage of a car accident and the Jaws of Death freed her. But now she felt naked and exposed. What was she supposed to do with her arms?

Chelsea steadied her as she stood. It wasn't the same rocking chair after all. Not anything like the one in the kids' nursery too few years ago. Her numb legs didn't respond to her brain's command for them to move. She might stay like that. What reason did she have to go home?

How was she going to explain all this to Liam?

~

Someone had left a cup of tea on the nightstand. How thoughtful. If only she could move her arms.

~

What was that piercing light? Oh, of course. The sun. So rude of it to intrude on her grief. She left her bed and padded to the window. When the drapes wouldn't stay overlapped, she walked into the master bath and grabbed a hair clip from the drawer. *Better take two.*

There. The sun couldn't reach her anymore.

~

Stop crying! Baby, you're going to wear out your vocal cords or make yourself sick. And then who's going to clean that up? Me? Yes, me.

Me.
I dry my own tears. I clean up my own messes.
And it's about to get real in here.

—

Today's the day she'd force herself to get out of bed and take a shower. Get dressed. Make conversation.

No. Too soon.

—

She smelled ripe and her sheets felt like wadded-up rags. Someone was going to have to deal with that.

People used to think Chelsea and Dylan were twins because of how close they were in age. Still did, because of Dylan's five-year high school plan. But they were strong enough to survive if she never emerged, weren't they?

No. Losing a third of your children doesn't mean you get to quit parenting.

So, maybe today. Today, she'd check back in to life.

This afternoon. Or this evening.

—

Mara opened a new document on her computer. In their ultra-calm, otherworldly way, the funeral home directors had been hounding her for days to provide Jeremy's obituary. Before she could think again, they'd posted some generic death notice that had little more than his name, the date, and "arrangements pending." That bought her a little time, but, like so many piercing atrocities surrounding their family, she had to find a way to deal with it.

She would not, would *not* consider their suggestion to have a combined memorial service for Liam and funeral for Jeremy. They each deserved their own. No lumping the two dead bodies—or one small body and a virtual pile of ashes—into a single ceremony for efficiency's sake.

She'd gotten no further than writing Jeremy's middle name on the obituary form before changing her mind. She couldn't imagine going through this twice. How could she stand there two different times for the obligatory line of mourners waiting for their chance to say, "I'm so sorry for your loss." As if it helped her to be reminded that her losses made other people feel bad. And the post-funeral buffet. Who invented that?

Where would you like the memorial gifts donated, Mrs. Jacobs? The Suicide Prevention Hotline or Deep Wells, Inc.?

If it weren't for the letter, she wouldn't have believed law enforcement's claim that Jeremy's death wasn't merely an overdose. Merely. What a horrible word. Dismissed as a statistic of the opioid crisis. "Tragically, too many first-time users have fatal reactions like your son's," they'd said. The way the two officers glanced at each other that brief second let her know they had as hard a time believing it was Jeremy's first encounter as she did swallowing the suicide idea.

Until Dylan found the letter in Jeremy's room. Handwritten. Jeremy's unmistakable leaning-backward penmanship with the letters *y* and *p* sporting extra-long tails—his signature style. She didn't doubt Jeremy wrote the words. She couldn't fathom, even now, what they communicated.

How could he have thought his father's death was his fault? Ridiculous. But he was so convinced, he apparently couldn't breathe. Couldn't think straight. Couldn't talk to her. Couldn't imagine living any longer with that distress haunting him.

The supposed suicide letter might have been his cry for help, the one that's intended to warn people who love him to take his emotional state seriously before something awful happens. But the awful happened. What he attempted worked too well.

She hadn't had a chance to tell Jeremy he was wrong. Dead wrong. The outrageous concept that he couldn't live with his grief and guilt was wrong. She knew that well. And guilt wasn't his to bear. How could he not understand? Had she neglected to talk to him about it? No. She remembered.

The stack of sympathy cards had mushroomed. The top one glared at her, its message simultaneously welcome and dagger-like: *Grief is just love with no place to go.*

No place to go. Love with no place to land.

Mara glanced up from her position at the kitchen island. She'd have to buy drapes to hang over the patio doors. When she looked outside, she couldn't afford to see the spot where Chelsea had found her little brother crumpled in their backyard. A bloodless death.

The opposite of when Mara's great-uncle had taken his life. Tortured by depression, or so the story went, and unable to function on his own, he'd moved in with her grandparents. Only once did Mara remember her grandmother hinting at how hard it was to make the decision to invite him into their home. To invite such irrepressible sadness and dysfunction to occupy that home known for its peace.

What must those days have been like? Grandma Lou would have wanted to help him pull free from what gripped him so tightly. She would have tried everything. Had she stopped singing when she worked in the kitchen or her garden? Had her life changed because Uncle Morton's disease bleached all the color out of it?

Grandpa had been gone the day his brother sat in the oak rocker in their fully restored Victorian farmhouse and silenced his tormented brain with a bullet.

One of her aunts relayed the story in tense whispers at a family reunion decades later. Grandpa and Grandma Lou never spoke of the specific incident, of how Mara's great-uncle's blood ran into the ornate floor grate under the rocker that day and into the furnace, which belched the smell and smoke of death until it had sufficiently spent itself. Grandma Lou did nothing for days but scrub blood splatter and bits of flesh from her walls and ceiling. She wordlessly tended to the fruitless task as if nothing else were more important, not eating or bathing or sleeping.

The scene could never be erased from her grandma's mind.

Mara knew the stats. If she hadn't seen them on TV, she saw them on social media, or heard about them at parent-teacher meetings. She'd gotten the big lecture about what to watch for after Dylan's first drug rehab "vacay." What parent didn't worry about suicide rates rising in teens and even younger? Some said by as much as 56 percent in recent years. She remembered the statistic. She'd never thought it would apply to her Jeremy.

Mara needed drapes on that sliding door. She couldn't scrub away the invisible shadow of her twelve-year-old son's form.

Jeremy's midnight-blue constellation comforter still hung on the clothesline. She'd washed it the day he'd stayed home sick. How long ago had she draped it over the line to let it finish drying?

Long enough for the colors to have faded in the sun.

She should eat. But everything tasted the same and nothing seemed worth the energy it would take to chew or swallow. Grandma Lou hadn't eaten or slept or bathed. *I get it.*

The house was as empty as a discarded cardboard box. *If my heart stops beating, can I give myself CPR?* She slid off the stool at the island and snatched a permanent marker from the junk drawer. Standing in front of her bathroom mirror, she pulled the neck of her slouchy sweater low enough to write the letters DNR over her heart.

Do. Not. Resuscitate.

She capped the marker and stared at what she'd written. The N was backward. Figured. *Can't even successfully pretend to give up.* Mara soaked a tissue in fingernail polish remover and rubbed at the letters until all that was left was a red-rimmed bruise of black ink.

When Jeremy felt himself slipping away, had his brain screamed "Abort! Abort!"? Did he realize how far a bloodless death could splatter?

It's not that I don't understand guilt, Jeremy. Well familiar with it. But that was a stupid, stupid thing to do. If you were still here, you'd be grounded . . . forever.

I know what it's like to wear The Guilt Quilt. At first, it feels like what we need, or deserve. It's big and wraps all the way around. But you can't live in it. It's not like yoga pants. Or those long basketball shorts you like. Liked. You don't wear guilt for very long before you start tripping over it. It's a deceptive comfort. Guilt Quilts are made of fiberglass threads.

You're probably too young to know what fiberglass threads are like, aren't you? That analogy must have been for me. Take my word for it. It itches and leaves a rash of embedded shards of glass.

Your guilt was completely misplaced, buddy. If anyone was responsible for your dad's death, it was me. He knew you loved him. I'm not sure he knew I did.

And a river isn't like a hungry lion. It doesn't lie in wait to attack, looking for potential victims who are limping, emotionally. Your dad's death was an accident.

Telling that to the mirror was getting her nowhere. She had an obituary or two to write.

nine

Official ruling. Jeremy may or may not have intended to, but he took his own life. Who knew that there's no standardization for suicide determination among medical examiners, or that many suspected suicides are later classified as accidental or undetermined. Accidental suicide, the oxymoron to end all oxymorons.

The authorities didn't have enough evidence to tie the lethal dose of drugs in Jeremy's system to his big brother's on-again/ off-again habit, despite Dylan's initial confession to her that it must have been his. So no further investigation was warranted. Mara might never know if Dylan was telling the truth when he approached her days later to say he'd been wrong. His stash had been there in his bag, caught under a pocket flap.

He'd even shown the small, innocent-looking packet to her. His last act, he'd said, as a user was to show it to her and discard it. He was clean for good now, he'd said. She supposed she should look at that as a bright spot in the murky sludge of the tragedy. But if that's how God answered prayer, she had to be more careful what she asked for.

Jeremy must have found another source that day. It wouldn't have been hard. Even in small-town America. Dylan pled with her to believe him. The drugs weren't his.

Chelsea believed him.

Mara might never know for sure.

If she laid aside her suspicions and embraced Dylan as if he had nothing to do with it and it turned out she was wrong, what a fool. If she held back her love for him and it turned out she was wrong, a bigger fool.

"Lord, help me love Dylan without restraint. I can't do it without thinking about . . . I can't do it." She thought back over the prayer, checking it for potential trouble if God answered. She let it stand.

Mara's combo mom-radar/lie-detector had been misfiring lately. She couldn't trust it. Chelsea was gone more than she was home. Said she was hanging out at the library. No reason on earth to doubt that claim, right?

～

On the day of the ceremony that they'd decided to call a memorial service for both Liam and Jeremy rather than a double-decker memorial and funeral, clouds hung so low and gray in the sky that it would have felt like breathing through wool if it hadn't been so cold. Second week of November already. How had that happened? When they pulled everything together in preparation for leaving the house, Mara reminded Dylan and Chelsea to bring a coat warm enough for the graveside ceremony.

Earlier that morning, she'd burned a bunch of envelopes from sympathy cards to create enough pretend Liam-ashes to sprinkle over Jeremy's casket. The ashes were ready. Waiting to play their role.

They'd get through this. How many people actually die from funeral stress? Probably not a good idea to google the question. Most people lived through it, didn't they?

Did the American Medical Association mention the level of tiredness that ate at Mara's bones and made it seem as if gravity had ramped up its pull by 50 percent? How could she be losing this much weight and feel a hundred pounds heavier than she'd been a couple of months ago? Was NASA aware of this weird gravitational thing?

Dylan had showered that morning without her pestering him. God bless him. Now he'd asked a question she must not have heard.

"What was that, son?" Small victory. She'd managed to call him *son*.

"Did you want me to drive us to the church?"

No, I've got it. I'm okay. The response formed just behind her teeth. She stopped herself. She did not have it. She was not okay. And Dylan probably needed to feel like a hero for five minutes. "That would be great. Thank you."

Chelsea hugged her elbows as if already cold, her eyes questioning Mara's answer.

"Let's go, kids." She drew a breath and blew it out with enough force to knock down a little pig's straw house. Jeremy's favorite story as a toddler. He preferred the Christian comedian's version by the time he was in school.

"Mom, don't forget Dad."

Mara snatched up the half-pint canning jar of ashes and stuffed it into her purse, then handed Dylan the keys. He was old enough to be out on his own, providing he graduated in the spring. And Chelsea wouldn't be far behind him. Mara would soon be more alone than she was now. Imagine.

After they got through this memorial service business, she'd start thinking about downsizing.

~

Mara had to give the minister credit. He did not balk when Mara insisted that he not ask for people to share their personal stories or remembrances about Liam or Jeremy during the service. He must have either respected her wishes without question or innately understood that it would have been so heavily weighted to memories of the forty-three-year-old father because his son had only been alive since the iPhone 3G.

Did she have a favorite passage of Scripture she wanted read? No. He could choose whatever he thought appropriate.

When Chelsea volunteered to choose music for the service, Mara had been happy to roll that task onto her. Good move. It wasn't all organ-y and dark. Not that their church had seen an organ recently. Or that Mara had seen the inside of the church recently, either. Liam's demise had changed so many things.

Chelsea said she'd consulted with the new worship team leader. Mara didn't even know they had one. So, it came as an even bigger surprise that it was Logan, Dylan's peer counselor. Logan and library start with the same consonant. Connection?

During the service—about as lovely as a double tragedy memorial can be—the few lyrics that registered in Mara's mind spoke of hope and peace and the hard one—God's faithfulness. True, true, absolutely true. Hard to hear in this setting, though, a service for a small boy and a father who hadn't shown up. Except for the jar in her purse, which honestly couldn't really count, could it?

The collection of family, friends, and community members, including teachers and students from Jeremy's school, blurred into one blob of humanity. Before and after the service, they swam like a circle of silver fish around her, each one identical, moving at the same pace, saying the same words, expressing their deepest condolences. The church had been near capacity. An occasional stray voice would reach her. Jeremy's English teacher, her tears falling fast and hard. A boy Jeremy's age—a classmate no doubt—who didn't say, "Sorry for your loss." He choked out, "I'm sorry," then disappeared into the swarm.

A contingent from Deep Wells attended. She appreciated that they stayed on the fringes. And that they made a sizeable donation in Jeremy's memory to children's cancer research. Way to throw off the gossips. She'd tucked the donation check into her purse right next to the now empty jar that had contained his father's stand-in ashes.

No number of layers of outerwear had been enough to ward off the chill of the graveside ceremony, short as it was. Although the service was billed as family only, Chelsea had asked if Logan and his father could attend too. She said Logan could play a song on his guitar. Mara didn't have the energy to object.

Logan had a dad? Did she remember that? Of course, he did. Most people have dads. The blueberry pie guy. No one else huddled around the hole in the ground had a dad though, except maybe the pastor or his wife.

Gloveless, Logan played and sang a sweet song about being safe in Jesus's arms. Nice. She'd remember that one. And she'd remember the casket spray shivering in the wind. And Liam's faux-ashes flying every which way when Mara and her two remaining children tipped the jar. And the moment after the final amen when they turned their backs on the scene to walk back to their cars.

She'd remember the compulsion to run the other way and fling herself into the grave. She'd remember Chelsea's hand tightening on her left arm and Dylan's on her right. Did they sense her wild thoughts? Or were they holding on to her to keep their own at bay?

Too few minutes later, they were back at the church, reaching for food on the buffet table. With no appetite to motivate them, they filled their plates for the sake of the kind people who had donated cabbage salad, fruit salad, ham sandwiches, and chocolate cake.

A thousand people, more or less, asked if she needed a refill of coffee or water. *Anything but water, please.*

Minutes ticked by at such a slow pace that she assumed the

clock on the wall of the fellowship hall had run out of batteries. She'd look up an hour later and the time hadn't changed.

Eventually, the crowd began to thin, offering the first breath of hope. It would soon be over. Not the agony, but having to share it so publicly.

"Mara?"

She turned at the voice. "Ashlee?"

"Can I give you a hug?" Ashlee Eldridge didn't wait for an answer.

"What are you doing here?"

"I follow Chelsea on social media." She leaned close to Mara's ear. "Helps me know how to pray for that girl. Heard about all this through her. She posts more than you do."

Mara couldn't help but release a stress laugh. "Understatement. You came all this way for the service?" Now, that was a forever friend.

"Don't give me more credit than I deserve. I live about six blocks away from you now."

Mara took a good look at the face of a friend she hadn't seen for more than a decade, and even then, only for a few minutes. Same kind eyes and soft smile. Same authenticity. She was serious. "Six blocks?"

Ashlee looked behind her, as if checking to see if other mourners were waiting to talk. Clear for the moment. "I'm renting for the time being. Not sure about buying. I needed a change of scenery."

"From Arizona to Wisconsin? Who does that?"

"Honestly, I knew our zip codes would be the same, but I hadn't calculated how close my rental is to your house until I drove past the other day."

"You really do live here? Why didn't you tell me sooner? Wait, you drove past without coming in?"

Ashlee's eyes clouded. "Was I wrong, thinking you needed some space?"

Mara couldn't imagine anyone who understood her better than this woman. Distance hadn't weakened their bond. Mara's silence the last few weeks might have. "No, you weren't wrong."

"I wasn't certain I should impose myself into today. But I couldn't imagine not being here."

Mara leaned toward her ear. "Can you save me from these people?"

Ashlee leaned back. "You mean all these people who love you and care about what you're going through? All these people who gave up part of their day—some of them missing work—to mourn with you and pay their respects?"

"Yes."

"Sure." Ashlee stood to her full height. All five feet of her. "Follow my lead." She approached a couple and extended her hand. "I'm Mara's friend Ashlee. Thank you for coming. I think I'd better get the family home now. It's been a hard day."

To another, "Thank you for coming."

And another, "Thank you for coming."

Soon it was Mara extending her hand. "My friend Ashlee's giving me a ride home. Thank you so much for coming. Dylan? Chelsea?"

"Right behind you, Mom."

"Can you two ride together, kids? Oh, we should thank the pastor."

Chelsea stepped closer. "Already did, Mom. The funeral director wants to know what you want done with the flower arrangements. And before you say 'I don't care,' I should let you know that Logan and Dylan took pictures of all of them and their little tags, and that Logan and his dad said they'd be happy to load them up and bring them over later. And yes, you do care. Or you will."

"That girl has leadership potential," Ashlee said.

God, you're here, aren't you? The awfulest of all the awful days. And you're right here in the middle of it. You sent Ashlee. Chelsea has leadership potential. And Dylan isn't in prison. She shook her head in disbelief that leaned heavily toward belief.

Jeremy loved nature.

"Yes to the flowers. I'll see you at home."

ten

The sun was tardy that day. It hadn't had the courtesy to show up in time for the memorial service, or the interment at the cemetery. But now, when it was all over, the two women had to lower their visors in Ashlee's SUV to keep from being blinded by it. The same rude sun had bleached out the color of Jeremy's comforter and the patio cushions. It would have meant a lot if it had shown up at the gravesite, maybe warmed the casket spray a little, or Logan's fingers on the guitar strings, or the tips of Mara's ears.

She'd worn her hair up. Mistake. Wouldn't it be sad to get frostbite on the day you bury your son? And scatter the memory of his father?

Mara covered her ears with her gloved hands. She glanced at Ashlee behind the wheel. "How are you not freezing? You're acclimated to a desert climate. November in the Upper Midwest is not the same as November in Arizona. Or so I've been told."

"You always had a standing invitation to come visit me, Mara."

"So did you."

Ashlee signaled and turned without needing directions. How long did she say she'd been in town?

"I guess life got in the way for both of us," she said.

"Life and finances."

"Death and taxes."

"Your Robert's illness." How hard that must have been for Ashlee. Some friend Mara had been. Two years of his battle with cancer. Eight years of Ashlee's aloneness. Mara had called—what?—twice for every six times Ashlee called? Sent a card. Or had she ever mailed that?

Ashlee pulled into Mara's driveway and parked to one side of the double garage door. "This spot okay for now?"

"Mmmhmm." Mara had a headful of tears she'd been waiting to discharge. And she wasn't about to do it in front of Ashlee the Strong. "Thanks for the ride home."

Ashlee paused with her hand on the door latch on the driver's side. If she was waiting for Mara to invite her in, she'd be waiting a long time. It was great to see her. But it would not be great for her to see the mess grief had made of the house, or the full view of the mess grief had made of her.

"Anything I can do for you, Mara?"

"No." Nobody had the power to do what Mara really needed. Time hadn't traveled backward since that incident in the Bible when the sun retraced its path down the steps. Or was it up?

"I'll call you tomorrow to check in," Ashlee said.

"If you want to."

That wasn't pity on Ashlee's face, was it? No, compassion. Ashlee knew at least a measure of the pain choking Mara.

"I'd like to have you over for coffee when you're up to it," Ashlee said, as if Mara were recuperating from major surgery. Metaphorically speaking, scalpels had been involved, slicing open Mara's heart.

"You're the one who's new to the neighborhood. I should be the person inviting you." *Mara, stop talking. Stop self-talking, while you're at it.*

"I still make a mean sour cream coffee cake." Ashlee's eyes smiled.

"That's *my* recipe, as you'll recall."

"Didn't it come from your Grandma Lou originally?"

"How do you conveniently remember these details?"

Ashlee faced the garage door. "I care."

What was one more impossible thing in a day full of impossibles? "Did you happen to bring any of that coffee cake with you?"

"Backseat."

"Do you promise not to judge my housekeeping abilities?"

Ashlee unbuckled her seat belt. "I fancy myself more an attorney for the defense than a judge."

"Will you try to force me to talk about my *feelings*?"

"No."

"You might as well come in, then."

───

Ashlee was as true to her word as she'd ever been. She didn't press for information once in the house. Mara didn't offer any. Couldn't.

How much did Ashlee already know? Mara scrolled through Chelsea's social media posts while Ashlee took a bathroom break, and likely took it upon herself to tidy up the sink and a few other things, knowing her. Chelsea's posts had been in compliance with Mara's wishes—bare facts only. No rant about her father's pretend ashes. No hints of Jeremy's cause of death.

Not that it should be an embarrassment or a secret. Or maybe those were exactly Mara's issues. Potential embarrassment. Or worse—pride. If she'd been a better mom . . . If she'd been more aware . . . If she'd paid attention to his pain instead of wallowing in her own . . .

She couldn't protect him from taking his life, and try as she might, she couldn't protect him now from rumors or from those who, if they heard, would think less of him.

Did his classmates suspect? That little boy at the funeral. The sorry one. The community might have no legitimate right to hear the full story, but did they have a need? Was she going to have to make sure they understood that suicide solves nothing? It just transfers the pain to others.

Like her voice mattered. It took all the courage she had to use the word suicide when talking to *herself*. Hardly spokesperson material.

Ashlee emerged from the bathroom smelling like lemon-scented Lysol. Mara didn't blame her.

"I'm going to warm up the coffee cake. The butter will melt better if we do." Ashlee opened a cupboard door she must have instinctively known would hold small plates and pulled down four.

Mara was grateful someone in the room remembered she had two more children who would be home soon. "I'm not really hungry."

"Doesn't matter."

"And I've been trying to eat fewer carbs."

"My guess is that you've been trying not to eat at all."

Mara would have bristled if anyone else had said it. Ashlee knew her so well, despite the decades between their visits. "But—"

The microwave dinged. "You don't need it for the calories. Well, you do. But more importantly, you need this for the taste. You need to taste something. Feel something other than the waves of grief battering you. I don't mind eating your piece too, if you think I'm wrong about that."

Kick her out of the house or listen to the woman? "You're not wrong. Hand it over."

"Allow yourself to eat it slowly, my friend. Savor every bite, every crunch of the topping, the moistness of the cake layer, the warmth and the sweetness . . ."

"You think pretty highly of your baking skills, don't you?"

Ashlee smiled and tore off a half-sheet of paper towel for each of them. "Again, your grandmother's recipe."

"Mm. This would go great with a cup of—"

Ashlee had already turned on the coffeemaker and flipped it to the carafe setting.

Mara let her fork slide slowly through the crumble crust and into the soft, almost creamy cake. She worked on savoring the bite. And it was work. Her taste buds hadn't cared about anything for too long.

"I usually make this with kale," Ashlee said. "But not this time."

"Kale? Really?"

"No. What? Are you kidding me? Kale? You think I'd adulterate your Grandma Lou's recipe that way? Hey, Mara. Kale's nothing to cry over. I was joking."

Her throat too tight to answer, Mara waved her fork, begging a moment.

"If you want me to leave . . ."

She shook her head no.

"If you want me to be quiet . . ."

She nodded her head yes and let tears fall into her paper towel. And the second one Ashlee handed her when the first one was adequately soaked. The wave passed. It would be back when she least expected it. A pattern these days.

"Blow your nose, Mara."

"I'm fine now."

"No, seriously. You've got something—" Ashlee waved her hand near her nose.

"Oh." Mara took care of it. "Do I have kale in my teeth too?" She exaggerated a toothy smile.

"You're good on that front."

"Ashlee, I'm not good on any front right now." Fork abandoned, she dropped her hands into her lap, shoulders reaching for her ears. *I must look like a train wreck. A scared train wreck. And she doesn't mind.*

Ashlee's hair had changed since they'd last seen each other. But the peace she wore on her face like high-priced foundation hadn't. "Remember when we were kids and we'd race our bikes in Grandma Lou's gravel driveway?"

Mara nodded.

"In shorts."

She nodded again.

"And flip-flops."

"I wonder if Grandma Lou ever thought about having our IQs tested."

Ashlee smiled. "Adventure and bandaged knees go together."

"They do."

"Are your knees okay?"

Mara tilted her head. "Well, they're older, but yes. That's not what hurts right now."

Ashlee seemed to ponder her next words, as if struggling with the decision to say them or not. Finally, she quietly said, "The adventure of loving is like riding a bike on gravel in shorts and flip-flops. Pain is inevitable."

The garage door started its slow growl.

Ashlee said, "Sounds like your kids are home. I'll take my piece of cake and my coffee to go. I'm keeping the mug and plate until we next get together." She looked Mara in the eyes. "See what I did there?"

She did. "Ashlee, you don't have to go just because Dylan and Chelsea are home."

"I'm six blocks away. And I'm in this insomnia phase. So text or call if you need me. Day or night. I mean it."

"I know you do."

At the door, Ashlee turned and said, "Don't be afraid to let those kids feel all the feels, Mara. And don't be afraid to let them step up, either. They're trying."

"Yes, Sarge."

"And make your bed tomorrow morning. It'll help. Trust me."

If it were anyone but Ashlee . . .

~

What was that cloying smell?

Mara threw back the covers on her bed and padded out of her room in search of an answer. In the morning light, the family room and kitchen looked like a florists' convention and smelled like lilies, carnations, roses, eucalyptus, and unknown green fronds of jungle growth. Sun poured through the double doors to the patio, intensifying the fragrance cocktail. She retreated to her room, more than ready to climb back into bed, when she heard Ashlee's voice in her head.

She made her bed. Throw pillows and everything, smoothing the quilt and making sure it hung evenly. Then she stood back and surveyed her work. It helped a little. A spot of tidy in the chaos that defined her life. Currently floral-scented chaos.

Jeremy's bedroom door had remained closed since she'd been forced to go in there and pick out his burial clothes. No mother should ever have to do that. He'd looked so handsome in what he wore to his former teacher's wedding last summer. She'd chosen that—the pale blue no-iron shirt and black pants. At the last minute, she decided he needed the navy blazer too. But as she stood over his open casket before the service began, she realized she'd made him look like a preppy version of who he really was. If dead people can cringe, he probably did.

What was she thinking? He should have been buried in those droopy basketball shorts and his one and only officially licensed Packers jersey.

A twelve-year-old shouldn't have to be buried at all.

A shaft of light shone from under his door. She didn't remember leaving his window shade up. No. She'd left his light on. Mara reached to flip the light switch off but recanted and

95

left it as it was. It seemed fitting somehow that part of Liam's life insurance would pay for an unnecessarily high electric bill.

And his son's funeral costs.

Jeremy had talked about having written a letter to his father. Could she find it? What if she could read her son's last communication with his dad? Would that help make sense out of the senselessness?

A real letter. With a postage stamp. His teacher had mailed it to Uganda for him. Maybe the teacher had read it first, corrected the grammar and punctuation, graded it for originality or sincerity or creativity. Mara needed to call her for information.

What was her name?

Funny how the loss of someone important was accompanied by what Mara hoped was only temporary dementia. Hearing voices. Forgetting names. Forgetting how to breathe. Choking on the scent of flowers.

Without looking it up, she already knew the answer to the question about how long it takes to get over the death of a child. Until forever and then some.

Death of a spouse? Pretty much the same answer, no matter how healthy or unhealthy the marriage.

Remorse—so much remorse—complicated both of her losses. Remorse, she'd learned quickly, is relentless. It doesn't give up hounding. It exhausts its victims but doesn't tire. The ultimate villain.

"Apparent" suicide. Deemed such, it compelled law enforcement to do that initial investigation. With a child as young as Jeremy—sadly not their youngest suicide victim to date—the investigation consisted of searching his room, his locker at school, and both his laptop and cellphone. They found no inappropriate or suspicious phone calls. No suspect web searches. No repeated visits to dark or destructive websites. No online conversations with sketchy people. They found that Jeremy had received what the officers described as no more than the average bullying.

CYNTHIA RUCHTI

Average bullying? Had it come to that?

And who was bullying her son?

The authorities hadn't scrubbed his phone and laptop clean before returning them. She could see everything they had seen, if she chose to. Not today. The sun was too bright. As heavy as the flannel blanket of gray clouds had felt yesterday morning, today's bright sun created an atmosphere of vulnerability. She caught herself shielding her eyes from it while indoors.

Ashlee texted a morning greeting. "?"

Mara sent her a photo of her neatly made bed.

eleven

With Ashlee nearby, it wouldn't be as easy to crawl in a corner until someone noticed the odor of her flesh rotting. Ashlee was more persistent than remorse.

Gentle. Most of the time. But persistent. She'd reminded Mara that if she needed God's comfort, she was going to have to look in the Book where he stored it all, whether she felt like it or not. "Faithfulness first, feelings follow," she'd said. Sounded like a meme idea Ashlee had swiped from Pinterest.

But Mara had tried, because, you know . . . Ashlee.

This morning's gem of soul-salve? Mara had played Bible roulette—see where the page falls open. Isaiah 21:10—"O my people, crushed on the threshing floor . . ." Okay, so, yes, truth. But not what anyone would call soothing. She closed the Book and dragged her crushed self to the toaster for a threshing floor bagel.

Dylan and Chelsea insisted they were ready to go back to school. She would have been more than happy to give them a pass for a couple more days. And the suddenly empathetic principal had agreed. But her kids were adamant they'd be okay. The toaster spat her bagel out with an idea attached. Maybe they hadn't gone to school because they were that strong. Maybe they just needed to be somewhere other than the house of doom and the pall of their mother's sadness.

It still smelled like a floral convention in there, even though with Logan's help they'd found places for most of the arrangements to bless other people. The kids had taken flowers to the first responders who had handled Jeremy so tenderly, including the ones who weren't afraid to let tears fall while they worked on him. They delivered another bunch to the hospital ER staff and to an assisted living facility. No personal connection, but Logan had suggested it.

Every neighbor who brought food took home flowers, the Jacobs version of "If you visit, you get a free kitten from Fluffy's latest batch." Despite Mara's inability to respond with more than a minute of conversation, despite her mood swings that sometimes closed the door in their faces before she could stop herself, friends and neighbors kept reaching out with help. How long would that last?

The stink of sadness still hovered. Mara considered a professional disaster cleanup crew. For a nanosecond. Nothing of a chemical, natural, or mechanical nature could dissipate the odor grief leaves in its wake.

With her bagel abandoned untouched, she stared at the growing mound of paperwork, knowing full well it wouldn't have shrunk a bit by day's end. The sun had risen on misery and it would set on unchanged misery. It was a truth universally accepted.

Could she at least get those drapes ordered so she didn't have to look at the patio every time she stood in the kitchen or sat in the family room? That would require measurements, which would require finding Liam's retractable measuring tape in the garage workshop. It was pale threshing floor comfort that she could—without seeming selfish—start calling it *her* measuring tape. In essence, she owned everything that had once been Liam's, and felt poorer for it.

What could have made Jeremy convinced he'd caused his dad's death? Of all the outrageous ideas! She'd thought the headache behind her eyeballs might fade if she and the kids made it through the memorial service. The headache remained. Tenacious. Exacerbated by flashbacks of the hospital scene, images of what Liam's last, gurgling—or seared—breath might have been like, the fear both her husband and her son might have faced.

Distract yourself, Mara. Emotionally, you're a panicked toddler being dropped off at daycare. Find something to distract yourself before you implode.

She stumbled toward the stack of paperwork on the corner of the kitchen island, slid one hand underneath, palmed the top page, and flipped the stack upside down. "There. I'm not utterly helpless. I managed to change something."

The bottom of the pile, now the top, was layered with papers and personal items Deep Wells had returned to her. Liam's "effects." Why were they called that? It was stuff.

His passport, as if that would ever come in handy again. Was it legal to throw a passport away?

She remembered asking a similar question after her dad died. Years after. She'd found his driver's license. Was it legal to throw it away? She guessed yes.

Liam's phone lay in the stack. She ran her fingers over the keypad where his fingers had been. No connection. Liam's immunization records and visa information rose to the top. A notice with an official Ugandan government seal, commending Liam for—huge surprise—his humanitarian efforts.

Underneath the commendation lay a rumpled envelope with familiar penmanship and a bunch of Forever US postage stamps.

She traced the leaning-backward pen strokes on the return address, strokes that had left slight indentations in the envelope as her son wrote his father's temporary address. She flipped it over. Still sealed.

Liam would have torn into it as soon as he received a letter from his youngest. She knew he would have.

Still sealed. Liam had never seen it.

But Jeremy took his life because he thought his words had wrecked his dad, made him careless, somehow caused the internal or external storm that overturned a canoe in a muddy river too deep to survive.

Jeremy! He didn't see the letter! You were not to blame, and you wouldn't have been even if he had read it. Your still-growing brain and sensitive heart betrayed you! You were not your father's cause of death.

Only your own.

The constriction at the base of her throat wouldn't let her inhale or exhale. How could a tragedy like losing Jeremy this way have grown any worse? But it had.

She retreated to her bedroom and pulled back the covers on her bed far enough to slide the still-unopened letter under her pillow. *Can't deal with this now. Can't know what he said. Have to know. Not now.* She smoothed the covers back into place. No lump. No evidence that underneath was a misunderstood weapon of mass destruction.

～

She'd washed her hands, but Mara's fingers still smelled like bacon, the residual effect of cooking a whole pound of thick-cut, hickory-smoked comfort and eating it in one sitting.

The bacon overload and two pieces of Ashlee's warmed and buttered sour cream coffee cake gave her a new reason for the ache in the pit of her stomach. It seemed twistedly wonderful to experience a distress unassociated with sorrow. She leaned into it, then realized to her dismay that she would never have eaten an entire package of bacon if it hadn't been for grief. It wins every contest.

Drive to the grocery store? Sorry. Grief won't let me.

Clean up that spill on the counter? Grief says I can't.

Hug someone? Nope. Grief has my hands tied behind my back.

Phone a friend? Grief says that would be a bad idea. Shouts it.

Reach out for help? Are you kidding me? Have you seen grief's right hook? It's a monster.

Answer the doorbell? Grief has me glued to my chair. Still glued. It can ring all it wants and I'm not going to be able to—

Oh, all right! Is there a more annoying sound?

She headed for the door, filling in her own answer. Her phone ringing—that was the only more annoying sound in the middle of grief. She held the door latch in her hand and peeked through the peephole. Stranger. She let go and started back toward the family room.

No. She'd seen this man before somewhere. *Grief, will you please let me borrow my brain for a few seconds to figure out—*

Logan's dad. What was his name? Sounded like a mafia name. Ah. Sol, short for Solomon, which didn't sound at all mafia-like.

She stopped. Retraced her steps. Opened the door. *Take that, grief. I opened the door.*

"Mrs. Jacobs, good morning."

"Is Logan with you?" She checked the bushes on either side of the porch as if that were logical. She made it a point to look both directions down the street. No Logan. No car either.

"I came on my own this time. Checking in to, you know, see if you needed anything."

You and Ashlee would make a great team.

"I have some passable handyman skills if you need any work done. Or if you wanted someone to mow your lawn one more time before the snow flies."

She was supposed to do stuff like mow her lawn. Totally

slipped her mind. Despite the two notices from the neighbor-hood homeowners' association in the stack on the island. Ashlee probably kept her lawn so neat and trimmed that the city used her as an example for recalcitrants like Mara.

"I'm fine, thanks." *Stupid grief. I do not like your tone of voice.* "Wait. Are you sure you'd want to do that?"

"I'm kind of between jobs right now. I'd enjoy helping out that way, if you're okay with it."

Between jobs, huh? Rethinking the "he's perfect for Ashlee" idea.

"I can't pay much." She had to say it, even though to be honest, she actually could pay him a fair wage.

"I don't want to or expect to be paid. I have the time and would like to assist, if I can. Your Chelsea means a lot to my Logan."

Did not need that tidbit of information right now. Once your Logan hears about Chelsea's "romantic escapades," he'll take off. Two more broken hearts. But, the lawn was a mess. None of them had interest in raking leaves or getting the exterior of the house ready for winter. Grief reminded her that she didn't deserve anyone's kindness, much less a stranger's. She turned a deaf ear for once.

"The lawn mower's in the little shed in the backyard. I don't remember the last time we checked the oil or filled it with gas."

"I can use Logan's. All the bells and whistles. Mulching ca-pacity. Built-in Wi-Fi."

"What?"

"That's a slight exaggeration. He has a cup holder where a person can set their mobile device and then use his Bluetooth headphones."

Interesting sense of humor. Ashlee might find it charming, if it weren't for the "between jobs" part of his resume. But then again, so was Mara. She'd officially resigned from her "position" at the cheese factory, despite the upcoming holiday rush. And it wasn't just because she couldn't park in a lot that an unkindness of ravens had once occupied. Leaving the house might never again make her list of life goals.

That's not my answer, is it, Lord? I should go back to work not for the money but for my sanity? You can't be saying that. Are you? Tell me I heard wrong. That's completely believable right now.

"So, Mrs. Jacobs?" Solomon Coppernall held his hat in his hands, his resemblance to a mash-up of a young George Clooney and a young Steve Carell evident. Kind eyes. They'd better be, if he was going to make the cut as a potential prospect for a woman like Ashlee.

"Mara," she said.

"Mara. Good, strong name."

She felt her face twisting. "My name means *bitter*. Thanks, Mom."

"Bitter? That's the pre-redeemed meaning, sure. But it also means strong."

Okay, this guy had better be more skilled at lawn mowing than he was at conversation. He didn't know what he was talking about. But free labor? Who was going to pass that up? Was it true that living in a chaotic atmosphere deepens grief? She considered the untended leaves blowing into her neighbors' yards, the garbage can she'd once again neglected to make Dylan take to the curb on garbage day, the spent flowers that now raised empty stems like skinny little grave markers to note where life once stood.

"When could you start working on the yard? I have . . . business . . . to attend to."

"Can't afford not to take advantage of beautiful days like this. I can be back with Logan's rig in, say, fifteen minutes? His house is right over there." He pointed across the street and three houses down.

Seriously? Logan owned his own house? And lived in the

neighborhood? That explained more of Chelsea's recent absences. Mara was sandwiched between her son's peer counselor on one side and her ebullient forever friend six blocks the other direction.

She wasn't a fan of sandwiches.

twelve

As Grandma Lou would have said, Ashlee "got it in her craw" that she and Mara should walk together every day. That was an automatic no. After all those years in Arizona, Ashlee may have forgotten that winter comes early in the Northwoods. How many Thanksgiving celebrations had been thwarted by ice storms or blizzards in their area?

Ashlee had said the weather was no obstacle.

Ashlee, Ashlee, Ashlee. You poor, misguided woman. I'm not going to do it.

We can't be friends anymore if you make homemade bread and scrapbooks. And if drop-in company doesn't panic you because your townhouse is always ready for anything. You play worship music while you weed your little flower beds. You weed!

And she walks. Every day. Oh, and is relentless.

Despite Mara's protests, Ashlee started showing up at Mara's front door at 6:30 every morning. This time of year, it wasn't even fully light at that hour. What was she thinking?

"Go home, Ashlee. I am not walking with you," Mara called through the storm door. "I'm still in my pajamas." Or what passed for pajamas these days. "In fact, I am going back to bed. So, sit here if you want to, but I am not going to walk for the sake of walking."

Mara marched past her kids getting ready for school, shut her bedroom door decisively behind her, and ignored the guilt with which she was on a first-name basis.

Rain or shine or sleet, there was Ashlee. Waiting. When Mara got up for the day, anytime later than 6:30, Ashlee was still there. Sometimes moving from foot to foot to keep warm. Sometimes huddled in a fleece blanket she kept in her backpack for that purpose. Sometimes stretching or doing jumping jacks right there on Mara's front sidewalk for all the neighbors to see and question.

Usually around 7:30, she left and headed home or wherever she went.

Most stubborn woman Mara had ever met.

If they texted or talked by phone later, Ashlee avoided mentioning how her day had started, but never failed to end the conversation with, "I'll see you in the morning."

After almost two weeks of this routine, Mara was roused by a desperate pounding on the door at 7:30. Her first thought was that her kids had locked themselves out, but they were already at school. Second thought, Ashlee. The woman had finally caved?

Let me in! Let me in!

Not by the hair of my chinny chin—Not the best analogy.

Mara flung the door open, ready to watch her friend admit defeat. But what greeted her was a taller-than-she-remembered Sol with his meaty hand clutching a fistful of Ashlee's turquoise down jacket sleeve.

"Is this woman bothering you, Mrs. Jacobs?"

"Excuse me?"

Ashlee's face wore a mask of rosy cheeks—could have been the nip in the air—and wide eyes. She squirmed theatrically. Sol tightened his grip.

"Among other things, I'm a retired police officer, Mrs. Jacobs. And I've noticed this woman camping on your doorstep day after day. If she's harassing you, or trespassing, it's within my authority to contact the police to have her detained and questioned. Or you could always file a restraining order."

He was not flinching.

What must he have thought when Mara burst into laughter?

The man who might be perfect for Ashlee moved up a notch to definitely perfect for her. And he had her by the arm—or coat—already. Next step, on his knees proposing. What a story it would make for their grandchildren someday.

"Ashlee, meet Solomon Coppernall. Logan's father."

"Oh," Ashlee said. She brightened and extended her free hand. "What a pleasure to meet you."

"And Solomon, this is Ashlee Eldridge, my best friend."

He dropped his hold on her jacket and stepped back. "Your best friend?"

Mara sighed. "Best and most stubborn friend. She's here every morning because she thinks it would be a good idea if I got into a routine of walking every day. More persistent than the electric bill and a nagging cough combined." Mara presented her recitation with all the excitement of an SAT proctor.

"Well." He rubbed his chinny chin chin. "Sometimes friends need restraining orders."

Mara laughed again. It was up to her to save Ashlee's reputation and her friend's potential relationship with the retired officer. "No restraining order for this one. You two want to come in for coffee? It'll take me a while to find my walking shoes."

⁓

Two refills later, each, Mara's shoes were laced, jacket, scarf, and gloves donned, and the two women parted company with Solomon to begin their long-delayed walk.

"The wind bites right through me," Mara said. "What's so great about this walking idea?"

"You'll warm up soon. The secret's in the layering." Ashlee's ever-present smile did warm the air a degree or two.

"How long will it take me to lose the pounds I put on while eating a steady diet of bacon?"

Ashlee's small backpack made a swishing sound against the fabric of her jacket. "You mean keto?"

"Not even close."

Ashlee shortened her stride and picked up the pace. Mara growled at her.

"I don't walk to lose weight, Mara."

"Of course, you don't. You have a BMI in the negative numbers."

"Not true. The secret," she said, lowering her voice, "is in the layering."

Maybe this walking wouldn't be the worst thing that ever happened to her. Something twisted near her heart. The worst thing that could ever happen to her already had. Should take off some of the worry edge about the future, shouldn't it? Why didn't it?

"You're convinced my exercising a too-tired body and talking through a worn-out grief will help somehow, aren't you?"

Ashlee slowed her pace until Mara could breathe without wheezing. "It helped me with mine."

Mara couldn't argue with that. Or could she? "Everyone's grief is different. All the literature says so."

"True."

"I wish I'd been there for you when Robert died."

"What makes you say you weren't? You were so kind to me during his illness and in the early days after his death."

Mara tried to match her arm swings to Ashlee's smooth rhythm. "Right now, I don't recall ever being kind in my whole life. And I meant, *present* for you, like you are for me. Even when I resist."

"Resist. Refuse. Rebuff. Restraining order . . ."

"Score one for the trespasser." Mara smiled at the reminder

of how close Ashlee came to being hauled to the station for loitering on her doorstep.

Ashlee's footsteps never wavered. Firm. Confident. High energy. Everything Mara was not.

"I knew you were there for me, even if we didn't communicate often," Ashlee said. "Physical distance isn't the barrier we sometimes think it is."

Eight time zones. "Yes, it is." Ashlee viewed her much more optimistically than Mara viewed herself, apparently.

"Watch your step."

Mara looked down. The sidewalk had heaved, creating a wide, uneven gap. Someone had marked it with orange fluorescent paint to prevent pedestrians from tripping. A more public version of her garage floor. "My point exactly. Sometimes a gap is a danger."

"Yet another reason why we're walking. Especially now—and this is personal experience talking—you can't afford a gap between you and God."

Mara would have ground her back molars if she didn't need her mouth open for breathing. "And you're the gap filler between me and God?"

"Goodness no. I'm the orange paint."

They walked in silence two more blocks.

"You're getting healthier, Mara."

"I don't feel like it."

"Get healthy."

"Get off my back," Mara singsonged.

"Forever friends camp on your back, Mara. We have your back. We call you back. It's a back issue."

Mara loosened the scarf around her neck. "Do we ever get to stop and take a break?"

"In a way. Grief is always there, always making itself known. But then, a grandchild is born or a work of art catches us with its beauty or a guy like Sol makes us laugh and we almost forget that we're in mourning. Almost."

"For the record, I meant while walking. A walking break. But you reminded me of something just now." Did Mara dare go there? Did she dare poke at that additional wound? She hadn't connected it until now. Maybe it would help explain why grieving a husband and son felt heavier than that earlier grief.

"What?"

If I wait long enough, maybe she'll forget I started this thread of conversation. No, she won't. "You were one of the few people I told the story to when Chelsea was pregnant and lost the baby."

"Those were tough days."

"You sent me and Liam a sympathy card. I still have it. I might not have allowed myself to fully embrace that I'll forever mourn the loss of my first grandchild. But you treated it as real."

"It was real."

Chelsea hadn't been ready to be a mom. It had been easier to focus on that truth than on the reality that her daughter had miscarried a child. A tiny child the rest of the world didn't know about. Mara's first grandchild. It had been easier to pick up and go on rather than let her mind linger on what might have been if the child had lived inside her daughter for six more months. The baby would be almost two now.

Mara couldn't afford to entertain the image of a casket smaller than Jeremy's, smaller than an envelope. Or that a casket hadn't been needed, the fetus was still so small.

Mara steeled herself against another layer of pain. "Chelsea better talk to Logan about it before they get too serious. He doesn't know who she is."

"Was. Who she was. Maybe he does. Maybe he's exceptionally good at grace and forgiveness and fresh starts."

Maybe Ashlee already considered him potential stepson

material. That would be weird, wouldn't it? If Ashlee were Chelsea's mother-in-law?

"What's on your mind, Mara?"

Not so great on the quick comebacks these days, Mara surprised herself with, "Relationships, lost and found."

"'I wish I could tell you it gets better. It doesn't. *You* get better.'"

"Bible verse?"

"No, a long-ago comedienne. Joan Rivers. Saw it on social media while I was shivering on your porch this morning."

"It beats what I read in my devotional time yesterday."

"What was that?"

Mara looked to the sky for help in recalling the exact words. "I think it was Isaiah something. 'Their fish rot because of lack of water and die of thirst.'"

"Playing Bible roulette again? Spinning the wheel to see where the marble drops?"

"Maybe."

"We need to talk."

Mara removed her neck scarf and stuffed it into her coat pocket. "Want to know my interpretation?"

"Because that would be a theologically sound approach," Ashlee said, her sarcasm not the least bit veiled. "Go ahead. I'm listening."

"At first I thought God might be trying to get me to empty my garbage and water my plants. But he may have been more concerned that I remember that Liam's efforts with Deep Wells mattered. To a lot of people. I complain about the taste of chlorine in the city water. The people he reached out to might have died of typhoid or cholera if he hadn't intervened."

"Interesting."

Mara dodged another crack in the sidewalk. "I should have gone over there when you called and offered to pay my way a year or two ago."

"Agreed."

She glanced at Ashlee. "Well, obviously, I couldn't, with the kids and the house and my job and my church responsibilities."

"Disagree," Ashlee said.

"But if I could have managed it, I might have gotten a better picture of the people, not the work itself. I understand the work and its importance. I think I missed connecting with the people."

"You got all that from rotting fish?"

"Do I detect an apology for my spin-the-wheel Bible reading technique?"

"No." She shook her head. "But I do have increased respect for God's ability to speak to you despite spin-the-wheel. That's divine love, right there."

Love? Is that what she called it?

Had the air turned cooler again? They'd gone several blocks beyond Ashlee's townhome, which Mara had picked out from the "Hope Lives Here" autumn-themed flag hanging near the front door. Mara abruptly stopped walking. "I need to get home."

"How about if we reach the end of this next block and then turn around?" Ashlee looked at her wrist. "I predict we can get in another two hundred steps if we—"

"Now. Please?"

"Okay."

"When we get to your house, I'll go on from there alone."

"I don't mind—"

"I do."

thirteen

Mara waited on the front porch, shoes tied and lightweight thermos filled with hot tea. The wind found her porch pillars no problem at all to work around. She shuddered at the chill and for what she'd put her friend through in leaving her waiting out here every morning.

She wouldn't blame Ashlee if she didn't show up this morning. Weather forecast notwithstanding, Mara had shown Ashlee enough cold shoulder to put a stop to her incessant attempts to . . . to walk with her. Listen to her. Be there for her.

But there she was, right on time. Dressed in hot pink athletic shoes and a coat to match.

"You're not my orange paint, Ashlee. You're my neon crossing guard."

"I'll have you know these shoes are too big, but they fit my thick socks, which I will be grateful for until we have to switch to boots in another few weeks."

"You don't have to come six blocks to meet me before we even start walking together. I could meet you at your house."

Ashlee smiled. "Yes, I do."

"I'll show up." Mara's voice sounded like Dylan's promises to be on time for his next probation meeting.

"Some days. Yes, you might."

It galled Mara that Ashlee was such a good judge of character.

"But I don't always walk the same route. Let's go the opposite direction today."

That would take them past Logan's house. Maybe his dad just happened to be visiting his son. Solomon hadn't specified where he lived. Mara assumed it was in town somewhere. He was never far.

"What are you planning for Thanksgiving?" Ashlee asked before they reached the sidewalk in front of Mara's glorified ranch-style house.

"Is it wrong if I answer, 'Being thankful both sets of grandparents are either deceased or out of the kids' lives so we don't have to go anywhere?'"

"Mara."

"And that means we can eat delivery pizza?"

"Come on, Mara."

Mara could quit any time. No one was forcing her to walk. "Don't start preaching at me, okay? I'm only here because I knew you'd never give up on me."

"Correct. I won't."

"Preach or give up?"

"Either. Here. Try these." Ashlee drew something from her jacket pocket and handed it to Mara.

"How are those gloves any different than . . . Oh my. Heaven."

"Heated fingers. I had a spare pair."

Mara caught Ashlee's glance. "Or you ordered another pair just for me."

"Po-tay-to, po-tah-to."

"Thanks."

"Thanks? And there you have it," Ashlee said, raising her fists in triumph. "You do have reasons to be thankful."

SMH. Dylan had teased her for weeks when Mara found out it wasn't a text language abbreviation for So Much Hate, but for Shaking My Head. Mara SMH'ed and nudged her friend. "Take a look. That's Logan's house."

"It's a beauty," Ashlee said.

"The only ultra-modern house in this neighborhood. It was unoccupied for a long time. A couple of years, maybe. I think someone bought it intending to flip it and ran out of money or steam or both."

"So Logan fixed it up, then?"

"Not sure," Mara said. "I don't keep up with neighborhood gossip."

"Kudos."

"Logan is one of the worship leaders. Did you know that?"

Ashlee turned back to take another look at the house they'd passed. "What else does he do? Worship leaders don't have money. Everyone knows that. Interesting."

Mara smiled. *Yes, isn't it? You can start practicing what it will be like to introduce yourself as his stepmother, Ashlee.*

"Chelsea seems to be growing up fast," Ashlee said. "She's turned into such a beauty."

"All October, her hair was the color of your shoes."

"Oh. How . . . festive."

"After we heard about her father, I asked her to dye it back close to her original color. She said she couldn't. Then, Jeremy's—And I didn't have the heart. But once in a while, I'd get a random wave of embarrassment that we were a family in mourning and my daughter had this mane of fuchsia hair."

Ashlee squinted. "It wasn't that way at the funeral."

"She dyed it back a few days before the memorial service. I hesitated but asked why she couldn't have done that right after her father died. Do you know what she said?"

"What? Want a juice box?"

"No. She's not a fan."

"I mean you," Ashlee said. "Would you like a juice box? I know you're avoiding the dreaded word *water* these days."

"I have tea. Thanks. Back to the story. Chelsea said, 'I had to wait until after October thirty-first, Mom.'"

"Why?"

"That's what I asked. She said, as if I should have already known, 'Breast Cancer Awareness Month?'"

"Oh, that darling."

"Uh-huh. That's one word for her. Then she added, 'And I lost a bet.'"

"A lot has changed for her in the last few weeks."

Mara had to admit it had. SMG. So Much Grief. "For all of us."

They rounded a corner, the wind now at their backs, which helped. Ashlee checked her wrist monitor and commented, "We're maintaining a great pace. I'm glad the sidewalks are still clear for us."

"I don't envision myself as a mall walker, if that's what you thought we'd move to after the ice and snow hit."

"How's Dylan doing?"

Mara drove her fingers deeper into her warming gloves. "You're going to ignore the mall-walking comment?"

"We'll cross that ice dam when we come to it. Dylan?"

"Clean, as far as I can tell. His random drug screens have all been negative. His probation officer has encouraged him to spend more time with Logan, so Dylan is helping with the sound system at church. I'm surprised they'll let him do that, considering his history."

"I'm surprised God will let any of us serve him, considering our history."

"Speak for yourself."

"I was," Ashlee said. She rolled her shoulders without losing a beat.

"Forgive me if—"

"You are forgiven," Ashlee said as if making a pronouncement.

She unzipped her jacket a couple of inches like she often did at this point in their walks, or conversation.

"I mean you—Ashlee Eldridge—forgive me if I have a hard time thinking your personal history is a problem with God."

She held her arms out, spread eagle, and twirled around completely. "Not anymore, it isn't."

"Have you ever even had a bad word float through your head, much less broken a commandment or pulled one of the kinds of stunts our family seems to be famous for?"

"True confession time?"

"I'm waiting." Mara steeled herself for what heinous revelation the impossibly wonderful Ashlee might confess.

She leaned Mara's direction, conspiratorially. "I once took a dime from the missionary offering."

Mara crossed her arms. It made it harder to walk, but seemed necessary. "What were you? Four?"

"Three. The point is that we all need rescuing from ourselves. For big or little things. It doesn't matter. And believe me, if this really were confession time, I would tell you I've had my share of evil thoughts flit through my brain. Some of them during Robert's illness. Some of them when I was a teen trying to figure things out, like Dylan and Chelsea are now. Our imperfections make it all the more of a miracle that God would love us, much less invite us to serve him."

Mara let her arms fall back into their walking stance. "And that's not preaching?"

"Testimonial," Ashlee said. "Race you to that rock, okay?"

"Nobody said anything about running!" Mara called as she struggled to catch up with her friend. "Need a break, need a break, need a . . . break."

"Breathing will help."

"Easy for you . . . to . . . say. I am not cut out for physical exercise, Ashlee."

"That's why we train. Because it doesn't come naturally."

Mara resisted asking her to explain. It could only lead to some deeply philosophical discussion her brain could not handle right now.

The rock at the entrance to the park was an anomaly in their town. Taller than a two-story building. Flat on top. Alone. Completely out of place in the otherwise bumpless terrain. A photo op for visitors and mischief-making promgoers.

"Let's climb," Ashlee said, already ascending.

"Let's not."

"Handholds and footholds, Mara. That's all you need. Follow my lead."

After this, she would never listen to Ashlee again. She intended to climb only high enough to grab Ashlee's ankle and insist they get themselves back on the ground. But once Mara started, she didn't stop until they were both standing on the plateau at the top.

"Great view, isn't it?" Ashlee said, her face glowing.

"Not a fan of heights."

"Me neither." Ashlee's smile remained firmly in place. "Let's sit."

Mara cringed. "Let's go back down."

"Okay, but that's harder."

"What?"

She was right, big surprise. Mara couldn't see the handholds and footholds as she descended. And she wasn't about to look down. So, clinging to the rock, she felt for each next step, testing the ledges that true rock climbers might have called stairs, and finally felt solid ground beneath her feet.

"Done. I'm done, Ashlee. Heading home."

"Give me a minute to collect myself."

"You? Collect yourself?"

Ashlee pulled two cheese sticks and a drink from her ever-present walking backpack supply kit. She handed one cheese stick to Mara.

"About Thanksgiving." Ashlee drained her juice box with an uncharacteristic slurp at the end. "My house. Noon-ish. Don't worry about bringing anything except Chelsea and Dylan. You know how much I love to entertain."

See, God? If this woman needs rescuing, where does that leave me? "Let me think about it."

Ashlee waited. Apparently she was looking for an alternate answer from Mara.

"I'll talk to the kids and see what they say."

Ashlee shook her head at that one too.

"Can I at least bring a can of cranberry gel? Gel, not sauce?"

"Yes! Yes, you can. Great idea. I hate that stuff."

Ah. A tiny flaw. Comforting.

⁓

For some reason, Mara was hungry at lunchtime after their climb. True hunger hadn't happened for a while. Her hunger-meter had misfired for weeks, causing her to crave nothing at all or anything not good for her and at odd times. Three in the morning. Four thirty in the afternoon. Eleven at night.

But here she was, eating a salad and sitting down to read her Bible without the roulette wheel. *Even I know the Psalms are supposed to be comforting.*

"Ask God to show you something before you start reading," Ashlee had said, which sounded a little *woo-woo*, but Mara couldn't find any real fault with the idea.

"Show me something, Lord." Short and sweet. Ought to do it.

She read for a few minutes, noting encouraging themes and nice words. But nothing stood out until her eyes landed on Psalm 61:1–2.

> Hear my cry, O God;
> listen to my prayer.

From the ends of the earth I call to you,
I call as my heart grows faint;
lead me to the rock that is higher than I.

Faint heart. Barely beating. Fading as the pulse at her grand-mother's neck that grew less and less discernable in her final moments. *From the ends of the earth.* It was entirely possible Liam had been crying out to God in Uganda while Mara cried out on the other side of the world, or that Jeremy cried out in his tortured soul with his mother a few feet away on the other side of the bedroom wall.

Dylan's resolve to stay clean had faded, fainted so many times in the past. Had he ever cried out, "Lead me to the rock that is higher than I"? Is that what was keeping him clean now?

Handholds and footholds, Mara. That's all you need.

New revelation: not all self-talk is unhealthy.

fourteen

The sun's path had changed with the season. The near-winter angle meant its light now fell on places not usually lit or sun-warmed. That included the crystal, heart-shaped Christmas ornament Mara hadn't taken down the year before. It hung by barely visible fishline from a hook above the sliding doors. As rays bore through its facets, spots of intense light danced with abandon on the walls and ceiling. Stirred by forced air from the heat vents, the heart moved, sending the bursts of light flying.

The new angle of the sun also illuminated the spot on the concrete where Jeremy had fallen. Mara watched, fascinated, as the shadows disappeared, replaced by pure light.

Maybe she wouldn't purchase drapes after all. Even if the phenomenon only happened once a year, or twice a year — would she see the same when spring turned to summer? — it would be worth it to watch it happen.

It was a gift that this November, notorious for its leaden skies, had been unusually sun-filled. A record year for sunshine in November. Mara didn't take that for granted. If she sat at Ashlee's Thanksgiving table with only one thing for which she was grateful, it would be this repeated pattern of sunny days and the way it chased shadows from the place where Jeremy breathed his last.

Full-on winter was around the corner. But she'd seen the sun-replacing-shade phenomenon. Had captured it with her camera. Had pointed it out to Dylan and Chelsea when they were home on weekend mornings.

Not that they were home much at all these days. They'd both gotten part-time jobs and were somehow raising their grades in spite of the hours spent at work and their volunteer hours at church. Logan invited Chelsea to sing on the worship team. Mara had heard her sing along with the radio or YouTube at home and in the school choir, which Mara assumed was Chelsea's attempt at an easy grade, but not like this.

She'd only heard her daughter on the team one Sunday so far, but Mara cried through the whole service. Her beautiful daughter with something that looked a lot like joy on her face. That clear voice blending with the other vocalists. The way Logan's every interaction with her was respectful and . . . cherishing.

Had any guy ever cherished her daughter before? Other than Liam? He'd missed the last three miserable years, but before that, in her early and midteens, he'd done everything in his power to make her feel treasured. She'd walked away from it, running to other arms rather than theirs. *Liam, you should have been there last Sunday. You would have been so proud. And relieved.*

The relationship between Logan and Chelsea was happening too fast by any parent's standards. But it wasn't PDA and googly eyes and whispering behind Mara's back. It was . . . sweet. Sweet, bordering on holy, two descriptors she never anticipated using with her daughter.

Dylan and Chelsea might actually graduate. The house might empty sooner than she expected. She'd never know now, but she suspected Liam would not have been content with one four-year stint building wells. On the hardest days, she imagined that after her two oldest left home for lives of their own—disturbing as she'd once thought those lives might be—if Liam did sign up for another four years, at least she'd have Jeremy. His bright personality would help hold her together. Now the loss of both Liam and Jeremy spelled a very empty future.

Almost noon. Time to go give thanks and force herself to eat.

She grabbed the cranberry gel, still in the cans, and her car keys. Dylan was working until noon and Ashlee had asked Chelsea to come over early to help her in the kitchen.

Mara hadn't minded being left out of that task. Ashlee was a good influence on Chelsea. Plus, Mara had been able to watch the sun chase shadows from the frosty patio.

—

"A table set for six, Ashlee? I thought it was going to be the four of us."

Mara set the cans on the counter next to the sink and dug in the drawer she thought most likely to hold Ashlee's can opener. Guessed right. "Please tell me I don't have to share an awkward meal with homeless strangers."

"Only one of us is homeless," a voice behind her said. A deep voice. Sol.

"And that's temporary. Right, Dad? It's tem-po-rary?" Logan laughed and deposited two contest-worthy pies next to the cans of cranberry gel.

Sol was genuinely homeless? Sleeping on his son's couch? In addition to his being "between jobs"? *Recalculating. Recalculating. You are not marriage material for my forever friend.* But Ashlee's eyes lit up when he came in the room. Although that didn't say much. Ashlee's eyes stayed lit most of the time. She didn't own a dimmer switch.

Thanksgiving dinner at Ashlee's moved from awkward to

awkwarder in under a minute. It had been a stretch for Mara to agree to a Thanksgiving meal at Ashlee's when it was a party of four, and Mara had given birth to two of those four. Now the Coppernall men had invaded. How soon could she excuse herself?

To be fair, she didn't know their whole story. To be unnerved, they also didn't know hers.

Okay, Mara. Think about this. Logan, who you first met at one of Dylan's probationary check-ins, has a thing for your daughter. But said daughter seems to be managing her grief way better than you are. And said daughter is also behaving herself in school, found a job, helps out around the house more . . . What's wrong with this picture? Nothing. Except you cannot sanction a relationship if you know practically zero about this guy or his temporarily homeless father. More investigation required.

She'd stay. But not because she wanted to be all thankful and hospitable. She had to gather intel. Which seemed like a lot of work to require from a woman who sometimes had to ask her friend to tie her sneakers for her.

"Mara?"

Oh. Someone was talking to her. What had she missed? "Yes?"

"It's a simple question, hon," Ashlee said. "Sol's filling goblets. Do you want sparkling cranberry juice or water?"

That is not a simple question. "Juice, please." *I can't face water yet. No offense, Liam.*

———

He's married. That has to be it.

Second round of the mashed potatoes and the Coppernall men had yet to spill a drop of anything juicy Mara could use against them. Imagination took over. *Sol is still married but his wife kicked him out. He's bunking with his son for the time*

125

being until he can afford an apartment of his own or he and the Mrs. reconcile, but what are the odds of that if he doesn't have a job and considers himself "retired" from the police force despite obviously being no more than four or five years older than Mara? Who retires that young? Unless they're compelled to leave.

And how could that scenario have played out? Mara had to know. Sol's fingers lingered just a little too long when he took the potato bowl from Ashlee. Their eyes met. Both smiled. *Ashlee, DO YOU KNOW HE'S MARRIED? Or might be. Or not.*

Sometimes a person has to come right out with it, in a clever, undetectable way. She waited for a break in the conversation that had been subdued but constant. "Logan, tell us about your mother."

Every fork around the table stilled.

"Moooom," Chelsea said, eyes wide.

"Did I say something wrong?"

Logan laid aside his utensils and wiped his mouth with his napkin, which Ashlee had probably hand-monogrammed. "Not wrong at all. It's a legit question. I'm not uncomfortable talking about it."

Rats.

Solomon, however, did squirm in his seat. Maybe she'd tapped into something important.

"Mom hasn't been in my life since I was a toddler."

"Ran away from home?" Mara knew that scenario all too well.

"Mother!"

"Actually, Mrs. Jacobs, that's not far from how it happened. I was too young to realize, of course." Logan picked at an invisible thread on the hem of his napkin.

Sol stared at his plate. A small part of Mara regretted having opened the can of worms. Maybe a not so small part of her. Too late now. They were crawling all over the tablecloth.

"I suppose I should pick up the story from there," Sol said.

Dylan stood. "I have to get back to work. Mom, can I take your car? Mine's almost out of gas. I have an empty can I can fill up on my way home."

Ashlee's face looked stricken. "We haven't gotten to dessert."

"Logan, man, can you save me a piece of the pecan pie?"

"My pleasure. I have a spare at home if we run out here."

"See you Sunday?"

"Sunday. Both services, if you can."

"Will do."

Their banter flowed so easily. They liked each other. This peer counseling idea had turned into genuine friendship. Or was that Logan's "my job is to be nice to you" persona?

A couple of months ago . . . Okay, the truth serum cranberry juice was kicking in. A few years ago, she wouldn't have been this cynical. She'd been burned by a hot African sun that had evaporated her husband's interest in their family. She'd drowned in her own muddy river of managing everything on her own, including these two children whose issues she was at least partly responsible for, and the child she was wholly responsible for being unable to keep alive.

"There's nothing you could have done," Ashlee and a dozen professionals would probably counsel her.

Oh yes, there was. I could have paid more attention. Recognized the depth of his pain. Questioned him about his letter to his father while there was still time to talk it through. Not let him stay in his room. Noticed he was gone from the house. Followed him. Stopped him. The list is more than six pages long so far. It'll grow.

Third helpings of Ashlee's world-famous mashed potatoes were abandoned in favor of pie. Conversation on hold, each of the five remaining chose a combo of pie and toppings and retired, as they say, to Ashlee's living room with tea or coffee.

Mara hadn't been there when Ashlee decided on this townhouse, hadn't even known she was moving so close. But if she had been consulted, she would have picked this place as the perfect spot for her forever friend. So many windows. So much light. Light gray walls, white trim, turquoise and coral accents. An only-she-could-make-this-work blend of modern amenities and carefully curated antiques. Curious art pieces on the walls and resting on low tables or bookcase shelves. It was so her.

"Another piece of pie, Mara?" Sol asked.

She hadn't remembered eating the first one. "No, thank you."

Thanksgiving Day. Why hadn't the guys complained about missing the football games? They hadn't asked where Ashlee hid her TV.

"You two aren't fans of football?" Mara asked in an attempt to say something both relevant and appropriate.

Logan sat on the dove-gray couch with his dad and Chelsea, close enough to jostle his father. "Big fans."

"We're also big fans of the ability to record the games so we can watch them later, so we don't miss time with—"

Family. He was about to say family. And if he did, Mara was crouched, ready to spring.

"—new friends. Mara, you asked about Logan's mom. She was a single parent."

Huh?

"And had a pretty serious relationship with heroin."

"I was a crack baby," Logan volunteered.

"I busted her half a dozen times or more, when I was on the force. One of the hardest—"

He choked up. The man choked up. Logan put his arm around his dad's shoulders, son comforting father.

Sol cleared his throat. "She'd been clean for a couple of years,

I thought. But one day, I found her on the floor of her housing project apartment. Her two-year-old—"

Logan raised his hand.

"—had fallen asleep against her body, wearing nothing but a diaper that had to have been three days old. Who knows how long it had been since the kid had eaten? There's more than one reason why I hate needles," Sol said, his voice nearly disappearing. "His mom didn't make it back from that one."

"Dad jumped through all kinds of hoops so he could apply for guardianship and eventually serve as my foster parent," Logan said.

"By the time they awarded him to me, I knew I wanted to go straight for adoption. That was a mess of legal red tape."

Try getting your husband's body home from a foreign country. Mara, you should be ashamed of yourself. This is his story. "But you succeeded?" Finally, a decent sentence out of her mouth.

"We made it work for a while with my mom helping out and good but expensive childcare options, although as you can imagine, Logan's needs were challenging."

"Crack baby," Logan reminded.

"Eventually, I quit the force. I'd been pretty frugal, but savings only lasted so long. Took on odd jobs."

"Tell them about the time you worked as a makeup artist."

"Logan."

"Come on." Logan leaned forward. "It's hysterical. Most clowns do their own makeup. But this one time, Dad got hired to help with—"

"I think that's plenty of details for now, Logan," Sol said. He patted his son on the knee. "Mrs. Jacobs simply wanted to know about your mom."

Logan turned first to Chelsea, then to Mara. "I would have loved to have had a mom who cared as much as you do, Mrs. Jacobs. I'm glad Chelsea has you."

Caring? That's the dominant feature the young man sees in me? I'm speechless. And internal-thought-less.

He wasn't wrong that she cared. Deeply. More deeply than any Deep Well. Would any of the last three years have knocked her so flat if she hadn't cared so much? *God, can you do anything with that? Start with the fact that I care excessively and bring me around to something I can live with? Something you can bless?*

fifteen

*D*umbest thing she'd ever done—recently—was tell Sol and Logan she didn't need a ride and certainly didn't need anyone to walk her home.

Not only did she miss out on gathering more intel that would aid her matchmaking efforts between Sol and Ashlee, but those few blocks felt like miles when mist started to freeze on the sidewalks. The boulevard of grass between the sidewalk and curb offered her a little traction. But it was treacherous going made more complicated by the mist in her eyes and freezing her cheeks.

Chelsea had stayed to help Ashlee with the last of the dishes. Logan promised to get her home safely after they grabbed coffee downtown. Wait. Where was Sol?

Across the street, about a half block behind her. He waved. She shivered and hunkered down, watching her feet for uneven ground and now-glossy orange paint.

Ashlee and Robert had often talked about adoption. That part of Sol's story must have perked Ashlee's ears up. Still had to investigate the homeless factor.

Sneaky of Ashlee to invite the Coppernalls to Thanksgiving dinner under the pretense of helping the grieving Jacobs family ease back into society. That part hadn't turned out so well.

But Ashlee got to spend quality time with Sol. She must be very pleased with herself. Those two were the answer to each other's prayers. Sweet.

Mara slipped on a patch of sleet-pebbles, but caught herself.

"You okay?" Sol called from across the street.

"Yes, I'm fine," she hollered back, sticking her hands into her coat pockets.

"Need any help?"

"No."

After a short pause, she heard, "I didn't think so."

So, Sol was trying to impress Ashlee by making sure her friend got home safely? Chivalry was not dead.

She turned into her driveway and said "goodbye" over her shoulder, should Sol be paying attention. Two footsteps later, she was flat on her face in the driveway. The good news was that the ice on the driveway gave her nose a head start to keep the swelling down.

Before she could get a firm grip to stand, Sol was at her side. "I looked away for one second," he said.

"Yeah, me too." Mara's eyes started to water. She touched the tip of her nose.

"Anything else hurt?" he asked.

"Knees."

"It's hard to break your fall with your hands in your pockets." He hadn't said it unkindly, but it irritated her nonetheless.

"Hard to keep your concentration," she countered, "when you're worried that the guy across the street might miss that broken piece of sidewalk."

He chuckled. "You might want to put some non-concrete-sized ice on that right away. Your nose looks kind of . . . bulgie."

Nice. Helpful. So helpful.

He checked her over. "Can you bend your knees?"

"Can *you* do cartwheels? Sorry. Trying to keep the mood—*oof!*—light."

He offered his arm to help her stand. "Yes, I actually can. But not now. It's sleeting out here. Let's get you inside."

"I'm fine. I don't need help."

"So you said. Frequently."

Chivalrous, but not without your own version of snark, huh? "I have a phone call to make, then I'll sit in a chair with ice on my nose and knees, if necessary, *Doctor* Solomon. Thanks, but I'm fine."

She unlocked the front door and let herself in before he could protest. Once a policeman, always a policeman. Always protecting, whether it was welcomed or not. Mara decided to text rather than call Dylan to let him know how bad the roads were. Then she texted the same message to Chelsea.

Chelsea responded right away. *"I know. Logan's dad called him. How's your nose?"*

And this is why she didn't need people in her life right now.

—

Definitely bulgie. Good way to describe her nose. Bulgie and red. But it didn't look or feel broken. Her knees were bruised but no protruding bones and the skin wasn't scuffed. With one more layer of chenille throw, she might be warm again. But the extra blankets were in Jeremy's second closet. And she wasn't about to go in—

She could do this.

Mara stood in the hall outside his room and gathered little bits of courage the winds of grief had scattered in their last gust. She reached for the knob but instead planted her hands high on either doorjamb and leaned her forehead on the door.

"Jeremy, it was a really nice meal at Ashlee's. You've never met her. But you would have liked her. Except it would have been like having a second mom. A neat one. Who cooks and does crafts and things. And doesn't mess up."

She lifted her head, then let it fall back against the door.

"Son, I'm sorry I laughed this afternoon. It wasn't because I've forgotten you. Or your father. I can never forget either of you." She sniffed back tears. "I don't know how to do this, how to carry this ache and carry on."

Mara bumped her forehead three times on the door, each time jarring the nerve endings in her nose. "I wish you were here so I could ask you how you figured I'd manage now. Everybody expects the baby of the family to have a hard time growing up, but you were more mature than I am in a lot of ways. You left me in the lurch here, buddy. I can't . . . carry this ache . . . and carry on."

She breathed that way for a while, but her nose didn't appreciate pointing down. She stepped back from the door and stared at the wood, shivering for lack of a blanket to wrap around her shoulders. For lack of a little boy's arms around her.

"I'm going to go now. I think I'll just stay cold. I probably deserve it. No, that's ridiculous. Or a sign that I really am going insane." She turned the knob before she could talk herself out of it, snatched a blanket from the shelf, and closed the door again behind her.

The scent of her son was slowly fading from the room.

Nothing she could do would stop it.

No school tomorrow. Thanksgiving break. Maybe Chelsea would help her pack up a few of Jeremy's favorite things to keep in storage. If Mara had her way, the room would stay just as Jeremy left it because he would be using it every day. But she didn't get to have her way. On most subjects, it seemed.

She could test-run the idea. Would putting his belongings in air-tight, water-tight containers in the basement allow her to envision anything and anyone but her youngest in that room?

Art. Or music. Or the ironing board. Maybe a place to toy with graphic design again. Anything except a shrine to a lost child.

Mara's phone dinged. A text from Ashlee. *"No walking tomorrow. Different plan."*

Mara already had a plan but read on.

"Wear decent clothes."

She glanced down at her gray heathered slouchy sweater and worn jeans. "I'm sure she didn't mean to offend you like that."

"Define decent," she texted back.

The three dots that signaled Ashlee was typing kept Mara from looking away from the screen. Eventually, the message popped up. *"Business casual. Have anything with a little color in it?"*

Not anymore. She didn't have to be told the version of blankness she wore daily didn't qualify as shabby chic or vintage and certainly not Velveteen Rabbit love-worn. It felt garish to wear bright colors, as if they stung both eyes and soul. And yes, she found bright colors offensive on others too, which was why she wasn't entirely comforted that Chelsea had drifted from her gothic—but not in a cool way—all black to jeans and flattering blouses with more color than Mara had seen her gravitate toward since she'd started middle school.

Before then, Chelsea's clothing choices had been more related to what Mara purchased for her than Chelsea's own preferences. *Something wrong there. Did I really dress her childhood self in styles and colors I liked, rather than considering what she liked? Out of love, of course. Or I thought it was.*

Ashlee had subtly suggested that Mara look online for some wardrobe updates. She'd pointed out a few things she thought Mara would look good in. *Because obviously I can't choose for myself?*

But I did. I chose faded. Drab. Lifeless colors, although I suppose some gray things do have life in them. Mice and . . . Maybe just rodents. Oh. Elephants. There. My fashion sense? Rodents with a hint of elephants. Nice.

Ashlee's subtle suggestion had actually started with her observing, "Mara, your color's not good."

"Maybe I'm anemic. I'll add it to the list."

"Not that color," Ashlee said. "The colors you choose to wear. Not good. Not . . . flattering on you either."

"Some would call them classic neutrals."

"That's the life you want to live?" Ashlee said. "Neutral? Is that how you numb away the pain?"

Mara shot back, "The gall of you to say that."

Ashlee retorted, "Even gall has a color. It's not beautiful, but it's a color."

"What are you trying to get at?"

"Remember the scene in *The Wizard of Oz* when the black and white scenes from Kansas suddenly exploded in technicolor?" Ashlee asked.

"I do. We watched that movie how many times in a row at Grandma Lou's?"

"When did that happen? The color? It wasn't just skinny striped leggings under the house that let Dorothy know they weren't in Kansas anymore. It was the flood of color. Because faded is lifeless and color is life."

Thinking on that conversation now, Mara realized how she'd been clinging to neutral. And why.

She'd held on to bravery for a brief moment, imagining herself able to empty Jeremy's sock drawer and clear the action figures and Lego creations from his shelving unit. But even though she'd have to dress "decently" and leave the house, she was willing to abandon the too-hard task with no more persuasion than Ashlee's brief *"Pick you up at ten."*

"Where are we headed?"

"Job interviews," Ashlee said before Mara's seat belt buckle clicked.

"What? Ashlee, unlock the door. Can I do that from over here? I am not going for a job interview."

"Oh, good. Me either. I thought the idea might soften the blow of where we're really headed."

Soften the blow? This could not be survivable. And in decent clothes, to boot.

"We're headed to an art gallery open house."

Mara sat for a moment, allowing her pulse to return to normal. "I might actually like that." She glanced at her black slacks and considered the black turtleneck she wore. "Do I need to change?"

"We all do, hon."

"Change my *clothes*."

"Oh. Let me see what you're wearing."

Mara opened her coat so Ashlee could see the only slightly worn sweater.

"You don't own any jewelry? Necklace or something?"

"Ashlee."

"Not to worry. I carry spares."

"Of course, you do. Where?"

"Can you reach my purse in the backseat while I drive?"

From the three options in the zippered pouch in Ashlee's purse, Mara chose an agate-looking pendant hanging on a leather strap. The agate slice was the size of an English muffin.

"Bold choice," Ashlee said, "but I like it."

"Bold? My other two options were orchid or Christmassy."

"'Tis the season."

"Please don't remind me." Mara paused. "Oh no. It's Black Friday. What was I thinking?"

"You were thinking how smart it is of your friend to take you somewhere other than a shopping center, big-box store, or mall today."

"Ashlee, it'll be a madhouse out there. As in, people everywhere."

Her driver braked hard. Stop sign. "Would I do that to you?"

"You made me climb a rock. You made me eat Thanksgiving dinner with . . . with . . . people."

Ashlee stepped on the accelerator. "Over the years, I've found that sharing dinner with pandas or koalas is conversationally less stimulating."

"Not funny."

"I wasn't trying to be. I was trying to offer you a safe place for the holiday yesterday. Your kids. Me. A young man who is obviously smitten with your daughter but a gentleman at the same time."

"And his father."

"Yes. Solomon."

Mara waited a tick. Would Ashlee reveal a budding interest?

"And pie," Ashlee said. "Don't forget the pie."

"I haven't. I'm sorry." Mara huffed. "I don't like myself very much at the moment, and sometimes . . ."

"You don't have to finish that sentence."

"I think I do."

"Can you save it, then? We're here."

The "here" was a cottage three blocks off Main Street in the historic downtown district. A simple but elegant "Art & Such" sign hung from a wooden pole in the front yard. The same design was etched into the frosted glass on the entrance door. Side parking beyond the building meant they made their way from car to entrance via a winding brick pathway that in spring and summer likely exploded with color. Now, all the leaves were brown, and the sky was gray, but Mara could imagine it in its glory.

The women were greeted inside by a hostess who took their coats and offered them clear glass mugs of hot apple cider. The hostess indicated they could start anywhere in the converted cottage, but recommended they begin with the exhibit just to her right in what had once been a small parlor.

Quiet background music did not assert itself but served as the accompaniment it was meant to be in that hushed environment.

"You let me know," Ashlee whispered, "when this Black Friday crowd gets to you."

"Again, very funny." They were practically alone in the gallery. "Private showing?"

"No. Good timing. Come look at this."

In the first room, at least, the images were all watercolors. Winter scenes. Delicate, but communicating both the harshness and beauty of the season. A faded red barn with a fieldstone foundation stood firm against blizzard winds. A stand of birch trees in snow, one lone cardinal providing the only break in an almost exclusively white and gray setting. A scene viewed through a frosted window.

"Did you notice this?" Ashlee said as they stood before the window watercolor.

"Notice what?" Mara leaned in.

"The petal on the windowsill. A rose petal. The scene would have been different months earlier, but the artist left a reminder of life."

Mara considered what might have been in the artist's mind. "Or death. Dead, fallen petal."

"Can't have death without life first," Ashlee said.

sixteen

*E*ach room in the Art & Such exhibit displayed the work of a different local artist, none of whom Mara had been acquainted with. She bit back regret. She'd distanced herself so far from the art community that she was unaware of the sculptors, painters, quilters, and watercolor artists in her hometown.

The newcomer—Ashlee—had been the one to serve as a bridge. As always.

They took their time strolling through room after room of wonder. A colorful blown glass ornament display. Tabletop-sized quilts with impossibly tiny stitches. Jewelry made from vintage silverware. Intricately carved birds.

Everything about the gallery open house soothed. Including the joy of watching Ashlee connect with the art.

"Wait, Mara! You have to see this!"

"It's lovely."

"Not just lovely. Take a closer look."

From a typical viewing distance, the large oil painting evoked deep emotion. A portrait of a well-wrinkled woman holding a sleeping infant. Her grandchild? Mara swallowed hard. She cleared her throat. "Beautifully expressive."

Ashlee tugged on her arm and drew Mara closer until both

of their faces were within six inches of the canvas. "Look at the tiny brushstrokes. Each one is tear-shaped."

A single sob escaped Mara's lips. Every brushstroke. The woman's thin, wispy gray hair. The infant's translucent skin. The baby's barely-there eyebrows. The woman's eyes.

"Those are your eyes, Mara."

"Thanks for making me feel young, Ashlee."

"The color. The shape. Those could be your eyes."

They did look like what stared back at her in the mirror every morning. Tired. Blanked with pain. "Let's go."

"Not yet." Ashlee pointed to the placard affixed to the wall listing info about the artist, the price, a short description of the artist's intent, and the title—"Tears for the One Who Did Not Live." She sighed. "Isn't that precious?"

"What's wrong with you? How could you do that to me?" All the peace Mara had collected as they'd walked through each room of the cottage now faded, dissipated, leaving hurt and anger in its place. She pivoted to face the opposite wall, lacking the will to search for the exit.

"Mara, I don't understand. I thought it would mean something to you that an artist found a way to express your pain, your loss. All your losses. The images that move us are sometimes painted with tears."

"It was a mistake to come here."

"Was it?"

The ceiling of this second-floor room showed evidence of water damage. *How fitting. That's what water often does—damage.*

Ashlee slid a velvet-covered ottoman toward her. "Sit."

"I'm not listening to your advice anymore." Her voice shook like it had in the hospital.

"I'll meet you downstairs. You sit here until you're done imagining you're the only one who feels the way you do. And I said that with love," Ashlee added. "And history. And my own waterworks."

Mara sat facing the portrait, taking in the finished product, imagining the artist on tear-shaped brushstroke number 3,602. Leaning in to add a baby eyelash. Persisting through her aching back and cramped hand to deepen the lines around the woman's mouth. With oil pigment tears.

Black Friday.

And Mara was about to spend four hundred dollars of Liam's life insurance on a painting.

⁓

Mara stuffed the receipt for the artwork in her purse before she could stare at the numbers long enough for buyer's regret to take hold.

What was the phrase? Feed a starving artist?

Time to feed the starving art lovers.

Finding a spot for lunch was easier than they anticipated. Restaurants weren't the draw the day after Thanksgiving. Ashlee and Mara chose a new Thai place neither had been to before. Not that Mara had gotten out much in recent years. Shrimp pad thai won both of their attentions from the hundreds of offerings on the menu. They added rice paper summer rolls to their order and sipped hot green tea while waiting for their food.

"You wouldn't think I'm stalking you if I started to come to your church, would you, Mara? I haven't settled in anywhere yet."

"Are you kidding? I'd love it." *And you'd get to keep an eye on Solomon Coppernall.*

"I only know the pastor from the memorial service, but he handled that so compassionately."

Had he? Mara couldn't remember any of his words.

"And with your Chelsea singing on the worship team . . ."

"Yeah, that was a surprise."

"It sounds as if what they're planning for Christmas is going to be powerful."

Ashlee must have gathered details while she and Chelsea were finishing the Thanksgiving cleanup. Mara hadn't seen much of Chelsea. Between school, her job, the worship team, and a certain worship leader . . .

"I'm not looking forward to Christmas, as you can imagine, Ashlee."

"This will be my eighth Christmas without Robert. It's still hard."

"Oh, that's encouraging." Mara refilled their teacups from the squatty cast iron teapot.

"You know that you and the kids are welcome to spend Christmas at my place, don't you?"

Her eighth Christmas without Robert, and two years of his grueling illness before that. "Is the invitation for your sake or ours?"

"Can't it be both?"

~

"Do you have a plan for where you're going to hang the portrait?" Ashlee asked on the drive home, her voice sober.

"No. But I had to purchase it." Even now, she was tempted to pull back the heavy kraft paper in which it was encased to drink in its powerful message one more time.

"Understood."

Mara loosened the place where her seat belt crossed her heart. "Ashlee?"

"Yes?"

"Could it hang at your house for a while?"

"My house?"

"I want to be able to see it when I need to, but I don't know that I'm ready for it to be right there in front of me day in and day out." Dumb question to ask. She should have thought of the "where are you going to hang it?" dilemma before she pulled out her credit card.

"Are you serious?" Ashlee asked.

"It's not that I haven't imposed on your last nerve of friendship before."

"True."

Mara shook her head. "I wasn't thinking clearly. Clearly, I wasn't."

"I know just the spot for it."

"Where?"

"On the wall in my reading corner," Ashlee said. "Perfect for it. You'll have to go there intentionally when you want to. But few others will see it."

"It's a private thing."

Ashley nodded. "For me too."

Oh. *Oh, Ashlee.* No children, despite her heart for them. And Mara had just asked her to hang life-sized childless tears in her home. *Mara, it's time to start thinking about somebody other than yourself as your default.*

Mara leaned against the restraint of her seat belt. "Ashlee, you don't have to do this. I wasn't thinking."

"Please don't take this privilege away from me. That's the child I wanted too."

Heartbreak has so many versions. Between Mara and Ashlee, they might have a corner on a high percentage of them. "Can we pull over?" Mara asked.

"Um, yes." Ashlee swung her car into a convenience store parking area. "While you're in there, would you grab me a bottled wa—a coffee? Any flavor. Any size. Doesn't matter."

"I asked you to pull over because hugging a driver while the car's moving is ill-advised."

～

Snow. Inevitable. A foreteller of a weather-word that would show up on her app off and on for the next five months, minimum. Its first appearance of the season, though, always brought with it a sense of wonder. It did today too.

They'd managed to get the portrait safely tucked in Ashlee's house before the precipitation started. For more than one reason, Mara volunteered to walk home. First snow was a big draw. Snow-kissed air. And she needed time to process a few things before she walked back into the house she'd allowed to grow so stale.

She turned the corner for the last two blocks and stopped, heart in her throat. Too-familiar red and blue lights flashed. Unless her depth perception was wonky, the lights were parked at her address. *Dylan, what have you done now?*

Mara, what have you done now? Assumed the worst about your son. A practiced response. But unfair. Until proven guilty.

The snowflakes had morphed from beauty to obstacle, obstructing her vision, keeping her from running. She felt the agate necklace thump against her chest as she walked as fast as she could to get home.

One block left. She dug her phone out of her purse and texted Ashlee. *"Pray!"*

The screen she'd ignored for the past couple of hours showed multiple recent messages from Chelsea. *"Mom, where are you? Dylan's in trouble."*

Sol greeted her at the door. Sol?

"What's going on? What are you doing here? Where's Dylan?"

He held her by the shoulders to slow her progress, which she did not appreciate. "Where is Dylan?"

"He and a couple of officers are having a chat. Mara, I think they're probably going to take him to the station for more questioning. Do you have a lawyer?"

"What did he do? I don't understand. Can I talk to him?" She shrugged off Sol's hands on her shoulders using a self-defense technique Liam had insisted she learn.

*Liam, you have missed two heartbreaking events already.
I'm . . . I'm glad you were spared all this.*

"I'm sure you'll have a chance to get his side of the story
later."

"Where's Chelsea?"

"She called Logan when the police showed up. I was at Logan's working on a project and thought maybe I could run
some interference for Dylan. Unfortunately, he's easy to profile
because of his history. And law enforcement isn't known for its
good grip on the concept of grace."

"Sol"—she worked to temper her rising frustration—"where
. . . is . . . Chelsea?"

"The officers wouldn't let her stay. So she's over at Logan's
now."

Mara's eyebrows must have raised without her conscious
thought, because Sol was quick to add, "With the rest of the
worship team and a couple of her friends from church. They're
a good support for her right now."

"What is it Dylan did to cause all this commotion? And why
does he need a lawyer?" His drug possession convictions had
been handled by public defenders. This was the same Dylan
who these days had his act together better than she did in some
regards. It made no sense.

He was the one who had talked her into turning off the light
in Jeremy's room.

"It's not the electric bill I'm concerned about, Mom," he'd
said.

No, you never have been.

His face had softened with a tenderness she'd rarely seen.
"It's you. It's like the light went out inside you, so you're trying to make up for it with LED bulbs. Seriously. You thought
that would work?"

That Dylan. That's the one being grilled in the family room.

Ashlee flew through the door before Sol could answer Mara.

The narrow foyer grew more claustrophobic. "What's happening?"

"I didn't mean you needed to come over. I needed you to pray."

"I am and can do that here too. Fill me in, somebody."

Mara staggered against the wall. Too much. It was all too much.

"What I know," Sol said, "is that Dylan found the guy who gave Jeremy the drugs that killed him."

"What? Where?"

"We'll get all those details later. Mara, the kid is in the hospital. It looks like Dylan messed him up pretty bad. Nothing life-threatening, but a nineteen-year-old pounding on a twelve-year-old . . ."

"It was a twelve-year-old?" The student at the memorial service who apologized to her? That kid?

"What do I do? What do I do now?" Mara's head swam with confusion.

"Keep loving Dylan. He's going to need it." Sol glanced at Ashlee. "Pray that none of the boy's injuries are permanent, and that the kid confesses. It's a big ask, but God's a big God."

"I need to get a lawyer for Dylan," Mara said. "Where do I start? Wait. Doesn't Dylan know he shouldn't say anything without a lawyer present?"

Sol dipped his head. "Mara, he was already talking when I got here. And he refused to stop when I told him to."

seventeen

Mara escaped to her bathroom for a few minutes after the officers left with Dylan in tow and in handcuffs. The hardware seemed excessive, but that might have been her opinion because she loved that kid despite his not always using his brain as it was designed. Rarely.

Except lately. He'd turned a corner. He was finding his footing. All that was gone now.

She leaned on the bathroom vanity top and tilted toward the mirror. "Do you have a personal vendetta against me, God? Is that it? This family can't catch a break."

It could have been her amped-up blood pressure or the headache throbbing behind her eyes again, but she thought she heard a Voice say, "Do you have a personal vendetta against *me*?"

No.

A small and tentative no.

Time to rejoin the troops in the kitchen. On a whim, she dug in the vanity drawer where she kept a few items of jewelry and extracted a beaded necklace Liam had sent her for their twentieth anniversary, for which he'd been AWOL. The beads, he'd said, had been made from recycled plastic bags and bottles by village women entrepreneurs. Most of the colored beads were brighter than Mara was used to wearing. But several of them picked up colors in the agate English muffin on a leather string around her neck. She looped the beaded necklace around her wrist several times until it fit like a bracelet. *There. Liam, you and I are going to the police station to check up on our son.*

After the red and blue lights left her driveway earlier—she'd sure field some phone calls from neighbors now!—Sol had said he might be able to help if he accompanied Mara and Ashlee to the station. Ashlee had insisted Mara not change out of her "decent" clothes. Standing up for her child in yoga pants and her favorite faded sweatshirt would not help Dylan's cause, in Ashlee's opinion. The situation called for business casual.

So Mara tamed a few stray hairs, brushed more from her shoulders, straightened her English muffin and plastic beads, and exited her bathroom sanctuary to face the music.

Or lack of it. She would have given anything for a moment of the kind of peace she'd felt in the gallery, the serenity of the calming music and stunning art. Instead, she and her friends were headed to the police station, a route she knew all too well.

She'd probably pay dearly for her evil thoughts. A small part of her was proud that Dylan had defended his brother, had acted—even with his fists—out of love for Jeremy, and maybe even to keep other kids like Jeremy from the same fate. A small part of her. To compensate, she sent up a quick prayer for the young boy lying in a hospital bed because her Dylan couldn't control his rage.

Zero points for that prayer. *Good thing God doesn't use the point system.* One of Ashlee's lines.

"Something isn't adding up," Sol was in the middle of saying when Mara returned to the kitchen.

"Lots of things aren't adding up," Mara said. "What are you thinking?"

"Dylan's story is that he punched the boy in the nose," Sol said. "And that would explain the blood on Dylan's shirt and the swelling in his hand."

Lord, another disturbing mental image I have to live with? Blood on his shirt?

"Granted, still assault," Sol added.

"Did he go back for another round?" Ashlee asked. "Sorry, Mara, for even thinking that."

"Something's not adding up." Sol shook his head.

The three left the house with heavy hearts and no answers. Mara rode in the backseat of Ashlee's SUV, texting Chelsea the latest, the short version, unsure she could hold her voice steady enough to explain it in a phone call. Chelsea begged to go with them to the police station. Mara thumbed words she never imagined using with her daughter. "Need you and Logan and the team there praying more than anything."

Chelsea replied with a crying face emoji and a thumbs-up. Strange combination, but what wasn't these days?

At the station, Sol seemed to intuitively know that Mara needed to take the lead in checking at the desk for information about her son. They were told to wait. And where. Not unexpectedly, they weren't the only people waiting.

Sol slipped away at some point. Part of the brother/sisterhood of law enforcement and ex–law enforcement, he chatted with the desk sergeant, who invited another officer to join their conversation. Ashlee and Mara had abandoned their own limp small talk in favor of watching Sol's interactions, although they couldn't hear what he was saying from that distance.

When he returned to the torture chamber of waiting, Mara asked what they'd been talking about.

"I can't interfere in any way, but I shared a hunch I had. I don't know if they'll run with it or not. God's got this."

"God gave you and Ashlee a double dose of confidence about that. I was shorted," Mara said.

"Handholds and footholds, Mara. That's all you need," Ashlee said. "Standing on the rock."

"Slipping off the rock."

Sol and Ashlee exchanged glances.

"We won't let that happen," he said.

Mara sat between them, which was awkward on more than one level. It wouldn't hurt those two to sit side by side. Plus, this way, Mara was surrounded by faith-talkers and those overly endowed with hope. It made her look like a slice of expired lunch meat between two pieces of fancy herbed bread. Homemade.

After an hour, Mara had exhausted her Google search for local lawyers. How was a person supposed to select a lawyer online? From a slick-looking website? Who had the best headshot? The fine print? *Lowlifes need not apply.* No website said that, specifically, but some law firms definitely targeted the rich and famous.

Here goes another big chunk of the life insurance money. If she hadn't just tamed her hair, and if Ashlee wouldn't have stopped her, she would have pulled out hanks in frustration.

Sol bought them all coffee from the vending machine. It wasn't as bad as it sounded. Any diversion was welcome.

"They can only hold him without officially charging him for—"

"I know the drill, Sol."

He nodded. "Right. You do."

"What's taking so long this time?" Mara squirmed like a kindergartener who couldn't get the teacher's attention to ask permission to use the restroom.

"Paperwork can be our friend sometimes," Sol said.

Whatever that meant.

Ashlee patted Mara's knee, then stood. "Want to get up and walk around? Work out some kinks? I do."

"Go ahead." Mara stayed put.

Ashlee sat again.

Mara stretched her neck from side to side. "I wish we could get an update from the hospital, but I know better than to hope for that."

"Yeah." Sol tilted his head back until it leaned on the wall behind his chair. "Yeah, me too."

"Look, you two," Mara said, her hands clasped in front of her, "I've been through this before on my own. Not this particular offense, but I'm familiar with how the system works. Why don't you go home? I can call if I need you."

Ashlee raised her hand toward Sol and said, "Wait for it."

Mara caved. "Okay, you're right. I already need you."

Ashlee lowered her arm halfway. She and Sol fist-bumped right in front of her.

Yup. Made for each other.

———

Mara crossed the tiled floor that had seen too much traffic and made another attempt to get information from the desk sergeant—a different one now, since the shift change.

"Still in processing," was the response.

In the Northwoods, that phrase is often associated with processing meat, especially during deer hunting season. Meat was deboned, sliced or chopped or ground, packaged, frozen. Processed.

Dylan wasn't the only one in processing.

A person could, it turns out, get in 10,000 steps pacing. Mara checked the face of her watch. A sparkly pink fireworks ring of light announced she'd reached her fitness goal for the day.

"Anybody hungry?" Ashlee asked, pulling what looked like leftover turkey sandwiches from her purse.

"When did you have time to do that?" Mara's stomach growled right on cue.

"Made up some this morning before we went to the art gallery. I intended them for the homeless on Water Street, but—"

"Except for the location," Sol said, "technically, I qualify." He took a plastic-wrapped sandwich from Ashlee and a takeout packet of mayo.

"I grabbed the mayo from your place, Mara. Hope that was okay."

That junk drawer came in handy once again. "Sure. I guess I should eat too. Sol, let's talk about the homeless issue."

"Such a hardship for so many," he said. "Returning veterans who can't find jobs. Single parents who can't make it on their small salaries. Those with cognitive impairments, some self-imposed, who have no place to call home. I can see why it's been deemed an epidemic."

"Sol, I meant *your* homeless issue." Mara opened her sandwich just enough to squirt mayo on the roasted turkey.

"Mara!"

Good going, Ashlee. Embarrassed enough for the both of us. I don't have the emotional bandwidth to add shame right now.

"I don't mind talking about it," Sol said, "if you really want to hear."

"We do," Mara said in sync with Ashlee's "Not necessary."

He chewed his bite of sandwich thoroughly before answering. "I could have gone back on the force when Logan was in school, certainly by the time he went off to college. I'd only been out of the game fourteen or fifteen years. But I went through a real soul-searching time. Even before I found Logan slumped against his overdosed mom, I'd grown so tired of catching people after they'd fallen. The protector part appealed to me."

No surprise there.

"But being part of the team that brought offenders to justice, that made sure they were punished for their crimes, drained me. Took all the life out of me. I had this burning in my gut . . ."

"Gut health is so important," Mara said.

"Mara!"

Ashlee's chiding would have held more merit if she hadn't spoken with her mouth full. So uncharacteristic for her.

"Cut me some slack," Mara said. "I'm the distraught widow

trying to distract herself while someone decides if her son is a felon or not. Go on, Sol."

"None of Dylan's other arrests ended in felony convictions?" Sol asked.

"No."

"Interesting. Might help his case."

"Carrot stick, anyone?" Ashlee extended a small plastic container with precisely even carrot stick leftovers.

"So, you had this burning in your gut, Sol?" Mara prompted.

"I wanted to apprehend people before they needed apprehending. Maybe intervene is a better word. I wanted to do something that made a difference to keep them from places like this, to keep families from distress like yours, Mara."

"Appreciated." Mara had to admit that Sol brought a sense of stability in the current crisis. Not that he could do anything, necessarily. But that he was there.

"So, I sold my house and chose to live in places like Water Street."

"What?" Again, Mara and Ashlee were in sync.

He slid his unfinished sandwich back into the plastic wrapper. "I lived among them."

"You went undercover?" Mara set her own sandwich aside.

"No. Not as an assignment. This was for me. I needed to know what it was like—for this one people group—to build my empathy. Help me understand the dynamics of what keeps someone in a state like that—financially, socially, emotionally. Spiritually too."

"How long?" Ashlee asked. "How long were you there?"

"When Logan moved here for his job, it was obvious he needed help finishing the endless reconstruction work on the house and help with some other big construction projects he has going. He asked if I'd move in with him until the work is done. Honestly, it was a tough decision. I still have so much to learn. But I must admit that approaching winter was the tipping point."

"And you're still 'between jobs'?" Mara hoped the kindness in her voice sounded like the concern it was rather than nosiness.

"For the time being. Carless too, you'll notice. I'm not yet sure what I'm supposed to do with this passion to help and this equal uncertainty about what it means, what it's going to look like. Once the documentary is released . . ."

Ashlee choked on her coffee. "What documentary?"

Sol stretched. "I guess I left that part out. An independent film crew heard about what I was doing and asked if they could make a documentary about my experiment. They promised they would film as unobtrusively as possible and with respect for the truly homeless, no matter what sent them there. And they did, I have to say. You may have seen one of the previews on a national news program."

"That was you?" Ashlee gasped.

Mara stiffened. How could she share Ashlee's enthusiasm? Another humanitarian? That's all she needed in her life.

"The last thing I wanted was attention," he said. "But if I can be a voice for awareness, I guess I have to use it. Wherever that takes me."

Or not. You can marry a good woman like Ashlee and love her well and stay around like a good man. Good men stay. No. That isn't completely true. Sometimes good men leave.

"Mrs. Jacobs?"

"Yes?" She was out of her seat like a bullet, which she edited to another analogy in her mind because of their current proximity to police officers. "Yes. You have news about my son?"

The desk sergeant referred her to one of the arresting officers, whose name Mara had already forgotten. He drew her aside. "Mrs. Jacobs, it looks like Dylan is going to be spending the night with us. You might as well go on home and get some sleep."

"Can I . . . post bail or something so he can come home with me?"

"We aren't that far in the investigation yet. But . . ."

"But what?"

"I don't want you to get your hopes up. I've seen Dylan in here before."

Every mother's dream.

"But he's changed," the arresting officer said. "I can't deny that. He's not the same young man who was always looking for trouble. I also can't deny that he's gotten himself entangled in a mess here. But, we have a new lead that—I can't say any more right now. Would if I could. I just don't want you to give up hope."

I have to have some in order to give it up, Officer Whatever.

"Keep hanging in there. Okay?"

"Okay." *No problem. Noooooo problem. My friends and I may go out for a little "my son's in jail again" celebration and then head home. I'll sleep like a baby and come back in the morning after my mani-pedi and we'll chat some more.*

Unfair. Unkind. Rude, even if they did remain *unspoken* thoughts. She squeezed her eyes shut but couldn't find an internal delete button. This isn't who she wanted to be.

She returned to her forever friend and the homeless guy and nodded toward the exit. "Time to go."

eighteen

Chelsea greeted her at the door at home with the kind of lingering hug every mom longs for from her legally-an-adult daughter.

"How did you stand that, Mom? All that waiting. At least I had people around me."

Mara's mind formed the words *I don't need people*, but her mouth said, "I had people. Ashlee on one side and Sol on the other." The concept didn't distress her. Huh. Maybe she was changing. All the more reason for those two of her "people" to figure out they'd make a good pair.

Then, the unimaginable. Chelsea took her mom's face in her hands and said, "I love you. You know that, don't you?"

Who was this child? "Yes?"

"You said that like a question."

"Not doubting. Curious where this is leading."

Chelsea held her face tenderly another moment, then stepped back a little and said, "I had to make sure you know."

Oh dear. What news was she about to drop? *Chelsea, not now, please.*

"I made supper for you."

"You did?"

"I wasn't sure you would have had a chance to eat yet."

Ashlee had insisted they stop at a drive-thru on the way home. But Mara wasn't about to tell her daughter that. "What did you make?"

"Chicken wild rice soup. I found Great-Grandma Lou's recipe. Logan and Lisa helped with some of it since I'm, you know, kitchen challenged."

Mara felt suddenly ravenous. "Smells delicious. Who's Lisa?"

"She plays cello in the worship band."

"Oh. Right."

Chelsea dished up two small bowls of soup. "Lisa thinks Dylan's hot, but whatever. She's a sweet girl. I like her. I'm kind of mentoring her."

Wait. What?

"Okay, granted, I'm only like a half step ahead of her in my faith, but it works."

Mara was still digesting the fact that Chelsea had hugged her and made dinner. And now she was using the word *faith* and herself in the same sentence. *Her* faith?

"Try it, Mom. See what you think."

Faith? Oh, she meant the soup. She took a spoonful. "I hear angels singing. Chelsea, this is wonderful. I hereby abdicate my apron to you, my child."

"Hold on there. You've never worn an apron."

"True."

Chelsea smiled. A beautiful sight. Like sunshine breaking through clouds. "And my culinary repertoire currently consists of PB&J, warming up leftovers, and this soup."

Burger and fries, move out of the way. I am eating this whole bowlful.

"We need to be honest with each other, right, Mom?"

She knows. She knows about the drive-thru. How?

"And that means I need to say something to you."

Here it comes.

"Sometimes, in the past," Chelsea started, "I did idiot things."

Mara nodded, but just a little. Not like, *Oh, baby, you sure did!*

"Sometimes, it was because I was afraid you'd leave too."

"What?" Mara dropped everything she was doing, including breathing.

"I know. I wasn't the smartest egg in the carton," Chelsea said.

"Eggs are supposed to be intelligent?"

"I was trying to use a word picture an older person would understand."

Mara tilted her head. "Old. Like me."

"Old-er."

"Honey, how could you ever think I would leave you?" Because their father had. Then he left for good.

Chelsea moved around the island and stood behind her mom, arms around her, head leaning against Mara's shoulders. "I don't think I even knew that's what I was doing. But I do remember wondering, *Why doesn't she just give up on me? Why is she still here? Why hasn't she kicked me out? What makes her keep hanging on when I do nothing but make her life harder?*"

"Simple answer, Chelsea. Love. That's what love does. It holds on." *Handholds and footholds, Mara. That's all you need.* "And hope, I guess. I didn't always have a good grip on it, but I had an underlying hope that we'd have a conversation like this someday."

Chelsea squeezed tighter. "Kind of like the discussion I've been having with God lately. I think that's why he didn't give up on me either, even when I gave him puh-LEN-ty of reason to walk away from me."

And the daughter becomes the teacher. "Well said, Chelz."

"Just Chelsea, Mom."

"Oh. I hadn't gotten the memo."

"I forgot to send it."

Mara bowed her head.

"You okay, Mom?"

"Savoring."

"I added a little bay leaf."

"Not the soup, Chelsea. You. This. The joy of loving you."

Chelsea pulled away. "Aww. Now it's just getting mushy in here." She returned to the stove, turned off the warming unit, and moved the soup pot away from its residual heat. "There's another thing."

Please, please, please let me have this moment a little longer. No "another thing."

"Two things," Chelsea said. "I need to get my driver's license so I can be a bigger help and not have to rely on somebody else to give me a ride to work."

"Oh. Sure. We'll set up an appointment with the DMV."

"I already did that. I know it's risky with the weather and everything, but I was able to get an appointment for the middle of December."

Would wonders never cease? *Lord, please don't let the wonders ever cease.* "So, you need me to take you out to practice for the test?"

"I don't want to lay one more thing on you, with all you're juggling," Chelsea said, brushing her Liam-colored hair out of her eyes. "Because I'm eighteen and he's twenty-two, Logan's been working with me on that."

"Ah." *Logan's twenty-two.* "Okay."

"And Logan's the other thing."

"I thought he might be."

"I'd like your permission to date him."

If Mara had dentures, they would have been swimming in chicken wild rice soup. "My permission?"

"He's, you know, older."

"Not like Mom-older."

"Right. Those four years won't make much difference when we're thirty-five and thirty-one."

160

She's talking future. With him. Long-term stuff. And she's asking permission to date? "You haven't been dating already?"

"When we're together, it's always in groups. Except for that one time when we stopped for coffee before he brought me home from Ashlee's after Thanksgiving dinner. Logan asked me out for next Saturday—a concert thing—and I want to say yes, but I also don't want our relationship to start with any secrets between you and me. This time."

The harsh, stinging glare of sorrow paled, if only for those few moments. Ashlee was right on so many issues. She'd told Mara she was convinced beauty and joy can ease the sting of grief.

"Yes. Of course, my answer's yes. I think Logan is, from what I know about him, a fine young man."

Chelsea smiled and exhaled. "Good. Me too. Oh, there is one more thing."

"Am I ready for it?"

"Dylan's going to be okay. I can feel it in here." She tapped her open hand on her chest, right over her heart.

Mara mimicked her move. "Me too."

And mimicked her tears.

"Chelsea, someday soon I need to take you to Ashlee's. She has a painting I'd like you to see. And it has a story with your name on it."

~

The taste and smell of coffee doesn't solve all problems, she discovered as she sipped and sniffed. Even the good stuff from a quaint little bistro like this one. Booths and tables that didn't match but still seemed related. Coffee posters from around the world adorning the walls. Coffee art everywhere she looked, including the coffee shop's name made out of coffee beans.

The conversation groups reminded her of pictures she'd seen

from a coworker's trip to Copenhagen and her favorite corner coffee shop there.

Despite her reason for being in this shop, Mara had a twinge of longing to pull out her graphic design background and help them develop a new logo that fit their brand better. A crazy thought. She pushed it aside and waited while the man across the table from her sipped and sniffed.

Did she really want a guy from church serving as her son's defense lawyer? Couldn't that get awkward on Sunday mornings? "Hey, there's the sound technician!" "Hey, there's my lawyer!"

She hadn't made the connection Friday afternoon when she'd dialed the spin-the-wheel attorney pick from her internet search. It wasn't until this morning at their coffee shop/bistro meeting that she realized the man with the heart-shaped bald spot often sat in front of her at church.

"Thanks for agreeing to represent Dylan, Mr. Lawson." *Lawson.* Had to be a good sign. Although, most lawyers prefer suits to buffalo plaid shirts and jeans, don't they?

"Your son has my full attention. I'm semi-retired but still have full credentials and take on cases of interest from time to time."

"Dylan's is a case of interest?"

"It's complex, to say the least. One piece of good news. His drug panel and alcohol screening came back clean, as we would have expected."

You might have expected. I'm deliriously grateful.

"There's still a question, apparently, whether he'll be charged with assault and battery or simple battery. In this particular jurisdiction, that's a possibility."

"The difference is . . ."

"Muddy. Which is why most court systems lump them together these days. And . . ."

"And what?" Mara had to ask.

Mr. Lawson took another sip of his well-doctored coffee. "Aggravated assault is not off the table yet."

The term turned Mara's stomach. Dylan could be mouthy, and when he had been high, he was a different person. But aggravated assault? "That would be a felony, wouldn't it?"

"Oh, definitely. What they call simple assault and battery can go either way—misdemeanor or felony."

"Mr. Lawson, I can't imagine—"

"Most parents can't. But you can trust that I'll make sure he's treated fairly throughout this process. The fact that the arresting officers are still forming their charges may work in our favor." He poured a sweetener packet into his coffee, stirred, and tasted. Added another packet.

Mara understood way too much about drug-related charges, both when Dylan was a minor and more recently. Her mind could recall the unique, claustrophobic, life-draining air inside a courtroom. But this was new and scary territory. "Don't they have to release him if he hasn't been arraigned?"

"The forty-eight-hour time window is a little wiggly in this instance, as it sometimes is. Not only is it a weekend, it's a holiday weekend. Not being able to get hold of a judge is a legitimate reason for them to delay without penalty."

She'd forgotten already. Thanksgiving. The time of giving thanks. Let us . . . give thanks. That also made it a major hunting weekend. The judge might be up a tree.

The mental image of black robes getting caught on thorny branches as the judge climbed a tree stand ladder, or alternately, a black-robed judge with a blaze-orange vest and knit hat, was almost funny.

"They're not going to keep him all weekend, are they?"

Mr. Lawson rubbed the top of his head. "I know this may sound like strange counsel, Mrs. Jacobs, but it could work to Dylan's advantage. I've gotten wind of new evidence."

"What is it?"

"Too early to voice it. I can't risk the fragile state your son's case is in right now."

"But I'm paying your fee." *Or rather, his dead father is.* "I apologize. That sounded not only unkind and rude, but not at all like a mom who is grateful you're on Dylan's team." Grateful. Gratitude. Thanksgiving. *Yay.*

He smiled in a way that reminded her of her grandfather. "It's a tense time. I'm used to that. But, for what it's worth, I believe Dylan's telling the truth when he says he did only one thing wrong—bloodied that boy's nose."

And yet, the boy sustained so much more than that. "Let's hope a judge believes Dylan too."

"A lot riding on it."

She'd told herself not to but had searched the internet. A sentence of one to as many as twenty-five years. Mara couldn't pin down the other questions swirling in her mind. They scooted away when she tried to corral them, not wild horses as much as wild amoeba. "Well, thank you. Oh, by the way, do you know how that boy is doing? Has he been released from the hospital?"

Mr. Lawson hesitated. "No, he hasn't. But that, too, is somewhat intentional. Believe me. I'll explain when I can. Hang in there."

Mara pushed her coffee toward the middle of the table. It tasted bitter. "People keep telling me that."

"It's not bad advice," he said. "Depending on what or Who"—he pointed heavenward—"you're hanging your hopes on."

She would have nodded more convincingly, but the stiff neck she'd given herself by trying to use Liam's pillow instead of her own restricted her movement.

Mr. Lawson leaned forward. "I know our pastor wouldn't mind if you felt you needed to talk to someone."

The door to the little coffee bistro opened right on cue. Ashlee and Sol.

Mara turned Mr. Lawson's attention toward them. "I already have two 'ministers' at my beck and call."

The newcomers wiggled their fingers Mara's direction. Same wave. Like synchronized swimmers. Perfect for each other.

"Sorry we were late," Sol said when they reached the booth.

Ashlee explained, "You know that 'I'm almost out of gas' dilemma Dylan had on Thursday? Today it was my turn."

Mara introduced them to Dylan's lawyer, who apparently had already met them both. They chatted like longtime friends, although both Sol and Mr. Lawson seemed surprised to learn that they shared a common interest in the law, albeit from different departments.

The lawyer slid out of his side of the booth to let Sol and Ashlee in. He was headed across the street to the police station to meet with his client again.

"Give him my love," Mara said. And meant it. "When can I see him?"

"I'll let you know," he said, leaving a twenty on the table to pay for their two coffees and a generous tip.

Mara turned her attention to the couple sitting across from her. She filled them in with what little she knew. Sol's forehead creased at the news that Dylan would likely be in jail for the holiday weekend, but the lines soon smoothed and he raised his chin as if the plan suddenly made sense to him.

Nothing made sense to her.

"I'm treating this morning," Sol said. The homeless guy. "Want a refill of coffee, Mara?"

"I'm switching to tea. Stomach's a little sensitive today. Could be the bitterness."

"Could be the circumstances," Ashlee countered. "But tea's a good option. They have a sun tea that is luscious. Had some the other day."

"Sun tea? With these temps? Isn't that called cold brew? Do they stick it out on the sidewalk to freeze?"

Ashlee studied the menu in front of her. "I've had it other places when it was named Uganda ginger tea." She looked up. "I think you should try it. Might settle your stomach."

Or it might remind me why my stomach's been in knots since mid-October. Uganda?

"Here," Ashlee said. "The description. 'In traditional Ugandan style, this soothing tea starts with boiling black tea leaves, milk, and sugar, then simmering with fresh ginger.'"

"I'll have that," Sol said.

"Me too." Ashlee caught Mara's gaze. "Make it three?"

Turning point. She was about to agree to try something new with Uganda in its description. "Okay. Yes. Make it three."

nineteen

*I*t promised to be a very long weekend.

Hovering around the police station would be counterproductive. Holing up at home would mean either cleaning or berating herself for not cleaning. Although, from what Mara could see last night, Chelsea might have burned off some nervous energy with a dust rag and a mop yesterday.

So when Ashlee invited Mara to her townhouse for the afternoon, Mara didn't ask why.

She should have asked questions.

"Welcome to art therapy." Ashlee spread her arms wide and welcomed Mara into a kitchen that had turned into a kindergarten craft workshop. Colored paper—various shades and textures, beads, bits of lace, dried flowers, leaves that looked suspiciously like part of the greenery from a funeral arrangement, paints and easels and brushes . . . oh my.

"Ashlee, I don't mind watching you do whatever it is you intend to do with all this. But I don't have the stamina or the brain power to be creative right now."

Ashlee brightened. Even brighter than normal. "That's exactly the best time to create. Where would you like to start?"

"At the finish line."

"Mara, this is going to be fun." She bounced, Tigger-like.

Mara groaned. Not that she had anything against Tigger in principle, or any of Pooh's other friends, either. Eeyore was grossly misunderstood, in her opinion. But, that said . . . "What . . . are we . . . doing?"

"Whatever we want. That's the beauty of it. If you want to sketch, you can sketch. Or make confetti. Or glue marbles together."

"We have marbles?"

"I knew something would excite you, Mara."

"That was a joke."

"Origami," Ashlee said. "Maybe that's more your style."

"Nope."

Ashlee drew a deep breath. "I don't suppose you'd like to make handcrafted Christmas ornaments for—"

"Definitely not."

"—the children's hospital." Ashlee drew out her final words.

"Oh. Maybe. Yes. I'd do that. For a while. I have some cleaning I should get home to."

Ashlee rolled her eyes. Like the good old days. "Okay," she said. "Do you need inspiration, or do you have enough already?"

"I'm lacking in the inspiration category. Spoon-feed me the ideas."

"Do you want something Jeremy-related or intentionally not?"

Mara crossed her arms. Zing to the heart. Jeremy-related. "You mean, something he'd enjoy or something that reminds me of him?"

"Whatever. You get to decide."

Lord, if you don't mind, I'd like to have a creative thought that has nothing to do with funerals or arraignment hearings or regret. If you don't mind.

She made the same request a few creativeless minutes later.

Ashlee was already deep into making angel ornaments out of

168

paper doilies. And frankly, they were cuter than Mara thought they could be. "Do you happen to have any Legos?"

"As a matter of fact, I do," she said, abandoning her project and heading for the hall closet. She returned with a wrapped Christmas gift.

"Ashlee, I'm not going to take a gift you bought—and wrapped already." It was two days after Thanksgiving and Ashlee had her shopping and wrapping done? How is it they'd stayed friends since they were in pigtails? Partly because Ashlee was the kind of person who would repurchase a gift so she could supply a tub of untouched Legos to a grieving friend.

"See? Unwrapped. All yours. I was rethinking my choice for my niece's twins anyway. They're probably a little too young."

"How old are they?"

"Not born yet."

"Then yes, Ashlee. They're too young."

"I wanted to be the good auntie who gives them their first Legos." She fake-pouted.

"Which you can do four years from now and it'll still be their first."

"Point taken." Ashlee smiled. "I wouldn't put it past God to have planted that idea in my head so I'd have them available for you now."

Funny thing. Mara had the same thought.

An hour later, Mara had created candy cane ornaments, several versions and color combinations of the word *Noel*, three different star shapes, and a miniature nativity set. One of the shepherds wore a Star Wars helmet, but still . . .

The left side of her brain had been worn thin by recent events. The right side of her brain enjoyed the spotlight for a while.

Ashlee spread her arms, the look in her eyes thick with compassion. "Look around you, Mara. The beauty didn't disappear when your husband did. When your son died. It's still here."

"Of all people, can you not see how offensive it is to appreciate beauty with all I've been through?"

"But beauty and love are what heal us. They're closely related, you know." Ashlee looked as if she wanted to say more, but didn't.

They worked in silence a while longer.

"What do you think of this angel?" Ashlee asked her.

"She seems a little . . . flashy. A fluorescent yellow sash?"

"Obviously, she's Crossing Guard Angel."

"Ah. My mistake. Everyone needs a crossing guard angel on their tree."

"Let's shift gears and do something else." Ashlee stood and cleared her side of the table.

"I was about to start on a fireplace with little Lego Storm Trooper Santa boots hanging down through the—"

"What I have in mind is a little more meaningful than that. One moment." Ashlee left the room again. Before she returned to the table, classical music floated from her living room.

"How atmospheric," Mara said.

"Exactly. Come sit beside me so you can see this better. Have you done cyanotype before?"

"No."

"I predict you will love it, and that it won't be hard for you to catch all the deeper meaning in its process."

The music helped. To Mara, "deeper meaning" right now sounded like a chore, an assignment, a "find the hidden images in this picture" exercise. Lately, she had to leave notes to remind herself to brush her teeth. Deeper meaning, huh?

"Ashlee, you know I love you. But I don't think you realize how fragile I am right now."

"Oh no," she said. "I'm completely aware. Yes. Fragile."

"How can you ask me to—"

"Mara. Can you do *this*?" She pinched her thumb and index finger together, then lowered her hand to the tabletop.

What kind of mental/emotionally unstable/early onset test was this? "You know I can."

"Show me." Ashlee repeated the action.

Mara rolled her eyes, then pinched her thumb and index finger and pretended to lay something on the table. "Happy?"

"Yes. And you will be too. You just proved you have the capacity to do your end of making amazing art. And you proved you have everything you need to reach out for your healing."

"Who said anything about healing?"

"Jesus."

Oh, here we go.

"Jesus met a woman one time who'd had all the life drained out of her. Everything faded away. Her friends, church family, physical energy, every relationship, everything she once loved to do. All of it was impossible. By that time, she was likely crawling on the ground, she was so done in. Then Jesus brushed past her, but she couldn't even call his name. All she could do was this." Ashlee pinched her thumb and finger. "All she could do."

Mara knew the story. "She caught the hem of his garment."

"That's right. And it was enough."

Mara sat in the stillness and the music for a moment. "And that made art."

"No, actually that made a miracle. But the art principle is the same. Watch."

Ashlee put a small cardboard box on its side on the table, the opening facing her. Then she opened a black plastic envelope and removed a letter-sized sheet of what looked like watercolor paper and set it on a thin board in the dark box. She placed a fern frond, three small seeds, and a bird feather on the paper, followed by a sheet of glass on top of the items.

"Come with me," she said.

Ashlee carried the box and walked slowly, every bit of her drama training in high school converging on the moment. She led the way through her back door out onto the starkly cold but sunlit patio.

"What are we doing out here? Shouldn't we have dressed for this?" Mara shivered for emphasis.

"Shh. Please. For the sake of the art."

"Yes, ma'am." Duly reprimanded, Mara vowed to hold her complaints.

Ashlee pulled the flat board and what rested on it from the box and laid it on a patio tile in the full sun. She tossed the box to the side and gestured for Mara to retreat back into the warmth of her kitchen.

"What do we do now?" Mara whispered, more than a little concerned that Ashlee might have tiptoed her into some kind of strange ritual in which she ought not to participate. Feathers and seeds, a little toad here, a little goat's blood there . . .

"We wait. Silence."

Five minutes ticked by. Six. The background music was nice. Vivaldi? As Mara was about to grab her coat and exit the craft center/twilight zone, Ashlee stood and waved her to follow again.

She retrieved the board and its contents from the patio tile and carried it to the kitchen sink. Ashlee removed the glass and tilted the board. The fern, seeds, and feather slid off the paper, revealing their shadows on the paper. No, the opposite of shadows. Light on now-colored paper.

"That's kind of cool," Mara said.

Ashlee raised her stop sign hand. She filled a dishpan with cool water and lowered the paper into it, agitating the water as if daring the faint image to remain despite the waves. The image grew whiter and the background paper darkened to indigo.

"Now, that's way cool."

Ashlee ignored her observer's comments that time, lifted the paper out of the water, added a capful of—*what was that?*— something that came in a brown bottle. Hydrogen peroxide? She moved the paper through the water again for several minutes, then rinsed.

"You may speak," Ashlee said.

"That's gorgeous."

"A cyanotype print. Art. Made by one of God's first creations, the sun."

"Stunning. The detail."

"It took me little more than my ability to pinch and lay down a sheet of paper, a feather, a seed, a stem. The real work was done by Creation, by a sun that both fades . . ."

Aha. The deeper meaning. Mara's patio cushions. Jeremy's constellation comforter. Her life.

". . . and empowers. Strengthens."

"How do you know all this?"

Ashlee clipped the paper to a cotton string hung between two cupboard knobs. "Someone demonstrated it to me during a time when I wondered if I'd ever again appreciate color or draw a full breath, ever care to be loved again."

"Who was that?"

"My Robert."

⁓

With music still playing in the background, Mara created a cyanotype print from an antique lace collar and another with her wedding rings while Ashlee began the art therapy cleanup.

"Have you thought about going into art therapy for real?" Mara asked her.

"Don't make a joke of it."

"I'm not. Have you? Seriously? Because I think you'd be very good at it."

Ashlee stopped gathering buttons into their plastic jar. "It would mean my going back to college."

Oh. That might delay the progression of the Ashlee-and-Solomon-sitting-in-a-tree plan. But delay didn't mean never.

"How many more credits would you need?" *Can you get them online? Working on it in the evenings when you and Sol sit by the fire sharing your hopes and dreams?*

"Masters degree, minimum. A lot more psychology credits. A true art therapist goes through an integrated program in psychotherapy and visual arts at an accredited educational institution. And then, I'd need to take the exam to be board certified."

"You took that info off the top of your head?"

Ashlee blushed. "I may have looked into it. A little. Or, as an alternate plan, with all these supplies, I could work as an aide in a preschool. There's that."

Mara laughed. "If you need a reference . . ."

"Is that your phone ringing or mine?"

"Mine, I think." She dug through the bins of supplies. One of the bins was ringing.

~

Mara held the phone to her ear, then said, "Hold on a second, please," pulled it away, and removed a static-cling bird feather. "Ashlee," she whispered, "could you turn off the music? It's Dylan's lawyer."

Heart, don't fail me now!

"Mr. Lawson, can I put you on speaker? I'm here with Ashlee."

"That's not the best idea right now, Mara. Some of these details are for your ears only until the testimonies become part of the court records."

Mara shook her head at Ashlee, her shoulders apologizing for her. Ashlee waved it off and signaled that she was praying. Mara took her phone to the living room. "Okay. I'm alone."

"Your Dylan caught the break we were hoping for."

"What does that mean?"

"Because of the delay for an arraignment, the investigating officers had time to follow a tip. Your friend Solomon is as wise as his name."

Wise and kind and protective. Perfect for Ashlee. Everyone could use a friend like—"Tell me the details, Mr. Lawson. I need some good news."

He cleared his throat. "It's not good news for anyone but Dylan, I'm afraid. Solomon suggested the doctors treating the boy look for old injuries. He had a hunch that if Dylan was telling the truth, the rest of his injuries might have been inflicted by someone with whom the boy was familiar, someone who heard about what the young man had done and tore into him."

"Who would do that? Old injuries? You mean, abuse?"

"That was the hunch. And unfortunately, it was true. The home had a history of domestic abuse calls. When the investigators heard about the evidence the X-rays showed, the multiple contusions that didn't follow the bruising pattern or timing of the nose injury, the spiral break in his arm that matched a similar but long-healed spiral break in the opposite arm, they spoke to the mother and father separately."

"Did the father confess?"

"Eventually. After the mother gave them an earful of what she and her son had been through with him. She'd reached her tipping point. She'd witnessed it. Said her son came home with a bloody nose, and that's all. When Dad got home from work, he wanted answers. The boy knew he'd be in trouble whether he told the truth or lied to protect himself, so he spilled it all. He explained why Dylan reacted the way he did when the boy smarted off about having made sure Jeremy had what he needed the night he died."

"Oh, my heart!"

"The boy had been the dad's runner."

"You don't have to tell me. I know what that means. I wish I didn't."

"So, of course the dad was furious that his son might have compromised his operation. Mom tried to stop him and has her own bruises and wounds to show for it, which she'd kept well-hidden until she was away from her husband and confronted by the officers."

"That poor woman."

"She has her own share of guilt, as you can imagine. But you and I have no idea how hard it is for the abused to leave their abuser."

If the mom hadn't spoken up, Dylan might still be facing a wrongful conviction. Prison. *Lord, thank you, but please help that little boy and his mom find the assistance they need.*

"Does that mean Dylan is free to go?" Mara asked.

"Obviously this development changes things. But even just punching a kid in the nose is a probation violation for your son."

"Oh, Dylan."

"If it helps, Mrs. Jacobs, you can look at it this way. How much longer would that boy and his mother have lived in fear and under the control of their abuser if Dylan hadn't done what he did?"

"It's doubtful the courts will consider that."

"You're right. But I do have a few negotiating skills in my arsenal."

Mara stretched the muscles in her neck. "So, we still don't know what will happen?"

"Correct. Likely, we won't know until Monday. But we do know he won't be charged with a felony he didn't commit. That should help you sleep better tonight, even if Dylan isn't back under your roof just yet."

"It will. Thank you, Mr. Lawson."

"Thank your friend for not keeping his hunch to himself. The man has instincts."

Yeah. That's what Logan says about his dad's pie-making skills too.

She clicked off the phone and fell against Ashlee's waiting shoulder.

twenty

How many other people walking at this hour of the morning were thinking thoughts like Mara's?

Time served, extended probation, and two hundred hours of community service, supervised in part by Logan. It felt like an early Christmas gift . . . with a few strings attached. And with a bonus—the judge's unofficial, unconventional, but personal thanks for Dylan's "cooperation" in helping bring a drug dealer and abuser to justice.

Could life get any more complicated?

Don't answer that, Lord.

They'd be together at Christmas—most of the Jacobs family. Well, three of them. Three out of five. Sometimes math isn't just hard, it's despicable.

Everything, every single thing made the numbers stand out as a reminder that two were missing. They now had enough stools for the kitchen island to not have to take turns. Mara could sit *with* her remaining children. The remainder. The remnant. She halved, but not quite, the pancake recipe she'd used when there were five of them home. One of these days, she'd need to invest in a vehicle, but it didn't need comfortable seating and elbow room for five. Just three. Within a couple of years, just one.

Most passenger cars weren't calculated like that, but sometimes emotional math counts differently.

Emotionally, Liam's three years on the field had been three to the power of ten. An exponent. The time zones were nine times a billion. The holes in her heart shrank by half on a good day and were the square root of something on others.

No wonder Mara and math weren't on speaking terms.

How emotionally dangerous would it be for Mara to hire Logan to paint several rooms in her house? Maybe if she freshened the walls, the atmosphere would improve too. How overloaded was his work schedule? And if Sol needed a place to exercise his handyman skills, she had a dishwasher and sump pump and a few other items in need of repair. It was time to invest some money in fixing the problems rather than grumbling about them.

Maybe these three weeks before Christmas were already booked solid for them. Or maybe work had slowed down because—unlike Mara—most normal people were decorating, baking, and shopping right now. It couldn't hurt to ask.

The danger might come in putting Chelsea and Logan together more than they already were. Would that be so bad? His influence on her daughter's life and on her faith growth spurt couldn't be ignored.

When had she ever considered one of Chelsea's guy interests a positive influence? This was a first. Everything about the respectful way they treated each other, the genuine kindness they showed each other, said that this was different. Liam would be so pleased.

Was it possible that at eighteen years old, Chelsea might have found her Forever?

Is it possible you're dreaming, Mara, because you so desperately wanted someone *in your life to have one?*

"You got lost there for a minute." Ashlee's voice broke through.

Mara straightened her walking posture and answered, "It's hard to get lost on an indoor oval track, my friend."

It had meant getting up even earlier in the morning to take advantage of it, but Mara was grateful the community college opened their indoor track facility for walkers looking to escape the increasingly colder weather. Inside, they found sure footing. It was windless, which saved them money in lip balm. The scenery didn't change much, but it was worth it to keep walking.

Worth it to keep walking? That didn't just come out of her mind, did it? *Mara, Ashlee's getting to you. Caution. Caution.* She felt the smile tug its way across her not-windburned cheeks.

"What would you think," Mara asked, "if I hired the Coppernall men to do some painting and repair work at my place?"

Ashlee wiggled every appendage. "Great idea. Brilliant."

"Trying to imagine paint colors that might work."

"Your whole house or a few rooms?"

"The kitchen and family room for sure. I'll wait to do Chelsea's and Dylan's bedrooms. Who knows how long they'll be living at home after they graduate? Which is looking more promising every day."

"Good start. The main living areas."

It was safe to test the next waters with Ashlee, wasn't it? "I don't know about Jeremy's room. I suppose I should do something with it."

Ashlee adjusted the trajectory of her path to step one track lane closer. It offered the two women less elbow room but made it easier to talk without being overheard by other walkers and joggers. "Wait on Jeremy's room too, until it's a want to rather than a should. You'll know when."

"Good advice. Thanks."

"And if you don't, I'll tell you." Ashlee put one lane between them again. "What overall color scheme were you thinking about?"

No getting out of it. Mara would have to pick colors. She

couldn't assign that to Ashlee or she might wind up with a Jelly Belly palette too bold for her taste. Although, Ashlee's townhome showed her sophisticated side and her restraint with light, neutral walls and a few pops of bright color in accessories and accent pieces. But it was a rental, so that might explain her restraint.

"What's the color of life?" Mara asked. "I'm tired of staring at death."

"Intriguing question," Ashlee said. "Life isn't one particular shade any more than death is painted in one color palette."

"Isn't it a little early for philosophy class, Professor Eldridge?"

The next few laps around the track could prove interesting. Now that Ashlee had a bone to chew on, they'd be down to the marrow before she'd let it go.

"Are the interior walls of your home black right now?" Ashlee asked.

And it begins. "No. You've been there."

"But it's felt like a place of death for months. Why?"

"Because it has been," Mara said.

"The color of life might be blood red. I give you Jesus."

No. The soil in Uganda is the color of dried blood. That's definitely not it.

Mara kept pace physically despite her mental gymnastics. "Yes, blood represents life, but as you'll recall, the blood part was restricted to before and during his death. So we're back to that again."

"Point taken. Let me rephrase, counselor."

"No more courtroom references, please." Mara had seen the inside of too many courtrooms. *Thanks, Dylan.*

"Another point well taken." Ashlee raised her index finger in the air with each point. "Does life exist in the deepest depths of the ocean?"

We're diving that far in this conversation? "Explorers say yes."

"But it's pitch-black down there. How do we know there's life?"

She'd play along. Reps around the track ticked by faster with something stimulating for her brain. "We know because deep-sea explorers have photographed them, filmed them."

"In the dark?" Ashlee sounded like she was prompting a first grader who already knew the answer but needed it tugged out of her.

"With special lights. And some of the creatures luminesce."

"Getting warmer."

Mara unzipped her athletic jacket. "Me too."

"Warmer as in closer to the *aha* moment."

"Which happens to coincide today with the perspiration moment," Mara added.

Ashlee peeled off her lightweight sweatshirt outer layer and tied it around her waist. "I had such high hopes for this conversation."

"I'm still listening."

"It's not color as much as light that reveals life. Chew on that." She pulled ahead and called back, "I'm going to kick into a run these last two laps."

"Fine. I don't run, you'll recall," Mara answered.

From a quarter of the way around the track, she heard, "I know."

I don't run, Ashlee. I overthink.

⸺

Cool down. Mara's favorite part of exercising.

Near the exit that the early morning runners and walkers used, she stretched her calves, hamstrings, torso, and shoulders as advised. She drank a bottle of chocolate milk, like the professionals, and because it wasn't water. And she focused on even, deep breaths.

"Did you ever think," Ashlee said, hugging one knee to her chest, then the other, as if that were even humanly possible, "that life might be the color of breath?"

"If your breath is coming out in different colors, you have a whole different problem than too much life, Ashlee."

"You've seen that image of the songbird in cold weather, haven't you?"

"Social media? Yes."

"You can actually see its song in the air because the moisture from its breath came out in a cloud," Ashlee said.

"Like it will for us when we leave this nice warm building. It'll be white, a vapor."

Ashlee planted her hands on her hips, stance wide. She leaned her head and upper body toward the side of her knee on the right, then the left. "Life is but a vapor. Now, where might I have heard that before?"

"So you're telling me I should paint the entire interior white?"

"Haven't you been listening? It may seem so in movies and fairy tales, but white is no more the definitive color of life than black is the definitive color of death. Life is light and breath."

"So, you're saying green, then?" Mara couldn't help herself.

"What?"

"That mint you popped in your mouth. Your tongue is bright green. I predict when we get out into those near-zero temperatures, your song is going to come out a lovely shade of—"

"Mara!"

"You started it."

~

A hulking form was waiting on her doorstep when she got home from the track center. And it wasn't a stack of UPS packages. It was Sol.

She let him in out of the cold. "When I texted you a half hour ago, Sol, I didn't mean it had to be right now. I'm merely exploring options for painters and handymen. Getting estimates. I'm not ready to commit."

"That's understandable." He paused for some reason. "But I need to see the broken appliances and get a close estimate of square footage to calculate how much paint and how much time it would take, should you decide to give the bid to the Coppernalls. I was available. So . . . I thought I'd pop by."

When was he not available? If a handyman is that unbusy . . .

"Need me to come back after you've showered?"

She unzipped her coat. "Do I smell that bad?"

"No. I didn't mean . . . You smell great." He cringed. "Also not what I meant. I just thought that's what most people do after a workout."

His awkwardness was cute, but she didn't need to follow her snarky instincts and make it worse. Instead, she said, "Not to worry. I took care of that one drop of sweat with a corner of a paper towel."

His face registered obvious relief that she hadn't handled it differently. "Can I take a look at the dishwasher? I already think I know what's wrong with the water faucet on the kitchen sink."

"You do?"

"That should be a simple and inexpensive fix."

She liked simple and inexpensive. "Great." She had skills. She wasn't helpless on minor home repairs. At one time, she'd had a reputation for being determined enough for four people. They'd had five in the family then. She wasn't afraid to tackle breakdowns. It was the energy and desire that had been missing for too long.

"This dishwasher, on the other hand, has seen better days," Sol said. "I can tear into it, if you want. But I assume all those other estimates you're going to acquire"—he paused again— "will tell you the same thing. The parts, if you can find them, will wind up costing more than it's worth. Manufacturers have made so many improvements in the past" — he opened the dishwasher once more — "twenty-five years. I think you can find something more efficient and energy conserving that won't put you into debt too far."

No debt. That blessed, interest-earning Deep Wells life insurance. Liam, I shouldn't have doubted that you'd find a way to take care of us. You always had a heart for it, even when you didn't have the means. "I'll move ahead with a new dishwasher then," she said. "In my mind, I figured that would be the best move. It's hard to make decisions like that when you're in the middle of —"

"Your exercise routine?"

Mara laughed. "I was going to say grief. I know you'll find that response shocking." *Watch the sarcasm, Mara.* "But that Ashlee of yours — of ours — was in rare form today, expounding on the philosophy of color."

A questioning look flashed in his eyes, but it quickly disappeared. "Speaking of color, are you talking about maintaining one basic color scheme throughout the open areas? The kitchen and family room?"

"That was my thought."

"Good. It'll make it feel more expansive, cohesive." He pointed his phone toward the floor and walked a path from patio doors to the kitchen cabinets and from one end of the family room to the other.

"Is that a laser measuring tape, or not tape, but —"

"An app. Makes estimating much easier. Especially when I'm working a jobsite alone. It has another setting where I can basically point and click. But I like to walk it. Get a feel for the space."

A handyman with soul. He's a riddle, wrapped in a mystery, inside an enigma. Mara mentally apologized to the memory of

Churchill, who first said it in an entirely different context, but there you have it.

"Logan's on a job now?"

Sol locked the measurements into the app feature. "Yes. A big project downtown. He specializes in historical restoration. I love when I can serve on his crew, but I have to admit I prefer the smaller, less intricate projects."

"Like mine?"

He looked up. "Everyone has their own interests, their own reasons for what they prefer."

"I guess we do. Coffee?"

"A little dark for your wall color in a room this size. Rich, but I think it would make it feel closed in."

"To drink. Would you like some coffee to drink?"

"Oh." He turned his attention back to his phone. "No, thank you. I need to, you know, get back soon. I'm working on getting more water pressure to Logan's second floor shower."

"That young man has certainly done well for himself."

"He has. Yes. And he's smart about how he's using it."

"You must have taught him well, Sol."

He glanced around the rooms as if he hadn't seen them before. "Is Dylan here?"

"Back in school."

"Right. He'd be . . . back in school."

Mara's gratitude for Sol's intervention on Dylan's behalf would never fade. "Has he had a chance to tell you how much it meant that you believed him and that you acted on your hunch?"

Sol's smile spread across his entire whiskery face. "No more than a hundred times. I just knew in my gut."

"Gut health is—"

"Yes," he interjected. "Very important."

"Tea?"

185

"Better," he said, "but I still think it's a little too dark for these walls." If anything, his smile broadened even further.

Ashlee did see all this wonderful in him, didn't she? His humility? His sense of humor? His genuine caring? Mara would make sure she heard about it.

"You worked at a cheese factory until recently? I'm sorry, but all I can think of when I hear that is 'free samples.' An ideal . . ." She shook her head.

He joined her. "*Not* an ideal job for every person. No. Not at all. Surrounded by all that cheese . . . Hmm. Could be tough."

Mara laughed. "I hear they're hiring, if you're interested."

Her renewed purpose in life—to find other people who wanted to work at the cheese factory.

She might have to spend a little more time thinking through renewed life purpose. And the color of purpose. She was pretty sure it wasn't cheddar orange.

"Well," he said, sounding a little like a cowboy hitching up his britches as he was "fixin'" to do something, "I guess I'd better get going."

"Great. I'll expect your estimate sometime soon, then?" Apparently, he wasn't in the mood for either coffee or tea. She led him to the front door.

"I'll talk it over with Logan and see what we can work out."

"Thanks so much." She opened the door. "Did you . . . need me to walk you home?"

"I currently live right over—" He indicated three houses down across the street, then stopped with his arm in midair. "Yeah, I see what you did there."

"Talk to you when you have some numbers to discuss."

"Will do."

The door hadn't been closed two seconds when she remembered she should have had him look at the sump pump. It could wait until next time.

twenty-one

Was there ever any question that she'd go with Logan and Sol? She didn't bother getting additional estimates. Who else would she trust to do the job without judging her for how badly it was needed? Who else would she trust in her house?

But committing to a color, and to picking out a dishwasher and—no surprise—a new sump pump took mental energy she wasn't sure she could muster right now. The wave of "Am I ready for this much change? Can I make a decision I can live with for a long time?" hit even before the estimate arrived, all professional looking and everything.

Maybe after the holidays, she'd tell them.

The pine tree in the backyard, Norway spruce if she remembered right, looked as cold as she felt. Its branches arched up rather than sticking stiffly up or out or down. Its lower branches were bare of needles, which gave it the appearance of standing barefoot in the snow with its graceful skirts held high.

You have a right to be cold, Tree. It's downright bitter out there. My thermostat on the wall says it's seventy degrees in here. I'd invite you in, but Lady, you must be close to sixty feet tall. You don't get inside much, do you?

The kids insisted it would be good to have a Christmas tree.

They'd help, they said. She wouldn't count on it until she saw the evidence.

And the tree would need presents under it. She'd managed to pull off a reasonable Christmas celebration for the past three, almost four years. By herself. She could do it this year too. Any day now. Any. Day. Now.

Ordering online hadn't been hard. Both Dylan and Chelsea had practical needs she'd put off, so that left her with plenty of options. She'd even managed to find something Ashlee might like. An electric mug warmer she could keep beside her reading chair. It could sense when a mug was in place by weight and would automatically turn itself off when a mug or cup was removed.

It was the celebration part that paralyzed her. Finding a tree. Putting up lights and ornaments. Except for one Lego Noel ornament she'd kept in Jeremy's memory, the rest she'd made on that bizarre craft day with Ashlee had been delivered to the children's hospital. Every other ornament she had in storage from past years seemed dipped in . . . what's the opposite of glitter?

Should she make it easy on herself? What was the point of trying to recreate a warm, memory-rich Christmas reminiscent of Christmases past? Should she start from scratch, a whole new batch of first-year-ever traditions and ornaments and food items? Would that keep Christmas from turning into "But remember when Jeremy was with us?" or "Remember when Dad was here?"

How did any widow survive a first major holiday? Time to consult with the widow she knew best. The one who skewed strongly toward optimism and hope. Ashlee also had empathy to spare and a historian's memory. If Mara asked for a blow-by-blow description of how Ashlee managed her first Christmas without Robert, she'd have an answer primed.

But she hadn't lost a son too.

She'd never had a son.

Sounded like a conversation they should have while sitting in view of the oil painting Mara had purchased at the gallery.

~

A quiet moment in Ashlee's reading corner. Who couldn't use that?

"Ashlee, what gives this tea its liquid sunshine color? Please don't tell me bottled mustard."

Ashlee snorted. "Turmeric. Just a touch. Beautiful, isn't it? And a health boost. How do you like the flavor?"

Mara sat erect, her pinkie in the air as she sipped and pondered. "Bracing with a hint of warm wool socks."

"Remind me not to allow you to write the descriptors for the cookie exchange."

"I'm not fighting you for that job. I figure I can't be more than six months away from getting half of my brain back. Tell me I will get my brain back after losing someone, correction, someones I loved."

"Yes to the brain question. You'll be *bahk*," she said, her Arnold Schwarzenegger impression not a 10, but somewhere in the 7 or 7.5 range. "As to how soon? It'll come and go for a long time, like a college student needing his laundry done."

"I taught them all to do their own laundry now."

"Good for you. See? You're not the world's worst mom."

The skin on the back of Mara's neck tightened. "Who told you I was?"

"Honey, you did."

"Ah yes. I remember now."

They sipped their tea in silence for a moment. Ashlee too, Mara noticed, couldn't take her eyes from the painting for long.

"I came here for a reason, Ashlee."

"You always do."

Mara cringed. "What does that mean? If you feel as if I'm taking advantage of our friendship . . ."

"No. Anything but that. You've always been so resistant to ask for help."

"I have? Always?"

"Pretty much your whole life." Ashlee sipped and leaned back.

"That explains a lot," Mara said.

"Doesn't it?"

"Now, I'm sure I should—"

Ashlee set her sunshine yellow tea on the antique side table at her elbow. "You most assuredly should, Mara. You can do it. Come on, girl. Ask for help."

Who could not love having this woman for a forever friend? "Okay. But it might be hard."

"I'm listening."

Mara could count on that. Ashlee would be listening whether Mara wanted her to or not. She'd pay attention. Weigh her advice. Not hold back. That's why Mara was there.

"Please tell me how a grieving mom and new widow manages to get through Christmas."

Ashlee leaned back again into her plush reading chair, a duplicate of the one in which Mara sat. "Mara, you make it sound as if Christmas is a gauntlet, corporal punishment. Enemies all around. Will . . . we . . . make . . . it . . . to December 26th?"

Mara waited for Ashlee's comedy routine to come to an end. She pursed her lips and gave Ashlee the Grandma Lou "Tell me you did not mean to say that" look.

Ashlee took another sip of her sun-colored tea. Fortifying. Bracing. "I'd be the last to make light of what a challenge it is for a grieving person to survive any of those firsts, Mara. And you'll find it isn't just the big holidays. It's the first time you see someone across a crowded mall and for a minute forget it can't possibly be your husband. Or your child. The first time—or the fifth—when you hear a song that meant something special to you two. The first time you save the burnt piece of toast because he always said he didn't mind."

"Liam hated burnt toast."

"Robert didn't."

"Still stings?"

"Always will. Not as bad, not as intense." Ashlee looked out the window. "Some days it'll be even more intense than the 'first' and it'll make you think you haven't made any progress at all in your grief."

Mara said, "I have no trouble identifying with that concept."

"I made the little-too-sarcastic-I'll-admit-it comment about the gauntlet," Ashlee said, "because of the way you linked the idea that Christmas was the enemy that had to be conquered. It's not that. And this part may help. It helped me."

Mara waited.

"It's a perspective change," Ashlee said. "Christmas itself is life-giving, healing, oozing with hope for us."

"Oozing?"

"I'll watch my word choices. But stay with me here. Christmas is *how* widows and grieving moms survive well. It's not something *to be* survived."

Mara glanced up at the portrait again. All she saw was brushstrokes in the shape of tears.

"The challenge is weaving our way through all the emotional triggers of a time of year known for family and celebrating and joy and . . ." She scratched her eyebrow. "And a lot of jingly, jangly activities that might be fun under other circumstances, but seem an offense to a person mourning the death of someone they loved."

"Yes. Yes, that's it." Did other people find such relief in knowing someone understood, even if they couldn't change anything about their circumstances? Who should Mara have been talking to for the past three years?

"But Christmas? It's our hope-giver. Our light-bringer. Jesus came into the world because people like you and me need him. He came because we *need* him. Both on that long-term, eternity spectrum and in the day-to-day when all would seem meaning-less without him. He brought the meaning with him when he arrived."

Mara sat back. "You don't feel at all passionate about this or anything, do you?"

"Did my voice get tight and pinched?"

Mara nodded.

"I didn't know it that Christmas eight years ago, after Rob-ert was gone. But Christmas wasn't my enemy. It was my hope. The trappings and the hoopla and the trivialities were what I needed to steel myself against. But the stunning com-memoration of Jesus coming to earth because I couldn't get to the Father any other way was my . . . my handhold and foothold. My leaning post. My anchor. My hiding place. My rock. My rock, Mara."

Mara tilted her head back but tears still pooled.

"I survived then by avoiding as much of the meaningless as I could and pressing into anything that honored my loss and reminded me of my Rescuer." Ashlee's facial expression revealed how deeply she was convinced of what she was saying.

"If I cried through the entire candlelight service at church," she said, "it was because I wished I could have shared the wonder with Robert. If eating his favorite Christmas cookie made me a basket case, I ate two, without regret. I savored the tenderness of that memory. If it ached to see couples holding hands while the snow was falling lightly on their shoulders and all was happy-happy, joy-joy in their world, I turned the channel."

Mara laughed at that.

"What's meaningful in your Christmas traditions that you

don't want to miss, even if they're raw and tender?" Ashlee asked.

"Going to the candlelight service as a family."

"Then go. Even though your family is smaller now here on earth."

"Hot cocoa in front of the fire on Christmas Day," Mara added.

"Don't miss that."

"Years ago, we'd go to a tree farm and Liam would cut down the tree we picked out. We haven't done that for years."

"You have a son old enough now to saw down a tree and start a new tradition in Liam's honor."

"I also have his death benefit money and could buy an artificial one that doesn't need anyone to vacuum up after it."

"That's true. Whatever works for you, Mara. No guilt. No regrets. It'll be hard. There's no way around that. But you'll get through the hard parts if you're leaning on the Strength-Giver."

"That does help."

Ashlee rested her hands in her lap as if her work were done for the day. "That and my ginger molasses cookies. Made a batch last night. I say we each have one with our second cup of tea."

"You sound like Grandma Lou. Ashlee, you're such a health nut in other ways. The walking thing, the kale . . . But you dive in if someone mentions cookies or cheesecake or sour cream coffee cake."

"Hence the walking."

Before I ever knew how much I'd need her, Ashlee was on her way here, wasn't she, Lord? Before I ever knew I'd need you, you were too. I'll think on that a little more while I'm taste-testing that cookie and this first Christmas without two of my loves.

She'd probably still be thinking about it while walking off the cookie tomorrow morning at the track.

—

"Let's add two more rounds today, shall we?"

"Ashlee, two more times around the track? That's not like asking for two more jumping jacks or two more lunges."

"We can do those, if you'd rather."

"We'll keep walking." Mara didn't try to hide her Eeyore voice.

"I have a favor to ask, Mara."

"Finally, there's something I can do for you. What is it? And keep in mind my current state of mental health, my lack of athletic ability, and my aversion to heights."

Ashlee turned her head away. "Oh, well, then . . ."

"Come on. What is it? I owe you."

"You don't owe me, but I'd appreciate this."

Mara nudged her friend with her eyes. "Don't keep me hanging. We only have one and a half laps left."

"Optimistically speaking."

"Ashlee . . ."

"I'd like to start attending a grief care group. A bereavement group. After the first of the year."

"You? Now? It's been eight years."

"Yes."

Mara slowed her pace. Ashlee matched it.

"Like, a support group?"

"A little more than that, but yes. It's faith-based. I've heard a lot of good things about the program."

"It's not just people sitting around whining about who or how much they lost?" Mara shivered at the thought.

"No. Not from what I understand."

"Then, go for it."

Ashlee was quiet for a moment, then said, "I'd like you to go with me."

Mara huffed. "You didn't really imagine I didn't already see that coming, did you?"

194

"I suspected you'd catch on. But I'm going whether you do or not because I have a few things to work through, and I want to do it in a spiritually and emotionally healthy way."

They'd finished their extra two laps before Mara thought of what to say in response.

"Okay."

twenty-two

*N*o stockings were hung by the chimney with care.

Dylan and Chelsea both said they'd outgrown the stocking tradition, as long as Mara stuffed the normal contents into a zip-top plastic bag or something. They did like the Oreo-flavored candy canes, the flavored lip balm. And yes, just for them, she'd gone to the cheese factory for their favorite taco-spiced cheese curds, which were in the refrigerator, not hanging near the fire.

The artificial tree was a nod to minimalism and its opposite, only a handful of carefully curated ornaments but with its extra strings of lights. Mara left the tree's lights on day and night, unless she was gone from the house or sleeping. She considered it one of the most beautiful trees they'd owned. And this one didn't have to die, lose every needle, and be discarded at the curb after the holiday.

Mara started a Christmas tradition of sitting in front of the fire every night to wind down before bed. When they weren't working, either Chelsea or Dylan or both—plus sometimes Logan—would join her. They rarely talked much. The communion of watching the flames together and feeling their bodies soak up the warmth was enough.

At first, she couldn't explain why she found the gas fireplace comforting, especially in light of the way Liam died. Over time, she believed it was related to the light within the flames—constantly changing color and shape but never consuming the logs in the gas fireplace. They're built to withstand flames and heat. They create no ash.

Some people argue that a gas fireplace isn't real. Or that an artificial tree isn't real. Mara knew better. It's the symbolism that matters more than anything.

Sol and Ashlee had helped her pick out a dishwasher, and Sol had the sump pump replaced and faucet repaired in the time it took Mara to decide where she wanted the tree to stand. When Sol finished tightening the new washer in the faucet, he stood beside her in the family room, used the wrench in his hand to point to the corner to the right of the sliding doors, and nodded once.

He was right. The perfect spot. Lights shone out the windowed doors onto the snow accumulation on the patio. They reflected off the glass, doubling their effect. And Mara could catch a glimpse of the tree whether she was coming or going. She'd told him to add a line for "tree location advice" on his invoice.

She'd allowed herself two Christmas events on her December calendar. The Women's Christmas Tea at church and the Christmas Eve candlelight service.

At the Christmas Tea, she sat at one of the exquisitely decorated round tables between Ashlee and Chelsea. Chelsea and her cello-playing friend Lisa provided the music for the evening. Elegance. Beauty. Music therapy. Her daughter. Plus her forever friend.

Ashlee insisted they arrive early so she could take Mara on a tour of each of the tables before the crowd arrived. What a display of creativity from the women who had designed, created, and decorated Christmas-themed tables with not one expected red-and-green color palette among them. Many women included candles or battery-operated lights in their tablescapes. The overhead room lights were kept low, which enhanced the small pinpoints of light all the more.

Something to marvel at, textures that invited touch, combinations that spoke of divine artistry, sound ambiance . . . Mara ticked off the boxes of what fed her soul and illuminated the shadowy places she could not escape.

Chelsea's and Lisa's music floated over her like silk brushing against her skin. Some songs were familiar Christmas carols mixed with classical music from an occasional cello solo. With Lisa accompanying, Chelsea sang of shepherds and angels, Love descending to reach us, heaven's breath holding us together, Light driving out darkness.

Mara would never tire of the transformation on her daughter's face, the way she'd gone from troubled teen to confident woman, with a song in her heart, in so few months.

Chelsea stood center stage for one final a capella song before the speaker was to take the spotlight. Her honeyed voice sang words Mara didn't recognize but wanted to. Ashlee leaned toward her ear and whispered, "Chelsea wrote that for you."

> And on a silent night
> And in a darkened stall
> The Sonshine of our souls
> Illuminated all
>
> He could not be denied
> This so-called helpless Babe
> And though betrayed, rejected,
> His is the Love that stayed.

The rest of the words blurred, but they washed over Mara like a baptism in slow motion, the lyrics falling from her face, her shoulders, her fingertips. The sensation was so vivid that when the song ended, Mara touched the back of her head to see if her hair was wet. She used both hands to wring out the hem of her black sweater. Nothing. But it had been that real, that sweet. Only her face was wet.

Was she breathing? Yes, still breathing. But each inhale seemed to fill her lungs with more than she'd invited in.

Chelsea resumed her place at Mara's side. *Lord, give me a faith like hers*, her mind whispered. Deep in her soul, a rumble responded, *I did. Step into it.*

If the speaker following Chelsea's song had started in a traditional speaker way, with a joke, or launched into a comedic routine about the smells in the stable, the sacred moment would have shattered. But she softly began with, "Let me try to express how much this Jesus loves you."

She had Mara's attention, and Mara could tell she'd captured others' attention all across the room. The speaker had dressed like the prophetess Anna, who, Mara had to be reminded, was an aged widow married only seven years before her husband died. Eight decades without her husband, but a woman whose name appears in the Bible, the speaker said—light in her eyes—because of her deep devotion to worshiping God. She'd served him night and day for eighty-four years *after* she became a widow.

Mara leaned toward Ashlee. "That would make me a hundred and twenty-six, if I follow the same pattern."

Ashlee leaned back. "I'm still eight years ahead of you."

With slow, sonorous words, the Anna character described how long her people had been waiting for the birth of the Child she'd just seen, then eight days old, how long they'd waited for their redemption.

Waiting for their world to change, for their pain to ease, for the promises they'd been given to be fulfilled.

Widows waiting to know love again.

Mara smiled. *Ashlee, if you would just give Sol the least little hint . . .*

Anna continued. "I have seen the Messiah with my own eyes. Who would know that having my husband taken from me so young would set me on a path of devotion to God? Or that the devotion God planted within me would allow me—*me*—a privilege afforded to few—to see our Messiah born to us.

"In the fullness of time, he came," she said. "For so long our people heard nothing but silence from God. So many questions, and no answers."

Mara couldn't take her eyes off the speaker now.

"We were shuffled like homeless children from one harsh master to another, mistreated, beaten down both by our circumstances and the silence. But now . . . now he is here. And I am yet alive to tell of him. What we thought was pain upon pain paved the way for the work of God."

How could a simple, elegant evening like this have succeeded in exposing the raw flesh of her soul to the air?

"Greek was forced upon us," Anna said, "but because it was, I can tell more people. Taxes were forced upon us, but because of our harsh masters' designs, the roads are ready for us to walk to tell of Messiah. Trade routes are well established so the news can travel more quickly. Even philosophers' debates have been set up for this 'fulness of time' with their desperation to know truth."

Desperate for truth.

"And our hearts are ready to be loved as only God can love, through this Child, this Messiah, this expression of the heartbeat of heaven."

The speaker paused dramatically. Candles flickered, but nothing else in the room moved. "Will you do as I did when I saw that Child? Will you lean close and listen for his heartbeat?"

She'd said more that night, Mara was certain. But Mara's mind had locked on to questions she could not even now shake. "If asked, I would say I love Jesus. Have I let him love *me* the way he wants to? Have I resisted even *his* help?"

Rather than disturb her sleep since then, the questions gently blew on what had been fading embers.

Yes, Ashlee, my friend. I chose only events and activities with meaning this Christmas. It is how I will survive.

Two weeks lay between that Christmas Tea and Christmas Eve. With a little help, she convinced herself she could pull off reciprocating the kindness she'd been shown by Ashlee and the Coppernalls. She offered to host Christmas dinner.

Against Ashlee's advice, Mara had refused their suggestions that everyone bring a portion of the meal. She could handle it. She owed those three people so much. And, frankly, Mara needed to nudge Ashlee to focus a little harder on winning Sol's affections.

With the new dishwasher installed, cleanup would be simpler than it had the past three years. With lights dimmed so the fireplace and Christmas tree lights would have maximum impact, no one would notice if she'd dusted recently. A traditional meal and a well-set table. That's all she needed to worry about.

She chose ham, because it would be easier than turkey, and because the meal couldn't look like a duplicate of what Ashlee had served at Thanksgiving. Mashed potatoes, the one exception. Grandma Lou's Endless Love fruit salad, a couple of vegetable sides, crescent rolls right from the can because come on who doesn't like those, and for dessert? A Christmassy cherry cheesecake. And a few other little tidbits. Having a project felt good. Ashlee's concerns about her attempting too much too soon were unfounded.

By Christmas Eve afternoon, the tremors started. She dismissed the thought that she'd made herself vulnerable by overdoing. Instead, she attributed the tremors to the Christmas card from Deep Wells, Inc.

Her hands shook as she opened the envelope. Of course, her name was still on their mailing list. But nobody at the office had thought to pull hers, apparently, when they slipped the quarterly newsletter inside. Maybe it was all mechanized, automated. She couldn't fault Deep Wells. They'd been thoughtful and caring. Going out of their way for her many times. But this? Not so much.

Among the traditional greeting and plea for support in the newsletter were news updates. Including the October "demise" of one of their own—Liam Jacobs—with a lengthy tribute. It included a picture of villagers from the area in which he'd been working. And an image of the charred truck.

She stared at it, hands still trembling, thinking about household after household around the world—all the Deep Wells contributors and partners—opening the newsletter to that image, that intimate deathly trauma scene.

Something smelled scorched. The newsletter wasn't scratch-n-sniff. The odor came from her oven. Cheesecake crust. How long had she ignored the stove's timer?

Chelsea shot out of her room. "Mom! What's that awful smell?"

Mara tucked the newsletter between pages of Grandma Lou's cookbook that lay open on the island. "I was about to get that. Must have set the oven temp too high." Why couldn't she move? What was happening around her? Action but no sound? She couldn't hear her own voice in her ears.

Chelsea opened the oven door a crack. Black smoke billowed out. "Take the battery out of the smoke detector, quick, or it'll be screaming at us."

Mara heard her daughter but wasn't sure what to do with the words.

Chelsea grabbed an oven mitt to extract the offending graham cracker crust and tossed it into a snowbank outside the front door to sizzle and cool down.

Mara briefly wondered how many homes on their street had blackened cheesecake crust decorations near their front door. She guessed no one else. What was that smell?

"Mom? Moooom? Why are you just standing there? Never mind. I'll get the battery out."

The smoke detector had already started its piercing wail. Chelsea silenced it.

"Are you okay?" she asked Mara.

"Yes. Sure."

"I have to get to practice for the candlelight services. Can you finish cleaning this up?"

Mara grabbed at the mercury beads of her sanity. "Yes. Yes, no problem. I was just startled, that's all."

"Okay. But text me if you need me."

"I won't. I've got this."

But she didn't.

She couldn't get her hands to work. They lay there as if they'd forgotten how to open and close. Her phone sat beside the stained cookbook. Sometime after dark, it flashed a message from Ashlee. "The service is starting. Where are you? Saved a place. Middle section, sixth row left."

Ashlee would keep asking if Mara didn't answer. Couldn't answer.

She stared at the phone as if it ought to know what she wanted from it. All it did was tell her the time.

An hour later, her door opened. Ashlee and Sol. *Good. Well, that's good.*

Ashlee ran to her. "Good grief, Mara, what's going on? Talk to me. Mara? There's a burnt pan by your front door. What happened?" Then, in a whisper, "Sol, this isn't good. Will you check if something's on fire?"

Mara opened her mouth. Two words tumbled out. "The truck."

"Hon, you don't own a truck. What are you talking about?"

"Everything fell apart."

"So it seems," Ashlee said. "Are you ill?"

Ashlee sounded worried. That wasn't like her. Mara should at least look at her. Couldn't turn her head.

Behind her, she could hear Sol checking burner knobs and the oven. He disappeared down the hall for a minute but was back before Mara could form another word or manage to process the activity around her.

Ashlee put a hand on the side of Mara's face. Mara could feel the weight of it, but her face was numb.

"How long have you been standing here, Mara?"

"What time is it?"

"A little after eight."

"Is that Central time?" No. That must not have been the right thing to ask. Ashlee twitched.

"Can you start at the beginning, Mara? Chelsea said she came out of her room on her way to worship practice and you were standing here, like this, leaning on the island, with the oven timer blaring away. She's worried about you. And so am I. Mara, talk to me. Sol, do you think we should take her to a doctor?"

Mara's eyes burned. How often is a person supposed to blink? Probably more often than this. She reached for the Deep Wells newsletter sticking out of Grandma Lou's cookbook, but her fingers couldn't close all the way. It floated to the floor.

Sol retrieved it. "Ashlee," he said.

Let them look. Ashlee might have one in her own mailbox, waiting for her.

"Oh, Mara."

She raised her eyes to look at Ashlee. Sol was pacing, running his hands through his hair. Ashlee's face looked kind. It was always kind.

"Ashlee?"

"Yes, hon?"

"Is it just me, or do you smell smoke?"

twenty-three

She'd survived Christmas Day. Two nights in the hospital on a unit she'd joked about needing, then really did.

They called it the Mental Health Care Refuge Center. She had a room that looked like a high-end motel room, not the padded cell she might have expected. Soft lighting. A weighted but cozy comforter on the queen-size bed. Tasteful decorations, though sparse. Soothing color scheme. She should have asked what paint color adorned the walls. Might be an idea for her kitchen and family room.

Her breakdown, if that's what it was, eased back to near normal within a couple of hours. Her medical team explained that seeing the image of the charred truck triggered a spasm in her brain as if it had been struck by lightning. Mara could almost trace the path of the jolt from the sore spot on top of her skull, through every cell of her body, and out through the soles of her feet—charred reminders along every internal inch.

She'd been evaluated, then mildly sedated, which not only helped her sleep but gave the spasming nerve endings time to untangle themselves so she could think clearly again. That was the protocol in layman's terms.

The nursing staff and the psychologist on call—holiday call, every doctor's dream—treated her with such kindness, it brought more tears. But all assured her that no one was surprised or put off by her weeping, or her meltdown, either. "Grief isn't a straight path," they said. "And yours hit a pothole the size of—"

"A truck?" she'd interjected.

"Something like that."

Christmas Day blurred in and out of quieting conversations and nap lapses. By that evening, the staff gave her the option of being discharged to go home or delaying until the next day. It was her choice. They deemed her "stabilized" but in need of follow-up counsel. She wasn't going to argue that.

Her kids were taking good care of each other. The Ashlee/Sol/Logan trio made sure of that. It felt decadent, but she opted for another night at the "spa."

She read, rested, and listened to a playlist of songs Chelsea had created for her. The music had an even stronger impact than the medicine. Words and phrases like *healing, shelter, strong tower, safe, power at the mention of his Name, holding on, freedom, his embrace* drove themselves deep into her soul through the earbuds. She'd set the playlist to shuffle mode, so the songs repeated but in different order, even as she slept.

Mara woke with a song in her heart. Not an "everything's gonna be all right" dance beat. A sturdy, stabilizing, soul-reassuring song.

And she woke with new understanding about how her mother's abandonment and her father's early death had contributed to her determination that she didn't need anyone's help—a toxic thought that brewed inside her long before Liam took the assignment with Deep Wells.

Liam hadn't *left* the family, a term Mara's mind had leaned toward since his decision to answer the call. Not like her mother who chose to. Not even like her father, who fought so hard not to leave her alone. Liam signed up for a temporary gig. He trusted her to handle things because she'd insisted she could.

And had been determined to assure him that she didn't need anyone's help.

She'd been left alone again now with Liam's and Jeremy's deaths. But not because Liam wanted it that way. And Jeremy was escaping whatever twisted thoughts messed with his mind, not intentionally leaving her. She—the music reminded her—had not been abandoned. Not for a moment was she out of God's sight line or reach.

The grief counselor she'd been assigned had commended her for all the healthy grief "management" tools Mara already had in place—a good relationship with her remnant kids whom she was falling more in love with every day, trustworthy friends, exercise to keep her body moving (Mara left out the part that Ashlee forced it on her), allowing space for her faith to grow, even the makeshift art therapy.

"All I need now is a therapy dog," Mara told the grief counselor. "And a bereavement support group, but apparently I'm already signed up for one of those."

The counselor pressed for more details.

"My forever friend's husband died eight years ago. She thinks she needs to join a grief care group, she said, and she's dragging me along. We can both see straight through that ruse, can't we?"

"So," the counselor had said, "you assume eight years is more than long enough to be done with a grief journey?"

Mara hadn't answered right away. When she did, she responded, "No. And I think that means I just had a major breakthrough."

———

The week between Christmas and the dawning of the new year moved at a slow, soothing pace. Everyone around her seemed bent on *gentling* her through her post-breakdown re-entry. She didn't resist.

How Logan and Sol had gotten the entire kitchen and family

room painted while she was hospitalized—during a major holiday—was a mystery. They claimed it was their own paint roller therapy, and they *thanked* her for the opportunity to implement it. Amazing friends, both of them. And she liked the color. Coconut milk. Perfect.

Ashley's touches showed up in Mara's sparkling clean kitchen, complete with brand new, artsy dishtowels, and in the not-too-bright but classy throw pillows that tied in the wall color and, regrettably, made her tired sectional look even more exhausted.

Mara shook her head at the idea that those three—with a little help from temporarily motherless Chelsea and Dylan—had to move the tree out of the way to paint, then move it back in place. They assumed she still wanted the option of enjoying the white lights on the tree in the freshly painted environment. They were right. The tree lights and her fireplace. And hot chocolate. And Ashlee's molasses ginger cookies.

Someday she'd have to think about replacing the carpeting too. Maybe hardwood floors instead, with a cozy area rug. For now, she'd enjoy the feeling of airiness in the room, and the evidence of her friends' sacrifices.

Who does that? Who thinks, "Mara's in the psych ward. I know! Let's forget about our Christmas Day festivities and move furniture and paint her house while she's gone"?

It was a pure-hearted motive, wasn't it? They weren't all just desperately tired of her indecision, were they?

No. It was their gift.

Mara tightened the fleece blanket around herself and sipped her tea, thinking what it needed was a shot of coconut milk.

～

Mara didn't have to be assigned Bible reading as part of her grief trauma recovery protocol. It seemed obvious for a woman who'd let her faith fade for too long. What wasn't as obvious to her was the particular passage from which she drew the most strength on the first day of the new year. The dawn of the new year.

The book of Ruth.

She remembered from long-ago classes or sermons or something that grieving Naomi intentionally changed her name to Mara. Why would a woman choose a name that meant *bitter*? And why would Sol keep insisting it had a double meaning? Strong, he'd said. *Seriously?*

The introduction in Mara's Bible noted that the concept of redemption occurs twenty-three times in a book only four chapters long. She sat on that thought until her tea had cooled. Verse-verse-verse-Redemption. Verse-verse-Redemption. Verse-verse-verse-verse-Redemption.

Like a worship chorus with a one-word refrain. *Sing it until you get it, people.*

Mara read the entire story, all four chapters, then started at the beginning and read again. Then she switched to "shuffle" mode and turned her attention to phrases and words that seemed to rise from the page, no matter their chronological order.

She couldn't read the ending for her own story right now. It hadn't been written yet, except in God's heart. But she could ponder Naomi's. If only Naomi could have known how often that beautiful, sacred, healing redemption chorus would repeat itself.

In a book titled *Ruth*, Mara focused on Ruth's bitter mother-in-law Naomi, who had lost her husband and shortly after both of her sons. *Mara Jacobs, you came so close to having one more grief in common with Naomi, if Dylan had been prosecuted.*

Mara was struck that despite those around who loved her, Naomi felt utterly abandoned by God, that an impossible grief load had been placed on her shoulders. She could no longer think of herself as Naomi—which meant *pleasantness, beautiful, gentle*—but insisted her community call her Mara—*bitter*.

Did Naomi know that carried the implication of strength? She should have had a Sol to tell her.

She should have had a Sol. A wave of gratitude swept over Mara that she did. She brushed it aside before it headed a direction she wasn't comfortable pondering.

Mara refocused on the pages in front of her. At the end of the book of Ruth, Naomi held her grandson Obed in her lap, a child she cared for as she would have cared for the sons she lost. A child who would grow to manhood and father a child named Jesse, who fathered a child named David.

Through Naomi's sorrow and uncertainty, God was working his plan for a kinsman-redeemer for her and her daughter-in-law, and eventually through that family line, a Redeemer named Jesus for the Mara reading about her story.

I can't know the end of my story, God. And I have to be okay with that, don't I? But I know your heart. Verse-verse-verse-Redemption. Sorrow-sorrow-sorrow-Jesus.

How many times over the years had people asked Mara Jacobs how she spelled her first name? She'd tell them. Inevitably, someone would ask, "Like the Mara in the Bible?" Inevitably, she'd toss back, "No relation."

But she was. And it was okay.

Her breaths came slow and steady. Peace-hemmed. It had nothing to do with the medication she'd been able to stop taking days ago. Someone with her name was well-acquainted with her distress. And the God who made sure that woman's story was told to the world infused uncommon strength in her name.

Mara looked up from her reading and into the fire, to the logs that wouldn't burn, that couldn't leave ashes.

The garage door opener growled. One or the other of her children was home.

School would be back in session the next day. The new year had dawned and Mara was facing it rather than hiding from it. Sol had been kind enough to drop off a bottle of sparkling pear juice on one of his trips past the house. Sparkling pear. One of Liam's all-time favorites. Mara and her kids shared the bottle and their traditional last-day-of-Christmas-break treat.

"More popcorn, Mom? Dylan?"

Their "no thanks" responses tripped over each other. His baritone, her alto. Same notes, but it still sounded like harmony. Mara's laughter took the lead. Her children joined her.

"Kids, I don't want you to worry about me."

"Okaaay," Chelsea said slowly. "You do know it's in my DNA to care, right?"

"Caring is good." Mara smiled.

Dylan plopped down on the sectional beside her. "Is there a reason we should be worried?"

Mara sat straighter. "Things like last week."

"Oh, that," Dylan said. "Your battery cable came loose. A night or two in the shop and you're good for another 50,000 miles."

"I appreciate the analogy, but it's more like recovery, Dylan. A day at a time."

"Oh. Yeah, I see that."

"You two are handling your grief magnificently, if you ask me," she said. "Much better than I am."

"Depends on the day." Chelsea tucked herself into Mara's embrace.

"Understandable. But I know it's a lot more like recovery than it is a destination. You're clean, Dylan."

"Yes, ma'am," he said with an air of confidence and humility combined.

"But no matter how dramatically you've changed, you know

better than to assume you can tiptoe close to the edge or entertain a thought that leads you to a dangerous place."

"I'm reminded of that every day. Grateful for grace, but keeping my guard up."

Mara leaned her head on Dylan's shoulder. "Well said, son.
Guard the dawn."

Chelsea lifted her face to look her mother in the eyes. "Guard
the what?"

"The dawn. Yeah, I know. I'm not sure what that means yet
either. But I feel like it will define this new year for me. And
maybe you two, as well. It's as if while I was in 'time out' at the
hospital, God handed me this phrase and said, 'Do *that* this year.
Guard the dawn,' without telling me what it meant."

Dylan snorted. "'That's for me to know and you to find out'
as Grandma Lou used to say when we questioned her about
something she wasn't ready to divulge?"

"Divulge? Dylan, your language skills . . ."

"What?"

"Never mind. I didn't hear an audible Voice, if you were
thinking I was listening to strange voices. It was an impression on my heart. I'm simply exploring what it might mean to
guard the dawn. I suspect part of it is to protect the dawning of
relationships, or renewed relationships like I have with Ashlee.
Or maybe I'm to focus on making sure my first thoughts of the
day are healthy ones that will set a tone I can draw from instead
of being drained by."

"I think I'll adopt that one too," Chelsea said.

Mara hugged her daughter. "It might have something to do
with that place where the sun rises eight hours before it does
here."

Chelsea leaned forward. "Uganda?"

"I don't know. Not seeing it as my enemy. Christmas wasn't
my enemy. Neither are the people your father felt compelled to
serve. The sun is so strong in Africa. For a long time, I thought

it was responsible for what had faded in my life. And now, somehow, I'm supposed to 'guard the dawn'?"

It would have been a good time for the fire to spit and crackle, if it had been wood that burned to ashes rather than the steady, unconsuming flame.

"Or," she said, "it might be as simple as not forgetting my reflective gear when Ashlee and I walk before the sun's up."

"Pretty sure that's a good idea, but not what God meant," Dylan said.

"I am sure, though, that he wanted me to get this one message loud and clear, kids." She drew them tighter. "I'm strong. I *am* strong. But I'm not self-sufficient."

twenty-four

By late January, they were back to their normal routines. Mara and Ashlee had missed the first couple of weeks of the new year session of the bereavement support group because Ashlee had been dealing with a rash of migraines. She'd refused to elaborate, and Mara didn't object to putting off joining the support group. She'd needed the nothingness of January to get her bearings.

Like an uninvited guest leaving hair in the sink and dirty paper plates in the family room, sorrow reminded her it was still there. Some days she could ignore it. Some days that's all she could smell.

So when Ashlee texted her the time and location of the next session of the grief care meetings, it didn't cross her mind to do anything but reply with, "Thanks. Pick you up?"

Mara had pictured a setting with metal folding chairs in a circle, 1950s linoleum, and Styrofoam cups propped next to a church basement coffee percolator. Maybe donuts. Instead, the room was Ashlee-like: bright and classy and warm. Inviting.

She tried to guess who the leader was as everyone took their turn at the high-end espresso machine. No one had that "I'm the healthy one but I do sympathize with all of you, so I'm here to help" look. As newcomers, Ashlee and Mara were directed to sign in on an iPad and encouraged to fill a plate with veggies and hummus, if they cared to.

Hummus.

She tapped Ashlee on her shoulder and said, "Are you sure this is a faith-based group?"

"Yes. Why?"

"No reason. Well, one. Where are the donuts?"

Laughter too was unexpected. But it made more sense to Mara now than it would have a few months earlier. Laughter had every right to be there in the middle of people working their way through grief. She cautioned herself to not get too comfortable though. At the first sign of "my grief's worse than yours," she was out of there. She'd warned Ashlee ahead of time.

"Ashlee?"

"Yes?" her forever friend answered, then dug into the hummus with a peapod.

"That thing I said about one-upping someone else's grief?"

"Yeeesss?"

Mara let out a purging exhale. "Forget I said that. Old me. We'll stay no matter what. It's not a contest."

Ashlee handed Mara a cucumber slice. "Well played."

The fiftysomething man in Birkies and socks—it was, after all, January—and sporting a magnificent mane of caramel-colored dreadlocks called the attendees to gather in what was better described as a conversation grouping than a circle. "We'll need to sit three to a couch tonight, it appears. So cozy up."

If he'd used the word *snuggle*, Mara might have—

Ah! Two "cozy" armchairs side by side. Mara power-walked to grab one and signaled for Ashlee to take the other. She set her purse on the cushion, in case anyone else had the same idea. *I'm here*, the purse said. *But I wouldn't say I belong yet.*

Introductions did not take forever, as anticipated. No one was required to report what or who they were grieving. It was beginning to look like Mara might skate through the evening.

215

"We'll start as we often do," Dreadlock Dan said. "With communion."

What?

"We come from a variety of faith and cultural backgrounds, so if this is uncomfortable for you, or you'd like to excuse yourself from this portion of our gathering, please know that is completely your prerogative. This is simply an invitation to join in communion, if you wish. It is the starting point of our true community. Elanna?"

A young woman—tall and elegant—stepped into the center of the room with a tray of bread and a pitcher of wine or wine substitute.

Dan explained, "We have three options for the bread from which you'll break off a piece. They're marked clearly, but as a point of reference, they range from light to darker: gluten-free, naan, and rye."

Mara whispered out of the side of her mouth, "Rye?"

"Large Scandinavian contingent here," Ashlee whispered back.

SMH. Should be interesting. *And breaking off our own pieces of bread? Did no one think about the fact that it is still flu season?*

Elanna began to hum a hymn Mara recognized as "Let Us Break Bread Together."

"Before you step forward to participate in communion," Dan said, "I'd like to talk about the song we're hearing. With its origins in pre–Civil War spirituals, it not only has a long history, but an interesting one as well. Some of the stanzas date back to the eighteenth century. Others have been added by oral tradition, which has led to many variations on the text."

His gentle but well-modulated voice made Mara think he could work as a voice-over actor for bedtime stories. The kind she'd love to listen to. Elanna's low humming—full in richness rather than volume—created an atmosphere that put Mara at ease and yet anticipating what might lie ahead.

"Depending on your denominational background, your cultural background, or the style of worship in your church, you may recall these words:

> Let us break bread together on our knees.
> Let us break bread together on our knees.
> When I fall on my knees with my face to the rising sun
> O, Lord, have mercy on me.

Elanna changed keys, raising the melody a little higher than it had been, though still quiet and flowing.

Dan continued, "The most notable difference in lyrics is that some hymnals and historical interpretations of the song use the phrase 'to the Lord of life' in place of what we believe to be the original version, which used 'to the rising sun.' Sun in this case was apparently considered a metaphor referring to God. As we sing together, we'll use the 'to the Lord of life' version in recognition that he is both light and life."

Hadn't Mara and Ashlee discussed that concept not all that long ago? What color is light? What color is life? He is both.

Guard the dawn, Mara. The rising sun. Rising life. Her heart took notes.

⁓

As soon as she got home from the first grief care meeting, Mara pulled out her laptop to conduct research to satisfy her curiosity. She'd grown up with hymns and now attended a church with a carefully thought out blend of old and new. But she hadn't remembered hearing the background Dreadlock Dan unearthed regarding the simple communion hymn she hadn't sung since she was a little girl.

The song hadn't been intended as a communion song, her research told her. It was part of the heritage of music that had been incorporated by the enslaved to direct one another—"with my face to the rising sun"—to secret meeting places and safe freedom routes.

Safe freedom routes. Music was still being used to do that, metaphorically. Mara still turned often to the playlist Chelsea had made for her, and it pointed her to peace.

How many millennia before and after the 1800s had people ended their prayers with, "O Lord, have mercy on me"? That prayer had been on Mara's lips almost daily for more than four months.

It had been a hard evening at grief care, but a good one. The twenty or so people in the room were there because they were broken by sorrow. She didn't know their stories yet, but she recognized the moments when a memory would change their facial expression, or when the light in their eyes would slightly dim. She'd told Ashlee she hadn't been having emotional blackouts but brownouts. Mara had often found herself not fully present in a moment because of having to come up for air after a wave knocked her off her footing.

Did anyone ever get kicked out of grief care for loitering? Or did they all eventually graduate, just at different paces? Like her two kids graduating this spring, even though they started kindergarten a year apart?

Ashlee said it was an eight-week program. How many signed up for automatic renewal? Would they?

Before Mara closed her laptop, she searched for an online version of the "face to the rising sun" song. She found a choral arrangement and let it fill the house while she waited for Chelsea and Dylan to get home.

⁓

Ashlee picked Mara up right on time—not surprisingly—the next week. On the way to their second meeting, Mara turned to ask Ashlee, "What are your goals for your care group experience?"

"Could that have sounded more clinical?" Ashlee responded.

"I know why I'm there," Mara said, redirecting the heat vent on her side of the car. "Two words—Christmas Eve. But this was more than just a way to force me to go, wasn't it? And it's not that you're struggling every day like I am."

"Oh. You think I'm not? You think I reached some kind of magical anniversary date and decided to delete all the memories, to upgrade seamlessly to a new operating system that doesn't have a Robert icon embedded in it?"

"Did you think that analogy through earlier or did it just come to you?"

"Just came to me," Ashlee said, a measure of accomplishment tingeing her voice. "But I am taking an online poetry class. I might have been inspired by that."

Mara watched the distance between them and the grief care group location shorten, fresh, wet snow making the roads "greasy," as Grandma Lou would have put it.

Ashlee glanced at her. "You still there?"

"I'm wondering how someone takes a poetry class over the internet."

Ashlee turned the vehicle into the parking area. "Line by line, Mara. Line . . . by . . . line."

Mara clapped her gloved hands. "I am so glad I know you."

"Likewise."

"What if your parents hadn't moved so close to Grandma Lou's when we were kids? I can't imagine never having a friend like you. And I can't imagine why it took me so long to realize what a gift you are."

"Took you so long?" Ashlee straightened her posture. "I'm not supposed to take offense at that, am I?" She rubbed her forehead as if pretending the words had stung.

"You know what I meant. You were always there, no matter how far away we lived. I was so consumed with survival that I wasn't always there for you."

"God brought us together again when we most needed it."

They headed inside. The elevator ride was short, just long enough for Mara to ask, "What made you decide on this town when you were looking for a 'change of scenery,' as you said? Of all the places you could have gone, why here? When did you make that decision?"

"The truth? The day I heard about Liam."

—

Ashlee uprooted everything to be here for me? What am I supposed to do with that? She's renting. Not sure if she'll buy. Is that what she meant? She's a traveling hug? She goes where the need is?

She moved halfway across the country because she knew I'd need a friend to walk me through this?

Ashlee, you are . . . an enigma wrapped in a mystery wrapped in a riddle. Same Sol principle, but different.

Dylan would be proud of her vocabulary skills. Did they teach that Churchill/Russia reference in high school anymore?

The meeting opened similarly to the previous week, but with a different song accompanying communion. It sounded more contemporary, but just as moving. Mara could see why the group had chosen to begin their gathering in that humbling, peaceful way.

Mara tensed, though, when the group questions started with, "What's the bravest thing you did this past month?" But she had an answer and volunteered to go first.

"I came here."

A murmur of agreement with an occasional chuckle made its way around the room.

"Anyone have something to add to that?" Dan asked.

A couple of tentative hands raised.

"I wrote thank-you notes for the memorial gifts. Especially

brave, since my daughter died six years ago and they're all more overdue than my library books. But I did it."

Another said, "I sold my mom's car." Applause ensued. "God was especially kind to me with the sale. It's going to a man who needed it so he can deliver meals to shut-ins. Mom would have liked that."

Dan nodded to Ashlee. "Yes?"

"I made an appointment for an MRI."

twenty-five

Mara slammed the passenger side car door harder than she intended to. "What was that all about?"

"I was waiting for the right time to tell you. It's likely nothing to be concerned about."

"But you need an MRI to know? Ashlee!"

Ashlee clicked her seat belt and gestured for Mara to do the same. "It's obviously not an emergency. The MRI department didn't have an opening until the end of February."

"What? No. We'll get you in to see a different doctor. You can't settle for waiting almost three weeks for an MRI. That's crazy."

"As I said, if it were an emergency, my doctor would have rattled a cage or two to get me seen earlier. He doesn't seem concerned."

"Is it . . . a back issue? Old football injury?"

"Thanks, Mara. I need your humor as much as anything."

"So, you *do* need me."

Ashlee backed the car slowly out of their parking spot, the snow now more of an issue than it had been. "I've always needed you."

"And that *does* mean it's serious." Mara crossed her arms over her chest. That probably read more defiant than she wanted it to. So she planted one hand over her heart.

Ashlee glanced her way. "Pledging allegiance, are you?"

"To you, yes. I'm here. And I hope you know you can trust me with whatever it is. I will not flake out on you . . . despite . . . you know . . . Christmas Eve."

Ashlee snorted. "If you keep me laughing, I'll be just fine."

"Are you going to tell me about it? Did you have a suspicious mammogram or something?"

The vehicle angled toward the curb, slowed, and came to a stop. Ashlee put her SUV in park and left the engine running.

That serious? Mara's heart felt as if it were headed for her ankles. "Talk to me."

"Mara, would you drive the rest of the way home?"

"Uh, sure. No problem. Can we talk first? You're scaring me."

Ashlee rubbed her forehead with her fingertips. "Don't be scared, Mara. Honestly, it's probably nothing serious. I've had a small lesion in my brain for several years."

"Oh, stop. Right there. 'Nothing serious.' 'Lesion on my brain.' What do those two phrases have in common? Nothing!"

"It might be the cause of the migraines I'm having . . . which, by the way, are exacerbated by people screaming."

"Sorry."

"No apologizing. Just take me home, okay?"

"Ashlee . . ."

"Please? I promise we'll talk. Right now, I need to close my eyes and stay quiet until the medicine kicks in. Do you think taking it with tonight's kombucha might minimize the medicine's side effects?"

—

Ashlee's living room looked like it was already prepared for receiving its migrained renter. The townhouse was quiet. Ashlee had left only two lights on—the nightlight on the kitchen stove, and a dim table lamp in the living area.

After Ashlee was settled, Mara turned to the task of settling herself. Her overactive imagination was no help. So she looked up the med Ashlee mentioned and kombucha.

"No known contraindications between kombucha and the prescription you're taking for the migraines, Ashlee." Mara turned her phone upside down on her thigh so the residual light from the screen wouldn't disturb her forever friend. *Little reminder, God. My* forever *friend. Okay?*

"Good to know," she said, eyes closed, head back, chenille throw wrapped around her like a shawl.

"Would you like to prop your feet up?"

"That would be nice."

Mara dragged an ottoman to where Ashlee leaned back, lifted her feet at the ankles, and positioned them carefully.

"My feet don't hurt, Mara."

"I didn't want to jostle you."

"Appreciated." Ashlee's volume told Mara all she needed to know about where her pain stood at the moment.

Mara looked around the darkened room, even the table lamp now turned off. What else could she do for her? "Would you like some water?"

"What did you say?"

"Would you like some—Oh. I asked if you wanted water."

"Not yet. Few more minutes. Need my stomach to calm down more."

Mara slipped into a chair near her. She shielded her phone with her body and texted Chelsea and Dylan that she was at Ashlee's and would get home later than expected. Dylan immediately replied that he'd shoveled the driveway, but snow was still coming down. He cautioned her to be careful.

She resisted responding, "It's six blocks, son." Instead, she thanked him.

A few quiet minutes later, Ashlee said, "I could use some water now."

"Got it." Mara navigated her way through Ashlee's living room by memory with a little help from what filtered through from the small nightlight on the stove in the kitchen. She grabbed a bottled water from the refrigerator, then another for herself, a little irritated that the refrigerator light was so bold.

Ashlee's eyes were open when Mara returned with their drinks. "Thanks."

"Anything. I mean it. Anything."

Ashlee's eyes drifted closed again. "Let's go to Florida."

"What?"

"You need a tan. We both need to be able to walk outside without dressing like polar bears."

Mara would have rolled her eyes, but there was no point if Ashlee wasn't looking. "Polar bears almost never wear clothes."

"You know what I mean. Wouldn't you like to ditch your boots for flip-flops for a week?"

"You're serious." *Keep your voice low, Mara. And your excitement. It might be her medicine talking.*

Ashlee sat up and turned on the small lamp on the end table. "I still have a condo near Bradenton. Beautiful beaches. Great food. Oh, what I wouldn't give for a fresh grouper taco right now. Well, not *right* now."

Mara leaned on the arm of her chair. "No offense, but Ashlee, does that med make you delirious at times?"

"Hear me out. Every year since Robert's been gone, I've spent the week of Valentine's Day at the condo. I'm going whether you do or not."

"Well, I obviously can't let you go alone this year." What was the woman thinking?

"If we asked nicely, do you think Sol would keep an eye on my place and your kids?"

Mara's heart started back toward her chest. Ashlee was thinking clearly. "Have you ever known him not to want to help?"

"Never."

"There's your answer, then. He'd probably move in while you're gone, if you wanted him to." That didn't sound right. She meant for the week. She'd correct her wording when Ashlee was more alert.

Ashlee closed her eyes again but stayed sitting upright. "I hope we can get a flight at this late date. It had . . . slipped my mind."

A flight. They'd be flying. And why wouldn't they? It would be a very long drive from the heart of Wisconsin to Bradenton. Likely with sketchy weather for a lot of the trip. People fly every day. *But not me. Not me.*

~

As expected, Sol didn't waste a second contemplating whether he'd say yes to keeping an eye on their two places while the women were gone. He also empathized when Mara told him it would be her first flight in a very long time.

"I don't blame you a bit," he said. "I hate to fly. Hate everything about it." He shivered for emphasis. "Flying, needles, and tiny spiders. Big ones, I don't mind. Don't ask me to explain that."

Mara had no trouble understanding the airplane and fear of needles part. But tiny spiders?

"Maybe we should get Logan to watch the two houses and your kids," Sol said, "and I'll chauffeur you there and back."

"It's kind of you to want to spare me the pain of planes, and win yourself a free trip to Florida, but is it a good idea to put Logan in charge of Dylan and the lovely Chelsea?"

Sol thought for a moment. "Logan's already supervising Dylan, but you're right. The way he feels about Chelsea . . ."

"You're okay with that, aren't you, Sol? That our kids are dating?"

"More than okay. Chelsea's amazing. Yes, I know she's been through some rough spots. We talked about it. But I think Logan is a very blessed young man to have her interested in him. I love her heart."

How much of "it" have they talked about? "She's the one blessed to have Logan. They have a sweet relationship. And I know she's an adult in the eyes of the laws of this state. But, she hasn't graduated from high school yet, so . . ."

"Agreed. I'm the chaperone of choice."

"And a long road trip? I don't think Ashlee is up to that right now. She's been having migraines."

"Yeah, I know. She had a doozy when we were painting at your place over Christmas. But she's getting help for them now, right?"

How much was she free to say? Ashlee seemed determined to play it low-key at least until after her MRI appointment, which couldn't come too soon for Mara's tastes.

Mara had to admit that having a distraction for Valentine's Day would be welcomed. She'd missed more than the one upcoming. But she sincerely hoped the distraction wouldn't include a medical emergency.

—

Ashlee's condo was on the seventeenth floor of a high-rise on the beach. So "on the beach" meant they could step out the door at ground level and step into sand.

At the moment, they were looking at the beach from seventeen floors up. Or, rather, Ashlee was looking down. Mara looked anywhere but down.

"You do remember I'm not crazy about heights, right, Ashlee?"

"Me either, but this view is spectacular." She would have

leaned over the railing, Mara was sure, if it hadn't been thick Plexiglass a good four feet tall.

"I'll look later. Think I'll unpack first," Mara said.

"I usually take the coral bedroom, but if you'd rather—"

"Happy with the beachy blue one. Two-bedroom condo? Posh."

Ashlee tore her gaze away from the scenery. "When we bought it, Robert and I thought it would be great for bringing kids and grandkids here someday." She sighed, but in a lung-clearing rather than a sad or tired way. "I've been tempted to sell it a hundred times—two bed/two bath right on the beach? But it keeps calling to me."

"I think I've seen pictures of this spot in some of your Christmas cards."

"Our happy place. I don't have any trouble keeping it rented out in winter. It paid for itself before we'd owned it five years." She turned back to the view. "Well, I'm keeping you from unpacking."

"Did you want to lie down for a while? Take a nap? How are you feeling?"

Another pivot to look Mara in the eye. "And that is your final act as my nurse, Mara. We're here to have fun and replenish our body's supply of Vitamin D. I'm doing fine. I've lived with this little BB-sized thing in my head for a couple of years. If I get a migraine, you'll know about it. And if I need help, I'll ask. Okay?"

"Okay. So, we can't take a nap, then?"

Ashlee chuckled. "*You're* the one who needs it? No better place to nap while in Florida than on the beach. Let's go."

A few months earlier, the sun had seemed an offensive, searing reminder of all that was faded in Mara's life. Now, it warmed all that had been frozen and stiff. Her skin was grateful. Her

228

soul was grateful. She let her body sink even deeper into the cushions of the lounge chair and let one foot stay in contact with the warm, sugary sand.

"Mara?"

"Mmmhmm."

"Do you realize we've experienced an eighty-degree difference in temperature between getting on the plane this morning and landing here? It was zero when we left Wisconsin."

"Mmmhmm. Not counting the wind chill."

"That's right," Ashlee said. "More like ninety degrees' difference."

"I'm enjoying every single degree right now."

"I'm glad." Ashlee lifted her sunglasses. "Sunset's in about an hour and a half. We'll need dinner."

"Your point?" Mara snapped her fingers. "Garçon! Bring us food!"

"It's not that kind of condo. We either cook our own or eat in one of the four hundred great restaurants within walking distance."

"Four hundred? Really?"

"Exaggeration. But we have lots of options. And my favorite — Look at me, Mara."

Mara opened one eye.

"My favorite is right back there."

She raised up on one elbow to see where Ashlee was pointing.

"Some of the best seafood I've ever eaten," Ashlee said, "with one of the best views of the sunset on this strip of beach."

"Sounds ideal. So, I can soak in the sun for another hour and fifteen minutes?"

"I don't know about you, but I'd like to clean up a little before we eat."

"Probably a good idea."

Ashlee looked toward the waves. "We haven't even dipped our toes in the water yet."

Mara assumed it was coming but thought she could avoid the issue a little longer. "I don't mind skipping that."

"Okay." Ashlee eyed her. "You're right. It'll be there tomorrow."

Mara watched an older couple walk hand in hand at the water's edge, kicking at the waves, their feet making impressions that disappeared as quickly as they'd formed. "Actually, it's not always there tomorrow."

~

Outdoor dining. Not what Mara would have been doing at home at this time of year. Grateful Ashlee had suggested she bring a wrap or sweater to dinner, Mara draped it over her shoulders as they waited for their dessert course. Mango sorbet.

"Nothing too heavy," Ashlee had insisted.

In light of the conch fritters, coconut shrimp, and platter-sized mounded veggie salad they'd had already, Mara agreed without argument. The crème brulee that caught her eye on the menu could wait for another day. Assuming . . .

Mara had only checked her phone once. As if reading her mind, Sol had reported in. "All quiet on the Midwestern front. Dylan working with Logan on community service. Chelsea is at a concert with Lisa."

Could Lisa be Chelsea's future forever friend? Ashlee and Mara were an anomaly. So few childhood friends maintain a lifelong bond. And they hadn't worked at it. Mara definitely hadn't. It was as if God had knit them together and said, "I have a gift for you. Enjoy."

Ashlee had grown quiet.

"You okay?" Mara asked. "And I don't mean that in a medical, nurse-like way."

"Enjoying. Remembering."

"Anything specific?" Mara opened her phone again and took a picture of the sunset colors enveloping the scene.

"Sunsets at your Grandma Lou's farm. Sitting on hay bales at the top of the ridge, watching the sun inch its way toward the horizon, guessing at what moment it would completely disappear." Memories and the current scene painted beautiful images in Ashlee's sunglass lenses.

"And the moment the porch light would come on at your folks' place, reminding you it was time to head home."

"I wonder why I always call it Grandma Lou's farm," Ashlee said. "Your grandpa was around somewhere too."

"He kept to himself a lot, though."

"True. Hard-working man."

"And he grew up not paying much attention to emotional cues. Grandma Lou kind of took both of us under her wing, didn't she?"

"Random thought," Ashlee said, then looked Mara's direction. "I must be hanging around you too much. Random thoughts are more frequent these days."

"I'm all about random thoughts. What is it?"

"In that beautiful old house, why was the living room floor not original? Everything else had those gorgeous restored pine floors. I've been curious about that."

Uncle Morton. That's why. Sometimes when a person takes their life, they destroy a whole lot more that can never be fixed. Right, Jeremy? Do you understand that now? I wish I could have told you.

His letter to his father had long ago been moved from under her pillow to the fireproof lockbox where she kept everyone's birth certificates and the deed to the house and her grandpa's silver dollars that he told her would be worth something someday. It seemed an invasion to think about reading it. A large part of her didn't want to know what he'd written, or why Jeremy might have thought it so devastating to his father.

"Well," Ashlee said, "I didn't realize it would be such a mind-boggling question."

"Lost in thought again."

"You're allowed." Ashlee turned her attention to the sunset. "I predict . . . right . . . now! Yes!"

The light wasn't gone yet. But the ball of fire had dipped its head under water. Mara opened the image she'd taken moments ago. She showed the screen to Ashlee. "Nothing can quite capture the glory."

"I have a feeling," Ashlee said, "it's supposed to be that way. You have to be here in person for the full effect."

Their sorbets arrived in long-stemmed glasses with an orchid bloom nestled at the glassware's feet.

"It wouldn't take long to get spoiled by these extra little touches." Mara examined the delicate orchid up close.

"That's another word I'd love to alter."

"What?"

"Spoil. It's hard not to think of it in negative terms. Spoiled meat. Spoiled toddlers in perpetual tantrum mode. Spoiling someone's fun. Diminishing the quality, like when a car horn spoils a romantic almost-kiss."

"You have an alternate word choice, my walking-thesaurus friend?"

Ashlee leaned back, her eyes reflecting the sunset's glow. "I think we're being treated to wonder all the time. We're not always observant of it, though. I want to live noticing the speckles in the orchid's throat, the cardinal in the branches of the birch tree in my backyard at home or in a watercolor, the hint of lime in the mango sorbet."

"Is that what that was? Nice."

"And receive it all as an expression of God's artistry and his love for us," Ashlee said, almost breathless. "We're not being spoiled. We're being freshened."

"You do know what freshened means in cow terms, right?"

"Refreshed. Better?"

"Much." Mara finished the last drop of now-melted sorbet.

"I probably used the word *spoiled* in regard to Liam's life insurance. As much of an answer as that first check was, the fact that it came at the cost of Liam's life made it feel like I didn't want to touch it. But I had to. This probably doesn't make any sense to you."

"Perfect sense. Now, get over it," Ashlee said.

"Subtle."

"You were blessed with provision. The proper response is, 'Thank you.'"

Thank you. Thank you, Liam. Thank you, Deep Wells, Inc., and thank you, Lord.

"I'm committed to letting you know if you're being foolish with the provision," Ashlee said. "But you're not."

"Except for impulse art purchases."

"Art therapy, my dear. Art therapy."

Mara made herself a mental note to see if she could locate the artist who had painted the winter watercolors with a cardinal in a birch tree. Ashlee's birthday wasn't far off.

twenty-six

Mara hadn't slept this late in a long time. Her alarm usually warned her that Ashlee would expect her to be ready to walk within the hour, no matter how dark it was outside. Or she'd been awakened by the clashing internal battle between regret and peace. Between grief and peace. Between worry and peace.

A Florida getaway and alarm clocks had no common ground. And a measure of peace had gotten the upper hand on many fronts lately, other than Mara's concern about Ashlee. What had awakened her?

The guttural sound coming from Ashlee's bathroom.

"Ashlee?"

Her friend retched, then said, "Door's open, if you dare."

"Oh, Ashlee."

"Good migraine morning to you."

"I'm so sorry."

"Give me a minute, okay?"

Mara retreated, dressed quickly, then moved through the main area of the condo closing drapes against the blinding light of the sun. She tiptoed to the door of the coral bedroom. "Is it okay if I make myself some coffee?"

"I'm not affected by smells, like some people are."

"Anything I can get you?"

"My sunglasses."

"I'll find them."

Mara sat in the darkened condo, praying for her forever friend to be just that—forever. How many migraine sufferers of the world longed for a diagnosis to explain their pain and at least give them a name to hang it on? Mara prayed Ashlee's MRI would either reveal what was hidden and treatable or . . .

What other option was there?

She heard her name.

Ashlee sat propped in bed, sunglasses still in place, but she looked less pale than she'd been. "Come closer so I don't have to shout."

Mara found a small chair in the corner and pulled it to the side of Ashlee's bed. "A little more tolerable now?"

"I measure in millimeters. Yes. Several millimeters."

"I'm going to call that progress." Mara straightened the items on Ashlee's bedside stand.

"You're trying so hard to keep yourself from asking me if I need anything, aren't you?" Ashlee said.

"So hard it hurts my teeth."

"I'll ease your pain. I could use an ice pack, when you have time."

"On it." Mara stood.

"Wait. Not right now. I have to get a few things said before I can't."

I've seen this in the movies. No, Ashlee. Don't do that. We don't need to have "a talk." You're going to be fine and we'll laugh about this next year when we come back. Maybe we won't laugh, but we will come back.

Ashlee must have detected Mara's unspoken hesitance. "Before I can't talk because the medicine makes me drowsy."

"Oh. Listening."

"Two big things. If the MRI shows something serious, I want

you to buy the condo from me and come here every year and love it like I have."

"Ashlee, stop talking like that."

"I'm not afraid, Mara. But I am sincere, here. If you don't buy it from me, I'll have to give it to you, and that just seems a little excessive, doesn't it?"

Still her Ashlee.

"We'll discuss that later." Mara turned Ashlee's bedside digital clock away so the LED numbers wouldn't aggravate her headache.

"Second," Ashlee said, "I am going to lie here for a while, but I don't want that to stop you from doing what you came here to do."

"What I came here to do? I came to be with you and just enjoy a little warmth for a change."

"Oh, my self-talking friend in denial. You came here to conquer. You came to put your face to the sun and feel it all. You're here to walk right up to the water's edge and then farther. Toes, ankles, knees."

"Sharks, jellyfish, stingrays."

"You came," Ashlee insisted, "to collect new items with which to make cyanotype art—crafted by the sun, to make art of what you have where you are. Life principle. What you have where you are. Here, it'll be shells. Sea glass. Seaweed."

"Sharks, jellyfish, stingrays."

"Mara. It's taking a lot out of me to have a discussion right now."

"Then it can wait," Mara said. "It'll always be there tomorrow, you claimed."

"So will the fear and regret, unless you keep collecting . . ."

"Collecting what?"

Ashlee rubbed her forehead. That wasn't where most migraines hit, was it?

"New memories."

Even with a gruesome headache, Ashlee thought more clearly than most.

Mara pondered as long as she dared, then answered, "Okay."

"Take your phone. I want pictures of *your* toes in *that* water."

Mara looked at her bare feet. "How will you know they're my toes? There are lots of people on the beach."

Ashlee's eyes were closed, but she lifted her sunglasses anyway, as if she could glare through her eyelids. "Yours need polish. How long has it been since you had a professional pedicure?"

"Never. Plus, what's the point if they're stuck in boots all winter?"

"Maybe tomorrow we'll rectify that. I want to head into the MRI with . . . with . . . Monet's 'The Artist's Garden' toenail art."

"Is that even possible?"

"Don't ask me hard questions right now."

—

As far as she could tell, no one else on the beach was miserable. Except for that baby getting his diaper changed on a blanket in the sand. Mara was the only other one, but she kept her wailing internal.

She stood on the hard-packed damp sand a good ten feet from where the incoming waves had crawled onto the shore. Some body surf when they go to the ocean. She body-*hugged*, wrapping her arms around her middle, upright and unmoving, like a stake planted in the dirt at the end of a garden row.

"I'm not afraid of water. I'm afraid of what it represents," she said aloud. "Clean water took Liam's heart to Africa. Muddy water took his health. Lack of water took his life. And an ocean separated us for far too long." The sound of the waves muffled her voice enough she could let her self-talk be exposed to the Gulf air.

She stood her ground.

"Liam's absence made Jeremy more vulnerable. His death made him inexpressibly sad. Jeremy's tormented mind made him think he was to blame."

She stomped her foot. "And you, waves! You're at the heart of it all!"

Mara couldn't back up fast enough. A single rogue wave, foaming and sputtering, chased her, overcame her, and drenched her to mid-calf before retreating.

She doubled over, first in shock, then with laughter. Lifting her face to the sky, she said, "God, you are so precise in your timing and relentless in your pursuit! 'You don't want to come to me, Mara? Okay, I'll come to you.' Nice one."

But now she had a problem. She'd have to recreate the scene in order to have proof for Ashlee.

She obtained her photographic proof the hard way. She asked a passing tourist to take her picture as she walked intentionally into an incoming wave. Then she walked the damp beach sand with a plastic bag looped over her arm as she watched for shells and coral and sea glass.

For years she'd kept a pottery bowl of sea glass on her bathroom counter. It had been from her "let's start here and redecorate with a beach house theme" phase but hadn't gone any further than that. Life got busy. And hard. She moved the bowl to clean the counter from time to time but did nothing with the pale aqua sea glass.

Many of the pieces had sharp edges, but what do you expect when you buy sea glass from the craft department at Walmart? The real stuff, she suspected, was in water long enough for its edges to be polished smooth.

As she walked the beach now, she recalled that when Jeremy was six or seven, she noticed he'd been in the basement a long time, too quiet. She sneaked down the stairs and found him trying to glue the pieces of glass together.

"Mom! I'm sorry! I don't know what this was before, but I knocked it over and broke it. I'm trying to put it back together like it was, but I don't know what it's supposed to be. A vase, right? I can't do it."

He was in tears by then. Such a sensitive soul.

She remembered pinching back her laughter as she embraced her repentant son. "Honey, it was a bowl full of broken pieces of glass. It wasn't anything. You can work all day and not find out which piece goes where."

"Maybe that's"—he sniffed twice—"why it's so"—another sniff—"hard to figure out."

Jeremy, you didn't break anything. It was a bowl of broken glass. And no matter how hard you tried, you weren't going to make a vase out of it.

"Yes, I'm listening, Lord."

~

She leaned low to capture a vignette of what had washed ashore. A leafy, almost lacy sea plant, a smooth piece of driftwood, and a starfish. She shielded her phone screen with her hand to see if the image came out as she hoped. Nice. It might make a great watercolor.

The phone buzzed. Ashlee.

"Hungry. Called in an order to our fave restaurant. Pick it up for us? Ready in twenty."

Ashlee, you are as sneaky as your Creator. You probably knew I'd be forced to run to get back "in twenty."

Something about the sea air and the warm-but-not-too-warm temperatures and the sun on her face made the jog exhilarating, as long as she stayed near the water. As soon as she left the water's edge for deep, soft sand, it was tougher going.

She rinsed her feet and hands at the outdoor shower spigot before slipping into her flip-flops and entering the restaurant through the beach access. Mara waited no more than a minute before the hostess brought her the takeout bag. Ashlee had paid by credit card when she ordered, which was good, since Mara hadn't thought she'd need to bring money to the beach.

She found her way to the condo building and to the elevator without incident, and without sneaking a peek at the mystery contents of the takeout bag. Ashlee had rarely, okay maybe never, steered her wrong.

Ashlee had glasses of iced tea waiting for them. The light-blocking drapes had been opened, but she wore her sunglasses and a floppy sunhat. Bright pink.

Mara deposited her beach-finds bag in the entry and the meal bag on the glass-top table between the kitchen and living area. "Want me to close those drapes?"

"I'm fighting the urge. So love that view."

"I know what you mean. Addictive, isn't it?"

Mara ducked into her bathroom to clean up, then joined Ashlee at the table. "Hey, how did you know how far away I would be? 'Pick it up in twenty'? Risky, wasn't it?"

"I knew how far away you *wouldn't* be," Ashlee said.

Can a person ever know you too well? "What are we having for our late lunch?" Mara opened the bag and extracted clam-shell takeout containers. Four of them.

"I ordered crab and artichoke dip with mega-veggies."

"Some of that sounds healthy."

"It does. Keep in mind you just ran on the beach. And crème brulee. It's tomorrow."

"It is." *And it's soon going to be today's tomorrow in Uganda.*

By evening, Ashlee's migraine had eased off enough for the two of them to sit on the condo balcony to watch the sunset. Mara planted her chair just inside the open patio doors and kept one hand on the doorjamb.

Seabirds and human-variety snowbirds cavorted near the

water seventeen stories below them, almost too small to recognize from that height. A breeze lifted the hair on Mara's arms.

"How does your brain feel?" she dared to ask.

"Bruised. The headaches are coming closer together. Not that it means anything," Ashlee was quick to add.

Like early labor pains. But Mara wasn't about to use that analogy with a childless woman. Someday, if there was time, she'd risk asking Ashlee why she and Robert hadn't followed through with their adoption plans. If there was time. "Still two weeks until your appointment?" Mara asked.

"Twelve days."

Ah. She was counting.

"How can you sit so close to the railing, Ashlee?"

"Because that's where the beauty is. Just a guess, but I'd say you haven't hiked the Grand Canyon, have you?"

"That would be a negatory. Have you?"

Ashlee peeked at her over the top of her glasses. "Many times. I lived in Arizona."

"Oh yeah."

"Remember other Christmas card backgrounds?"

Mara smirked. "I thought you were photoshopped into those. Honestly, how could you stand so close to the edge? I didn't see a guardrail. Do they not have guardrails?"

"Not in most spots. I think you and I should go there."

"Ashlee . . ." *You don't know it yet, friend, but I think God's on my back about another destination. He's talking. I'm trying hard not to listen.*

"We should go next fall," Ashlee said. "Maybe to honor the anniversary of Liam's and Jeremy's—"

Mara stopped her. "Weeks apart. Two anniversaries."

"We could stretch out the trip." Ashlee touched her fingertips together and spread them apart as if pulling highly elastic modeling clay. "I know. Train trip across the whole US. One coast to the other. That's an actual thing, and affordable, I've heard."

"I can't." Mara swiped a slice of raw zucchini through the crab artichoke dip.

"Predictable answer."

"Ashlee, not this year."

"But someday?"

The hope in Ashlee's voice shredded Mara. She knew better than to let herself read too much into the quiver, but that didn't stop her.

"Not this year. I think I'm supposed to go to Uganda."

twenty-seven

Ashlee hadn't so much as blinked when Mara announced her intentions to go to Uganda. As expected, and as Mara had counted on, Ashlee's response was, "Well. Okay, then. You can depend on me to be there for your kids."

She'd volunteered even before knowing Mara wasn't talking about two weeks or a month. Mara wanted in and out. A day's travel each way. A day to visit the village and seal the chapter.

And she'd said it as if the MRI was a mere blip and the migraines no hindrance at all. Ashlee . . .

"You don't think it's an insane idea, Ashlee?"

"I think it's brilliant. What's your motivation?"

"Now! There it is. Sun disappears into the water yet again."

"Oh. I missed it."

"Not to worry, Ashlee. There's another one tomorrow."

"The sun'll go down . . . tomorrow. Bet your bottom dollar that—Sing it with me, Mara."

SMH. SMSMH—so much shaking my head. "Did you realize we're missing the grief care group tonight?"

Ashlee propped her bare feet on the low wrought-iron patio table. "I'm not missing it. I brought a twentieth of it with me."

So did I. "This is so good for my soul."

"Mine too." Ashlee tilted her head back and breathed in far more than just beach air, Mara suspected.

"I wish you were feeling better," Mara said.

"Methinks you're avoiding my question."

Mara moved her chair an inch closer to the actual balcony. "Which one?"

"Motivation. You said you think you're supposed to go to Uganda this year. I do agree it's a good idea, but I wonder what made you decide to do that."

"It's a little more like a strong nudge from God than a decision on my part. But I believe I need to be in it. I've had only a virtual experience of the place that won Liam's heart, like looking at a photograph of an impossible-to-capture sunset or imagining what the Grand Canyon is like from paintings and a Christmas card."

"Not the same." Ashlee nodded. "You're right."

"I need to know what charmed Liam. The smells. The flavors. The look in the children's eyes that he so often talked about. I need to hold my hand under the flow from one of the wells he built. I lost two of the people I most loved because of Liam's attachment to the work he did there, the difference he made."

"Are you prepared to be disappointed?" Ashlee covered her feet with a beach towel. The air cooled as the sun's residual heat faded.

"What do you mean?"

"You may not feel what he felt. At one time I thought I was supposed to be an elementary school teacher, like my sister was."

Her sister, Jill, who died of a brain tumor!

Was Ashlee at the grief care group because of mourning her husband or her long-gone sister? Or both? How could Mara have forgotten about Jill and the medical family history connection?

"But," Ashlee said, "I got partway into my junior year and

thought, 'Nope. I'm not feelin' it.' All the other elementary ed majors were soaking it up and I was shriveling. What if you get to Uganda and think, 'Nope. Not feelin' it'?"

"I have to go anyway."

"Well, let me get through this MRI. You know the Coppernalls would jump at the chance to do a repeat of this week and keep an eye on everyone. After the MRI, we'll start looking at flights and paperwork and—"

"Ashlee?"

"Why don't you ever call me by my nickname—Ash—like you used to?"

Mara waited.

"Oh. Yeah, that should have been obvious."

"Ashlee, I have to go alone."

"Alone? Foreign country? Parts of it war-torn? You? Airplane? Alone?"

Mara patted her stomach. "I . . . just . . . feel it in here."

Ashlee looked out across the water. "Well, as we all know, gut health is pretty important."

"Thank you."

"Are you sure?"

"I think it's part of my 'guard the dawn' assignment, facing the sunrise. It's kind of like letting the searing sun seal that chapter of my life. Not so I forget, but so I can remember without regret."

"Maybe God meant 'guard the Dawn,' the dishwashing liquid. Don't let anyone take your dishwashing liquid." Ashlee's brow furrowed. She cringed. Always so close to the edge of pain these days.

Come on, MRI.

The lighthearted moment Ashlee attempted soon faded. Mara drew in a deep breath of Gulf of Mexico air. "And, I need to scatter Liam's real ashes."

⌒

"Was that Sol?" Mara leaned over Ashlee's shoulder to glimpse her phone screen, which wasn't hard, given the tightness of seats in the economy section of a plane full of tanned or sunburned tourists on their way home. "What did he have to say?"

"Frozen water pipes on my street. He checked my place. Nothing was flooding, but he made sure the heat was turned back up for when I get home. And he stocked the fridge and filled gallon jugs with water for me in case it's a while before the city gets the broken main fixed."

Mara smiled. He was taking good care of Ashlee.

"He said he did the same at your house, in case the temps drop any lower."

"Temps dropping lower. There's no place like home," Mara said.

"Except in January or February. Most of March."

The flight attendant interrupted for safety instructions. Within a few minutes, all devices were in airplane mode and they were climbing above the clouds.

"Ashlee, would you do it again?"

"Next February, Lord willing."

Mara kept her grip on the armrests. "I don't mean a getaway at your condo. I mean, would you ever consider getting married again?"

"No."

"That was quick and decisive." *And will be a grave disappointment to Solomon Coppernall.*

"I make a fine widow," Ashlee said. "Widowhood suits me."

"It does?"

She circled her face with one hand. "Look at this glow. Does that not say 'Happy Widow'?"

"It's sunburn, and it says, 'Should have listened to Mara when she told me to reapply the sunscreen.'"

"You may have noticed that I'm a bit of a free spirit."

Mara felt the plane leveling off. They must have reached cruising altitude, a phrase that struck her funny, as if she could look out the window and count the cruise ships flying by. "A free spirit I admire and aspire to be one day."

"You be you," Ashlee said.

"Oh, you have to stop having your morning devotions at the Pinterest meme board."

Ashlee laughed so loud the sound rose above the roar of the engines. Fellow passengers stared at the two of them.

"It's okay," Mara announced. "She's medicated."

"Mara!"

"Ashlee!"

"See me inserting my earbuds," Ashlee said. "I am going to listen to music as we wend our way back to the frozen tundra. Talk to you later."

Time to go home. Pay some bills. Set up another required home visit with Dylan's probation officer, Brad. She might even dust this time.

Time to think about planning a double graduation party. And find a job she could live with. And check on the status of her passport application. And decide if she could imagine going back to that condo if Ashlee weren't there.

~

Sometimes when light dawns, it blinds a person, like staring into a solar eclipse.

"Sol, you had no right."

"You aren't . . . pleased? When we worked on your kitchen and family room, you seemed to really appreciate it."

"This is different. This is an invasion of privacy."

He looked stricken. Good. He needed to be.

Mara's face burned so hot she couldn't touch it. And the heat had nothing to do with the Florida sun. She kicked her unpacked, barely-out-of-the-vehicle luggage out of the way. "How could you think it was okay to do this?"

"I . . ."

"You what?" She knew her stance must have made her look like a rolling-pin-wielding caricature or cartoon. She dropped her imaginary rolling pin. "What?"

"I was trying to help. Helping is what I do."

"This is too much helping, Solomon. Too much!"

She sank onto the leather loveseat where Jeremy's bed once stood. How much practice does it take to learn how to spit nails accurately?

"I hoped you'd like it." His words were barely audible. "Chelsea said you'd talked about converting Jeremy's room into a place where you could do art or music or—"

"And that?" She pointed to the accent wall. Somehow, he'd made wallpaper out of Jeremy's and Liam's penmanship. "Where did you find those notes?" She scanned quickly to see if any started with the dreaded, "Dear Dad."

"Chelsea and Dylan helped me pull them together." His voice wasn't accusatory. She knew he was trying to explain, tell the story, but this was altogether unacceptable.

"You should have known better."

"It was—" He turned his head to the blank, safe, almond milk wall—a little darker than the coconut milk kitchen and family room.

"It was what, Sol?" The fight in her had all but fizzled.

"A gift. A way to move forward but keep them close to you."

It felt like walking into a house that had been burglarized. Jeremy's room had been stolen. Yes, she'd wanted to do something with it someday. One of these days. Soon. But didn't she get to choose? Wasn't that her call, not his?

"Please leave. I'll deal with the kids later. Just go home, Sol."

She heard the click when the front door closed.

As much as she owed him for his kindnesses to their family,

even this past week while she was turning her face to a healing sun and he was going out of his way to check in on her kids and keep everything running smoothly, he had no right to do this.

She could hardly bring herself to look at the collage of notes in her son's and husband's handwriting. And yet, she couldn't look away.

Some of it looked like it had been taken from school essays or Mother's Day cards. Chelsea would have known where she kept them all. She tugged the chenille blanket Sol had draped just so over one arm of the loveseat and wrapped herself in it, then walked closer to the accent wall. Jeremy's back-slanting script. Liam's slanted at almost the opposite angle, his writing quick, never closing a *g* or *p* or *d* or *b* completely, which made his *b*'s look like *h*'s.

She recognized a line from a poem he'd written years ago for a college assignment. A story he'd created for the kids when Dylan and Chelsea were toddlers. A line from his first draft of their wedding vows. Where had they found that?

Mara touched the wallpaper lightly, tracing Liam's rushed words and Jeremy's that looked as if they were reclining.

Sol had no right.

Ashlee did not need a friend like him in her life. And Mara certainly didn't.

~

Chelsea and Dylan offered to change the room back. They'd saved everything in bins in the basement, just as Mara had planned to do. But reverting the room seemed more wrong than the way it was now. She'd learn to live with it somehow, until she had time to rip down that wallpaper.

Sol texted and emailed and phone messaged his apologies. She didn't respond. She supposed his heart was in the right place, but hers hadn't been. Her first thought was "too soon." But when would have been the "just right" time to let the house know that Jeremy wasn't coming back? Officially canceling the room reservation.

If Ashlee had known about this vandalism, she would have been on Mara's side, right? Just in case, Mara decided to wait a bit to tell her. She dodged Ashlee's questions about where Sol had been the last few days.

When a spouse or a child is no longer in the house, sorrow moves into the spaces they left. Mara could have decided to move. But decision-making had disappeared too. That meant walking past Jeremy's room multiple times a day. If the door was closed, her mind grieved what was no longer behind it. It was no longer a door, a room, a space. It was a hole.

What kind of person wouldn't appreciate having the hole filled in?

Liam once told her a story about ruffed grouse in winter. They'll burrow in deep snow for protection—like a grouse igloo. But grouse don't store fat well and have to eat daily. So if too much snow falls too fast and they can't break out of their burrows, their very protection becomes their grave.

All the sameness she thought protected something in her could become her emotional or spiritual demise.

If Ashlee heard that story, she'd probably land on the "eat daily" part. And she wouldn't necessarily mean food.

The day before Ashlee's MRI appointment, just after the two women had made arrangements for Mara to drive her to the clinic, Sol showed up at Mara's door.

"Kids at school?" he asked.

"Yes."

He lifted a black five-gallon bucket filled with tools. "I came to take the wallpaper down," he said. "It's the least I can do."

The sun was shining. In contrast to the last couple of weeks, temps were creeping close to the midthirties. It wouldn't last long. Colder weather would return with several attempts to discourage the spring-eager. But this day, the air was softer than it had been in a long time. Clear blue sky. Grace.

"Come on in," she said.

"Thank you."

"If you promise not to touch the wallpaper."

~

They shared coffee and very little conversation. At long last, Sol huffed out a breath and said, "I understand something about myself now."

"What's that?"

"When I was on the force, I was frustrated because I was policing without helping. And like many of us, I suppose, I flipped to the opposite problem. I've been helping without policing, without considering if my assistance was wanted or not, without restraint, without guarding another person's boundaries. And I am so very sorry."

She affected a Sol voice. "Like all the times you've asked, 'Do you need me to walk you home, Mara?'"

"Yes. Things like that. And . . . the room. The wallpaper."

"I can't imagine how much time and effort that took."

"It was a . . . labor of love."

What?

"With Chelsea and Dylan and me all working together. When we'd compiled the samples of their handwriting, their stories, and I sent it in to the wallpaper company, I felt as if I'd just been given a glimpse into who Liam and Jeremy were at their core. I really intended nothing more than to honor them and to bless you. And I messed up on both counts."

"You did honor them, Sol. For me, the blessing part had to wait until the shock wore off and I realized the kind of person *you* are at your core. Helping is what you do."

He pressed his lips together and sighed.

"We're not so different in that respect," she said. "For as

long as I can remember, I thought it was up to me to make sure everyone was okay. I volunteered too much. I worked myself sick. And I took it personally when my kids made choices that were unwise or unlawful or . . . fatal. You used the word *guard* earlier. I've been hearing that word too."

He nodded. "It would mean the world to me if you'd forgive me."

"Oh, Sol. I did that before I let you in the door. Now, let's talk about Ashlee."

twenty-eight

Mara did her best to wrap her arms around Sol far enough to get a good grip for the Heimlich maneuver. Her arms were too short. She pounded on his back with her open palm, which she then recalled was what you do for a choking infant.

"Can you talk?" she asked.

"Not . . . yet," he sputtered.

She raised her voice. "What can I do?"

"Stop . . . making . . . me . . . laugh! Mara, I choked on my coffee, not a chicken bone!"

"Oh." She returned to her mug and buried her smile in its depths. "Do you see the irony here? I was just trying to help."

"I do see the irony."

"You might want to be more careful about trying to breathe and do anything else at the same time in the future. See there? Helping too much."

He raised his hands in an "I give up" posture.

"About Ashlee," Mara said. "She's going to need us tomorrow. And we should probably set up our boundaries."

"Guard the perimeter. Right."

"I'll take the left flank."

"I'll take the right," he said.

"And by flank, I mean . . ."

"Side," he answered quickly. "Right side. Gotcha."

Mara noticed the palpable relief of conversing with Sol without anger or remorse between them. "And that will be after I get her home from her appointment."

"What?"

Mara set her coffee aside. "Sol, I think if we surround her, it'll feel like a bigger deal than she wants it to be."

"You're probably right."

"I have to be there. She requested a relaxant. Unless you wanted to use my car, but please say no because I really, really want to be there for her."

"Understood. You're the driver."

"But afterward, if she's feeling up to it, which I assume she will be, if she doesn't have another migraine, I think we should do something way normal."

"Normal. And by that you mean . . ."

"Weeeee . . ."—she raised her hands and arms to prepare for the downbeat—"eat."

"Yes. We eat. We eat what? Oh, I know."

Mara said, "Young man in the back with your hand raised. Yes, you."

"Chicken soup."

Mara shook her head. "That would indicate we thought she was sick."

"Yes. Good. Not good. Um, nachos?" he offered.

"Perfect."

"Unless it's bad news." His face darkened.

"Sol, she won't hear the results tomorrow. It could be as much as a week or more before she knows what's going on in there." Mara pointed to her head.

He was silent for a long moment, then looked up. "How are you handling it?"

"The MRI?"

"Your concern for Ashlee. I mean, you've had a pretty steady string of tough blows. If this thing with Ashlee is serious—"

"We'll walk through it together. I didn't think I needed another reminder that God is my only hope, and hers. But it's becoming my default thought now, rather than my last resort."

He folded his arms and rocked back and forth on the island stool. "I can see that. It shows in your face."

"That, my friend, is the work of the sun. Sometimes when you leave things out in the sun too long, they don't fade. They get brighter." *Cyanotype art prints.*

Mara's phone dinged. "I should look at this, Sol. It's from Chelsea's guidance counselor."

"Want me to leave?" He was standing already as if the answer were an automatic yes.

"You know what? No. I may need the emotional support. Most of the messages I've gotten from the school these past three years have not been day brighteners." She perused the message. "Until now," she said, turning the screen to face him.

He read aloud, "'Mrs. Jacobs, this is to inform you that your daughter has been selected for this year's Music Boosters' scholarship in the amount of $1,000. It will be announced at Senior Awards Day in May. More information will follow by mail.' Nice."

"I wonder if they've told her yet. I wonder if I'm supposed to keep it a secret. I wonder if that means I'll have to go to Uganda in April so I don't miss Awards Day in May. But I wonder if my passport will come that fast. Probably not. Might have to be June. I wonder what the temps are like in June."

"Uganda?"

"I may not have mentioned that. Sol?"

"Yes?"

"Are you free to pick up the nachos tomorrow? Will Logan loan you his truck for a while?"

"I can do that. He now has a second vehicle I'm working on buying from him."

"Great. And another thing. Lots of guacamole? It seems like it will be a guacamole kind of day."

"Uganda?"

The look on his face was priceless.

———

Dylan grabbed the bagel Mara had toasted for him and headed for the door. He stopped short. "Mom, what time is Ashlee's appointment?"

"Not until eleven. Why?"

"Want to know what time to pray. Oh, and I have news. A sweet new community service project."

"You sound excited about it."

"I am. And it would be awesome if you'd participate too."

"Me?"

"I created it myself. Both Officer Brad and the judge agreed to it."

"Bob."

"No, Mom. His name is actually Brad."

Mara felt her cheeks warm. "Oh. That's right. So, tell me about your idea."

Dylan glanced at the clock on the stove. "Okay, but real quick. I don't want to be late for school. I worked with some of the team from Deep Wells to create this 5K walk/run to help raise funds to build wells in Africa. A community service project with a global reach."

"You've been talking to the Deep Wells people?"

"Yeah. That's okay with you, right?"

Mara considered. "Sure. That's great. Are they going to send someone to be here for the race?"

"The run. Or walk. People can choose either. But it's not timed. It's just to raise money. People will get pledges per mile.

We'll have merch. Hats and water bottles and stuff. The mayor's going to be there. News outlets, if I can talk them into it."

"You need me to sponsor you, is that it?"

"No, I want you to walk it with me. We can train together. I hope Chelsea will do it too. And boom! A whole bunch of community service hours taken care of. Not to mention helping people have safe water to drink."

She felt good about all that, right? Of course, she did. "I'm proud of you, Dylan."

"Oh, what sweet words." He kissed her on the cheek and headed out the door.

⁓

Ashlee picked at a piece of lint on her pants and said, "You're going to participate, aren't you?"

"The 5K? That's like five K's, Ashlee. That's a lot of K's!"

"I'm aware of that."

"I'm not athletic. Do I need to keep reminding you?"

Ashlee clasped her hands in her lap. "A person could do a 5K with a walker, if she needed to."

"And I would," Mara said. "Not for my age, but the other reasons. Not in shape. Too far. Will collapse along the way."

Ashlee's sitting version of her hands on her hips almost made Mara laugh. Almost. "Do you know how many laps we usually walk at the indoor track?" Ashlee asked.

"Yes. Twenty." Mara well knew. Twen-ty. Every. Single. Time.

"A 5K is only five more laps than we walk every morning when we're able."

"Get out of here!"

"I'm serious. You're walking four-fifths of a 5K every day."

"I rock."

"You do."

Mara watched Ashlee clench and unclench her hands. "And you're going to rock this MRI."

257

"That wouldn't be good. I'm supposed to lie very, very still."

"Nice one, Ashlee."

"Thank you. I try. Oh. There's my name being called."

Mara squeezed her hand. "I'll be right here waiting."

"I know. And I'm grateful. See you later."

⁓

In some ways, waiting for Ashlee to emerge from her MRI testing was like waiting to know if Dylan was going to be sentenced. The future hung in the balance. Tipped one way, life would go back to normal, or as normal as Mara's and Ashlee's ever got. Tipped the other way, a path Mara didn't want to consider.

And in both cases, the hours of waiting would lead to more waiting. Judge's decision. The test's results.

Mara could work on seeing how high she could get her blood pressure to spike, or she could use the waiting time productively.

Prayer? Good idea.

Searching the web for info about low-key but high-gratitude double graduation parties that Liam would miss despite his promise to his children that he'd find a way to come home for that day? *That day, Liam?* Hard to focus.

Look for the quickest way to get from the Entebbe airport to a remote village in who-knows-where Uganda? Harder to focus.

Read? Always a good choice. She'd rediscovered the simple pleasure of a good novel. Ashlee had a hundred recommendations. At Ashlee's invitation, Mara had picked one from Ashlee's "favorites" shelves. Mara pulled the volume from her purse and opened to the spot where she'd fallen asleep the night before. Then she reread a few pages back, since clearly she hadn't remembered the scene before her.

Soon, she was lost in the story, her pulse slowing and racing with the pace of the words.

Mara checked the time when she reached the end of a chapter

and could look up without losing her place. It would be a while yet. "Lord." She'd already prayed through every detail. "Lord" was enough at this point, wasn't it? He was.

The next chapter led to the next.

"Mara?"

"Ashlee! You're done already?"

"All done." She sank into the chair beside Mara.

"How did it go?"

"Loud."

"That's what I've heard. Did you get to listen to music through headphones?"

"I don't know how I would have relaxed that long without it. What are you reading?"

Mara turned the cover toward her.

"Mmm. Love that one. Where are you in the story?"

Mara closed the book. "We can talk about that later. Good story, though. Right now, it's time to get out of here, isn't it?"

"I'm ready. Remind me about this later, though. It matters." Ashlee took a deep breath. Then another. "Yes, let's go."

—

Mara resisted offering to open the car door for Ashlee. She could do that for herself. Probably wanted to. The procedure hadn't taken anything out of her. It had looked into her. To the places that until now only God could see within the folds of her brain.

"No headache today?"

Ashlee smiled. "Now, that was a grace gift. No headache. But I am hungry."

"Got you covered. By the time we get to your house, Sol should be there with . . . let's call it a meal. No migraine on MRI day. Now, that's an answer to prayer."

"Mara, when I got back to the waiting room, you had just turned a page in the book," Ashlee said moments later.

"New chapter."

"Was the previous chapter written poorly? Not worth your time? Unimportant?"

Mara signaled and pulled out of the medical center parking lot. "Ashlee, you were the one who recommended this novel. You know it's a great story. It was a hard one to read, but I turned the page because that's what you do when you're reading."

"Little hint of sarcasm there," Ashlee chided. "The chapters build on one another. That's how it goes with all meaningful stories. A skilled storyteller makes the reader eager to move on to the next chapter, even if the previous one was their favorite so far. Or hard to read, emotionally."

Ashlee had a big old point she was trying to make, didn't she? Mara thought over what she'd just said.

"And that's you and me," Ashlee continued.

Mara glanced her way. "Figured that was coming."

"Robert was a beloved character in many chapters in my life. Now he's not in the scenes. But that doesn't mean they didn't happen. Or that they weren't meaningful. They were part of my story. And my next chapter may or may not have passages that are hard to read. But they matter."

"They matter to me too."

Ashlee said nothing more for several blocks of the drive home. Then, "Robert isn't thinking, *Ashlee, how dare you be happy? Did you forget about me? Didn't I mean anything to you?* He did. And I can't, nor would I want to, forget those pages. They helped tell my story. Shape it. Frame it. Make me the person I am today."

"Is our friendship part of your next chapter, Ashlee?"

"I don't know. I certainly hope so. But if it isn't, will your story go on?"

Mara pulled into a gas station.

"That shaken up, Mara?"

"No. I need gas."

"Oh."

"But, it does 'give me pause,' as Grandma Lou would say." She shut off the engine. Nobody else waited for her pump, so she remained where she was and turned to face her passenger. "Yes, my story will go on no matter what. But I may need to reread some favorite chapters once in a while."

Ashlee nodded her agreement. "They might not make sense on their own, without the rest of the story."

Neither spoke for the space of a mini-eternity.

Mara watched the movie in her head—the puzzle pieces converging into a more identifiable picture. "Liam and Jeremy."

"Yes. Some sweet chapters and some utterly heart-wrenching. All part of your family's story. And now, a new chapter, a sequel. Chelsea and Dylan getting ready to leave home. Maybe a long-term relationship between Logan and Chelsea. Maybe room for Sol?"

"Sol?"

"A possibility?"

"Ashlee, *you* have to take Sol."

"What? Why?"

"Because." Mara's mind sputtered. "Because that's what I've been praying for."

"*I* don't want him."

"Ashlee!"

She raised her hands, palms up. "What made you think I was interested in Sol?"

"He's perfect for you."

"*I'm* not taking him. He's a great guy, a wonderful friend. But, as you know, I'm not even sure how many . . . how many pages I have left. And I'm enjoying my life right now. Well, except for the medical part. Why would I want—"

Mara now knew the full meaning of the word *incredulous*. Mara was incredulous. Ashlee certainly looked incredulous. The view Mara caught in her rearview mirror showed that the guy in the car behind her seemed a mite incredulous too.

"Mara. Is that your phone?"

She pulled it from her coat pocket. "Yes. The nachos are waiting for us."

"Ooh." Ashlee rubbed her hands together. "Nachos."

twenty-nine

*I*f Sol noticed their weirdness around him during Nacho-Fest, he didn't mention it. Mara hoped he attributed it to post-MRI-but-pre-results concern. A gentleman as always, he simply served and met needs and treated both women with kindness and respect.

One of these days, she and Ashlee would have to look up that documentary he'd talked about. Somebody had made a film about his homeless experience? No, he'd called it his experiment. And yet, technically, as he said, the man was still homeless. But living across the street and down three houses. A lot of anomaly going around.

All through Nacho-Fest, he stayed a reasonable distance from boundary markers. Mara and Ashlee had a harder time, wide-eyed and ultra-incredulous—their new favorite emotion, apparently—behind his back. It was a silent volley of Mara's "You don't want him? How could you not want him? He's perfect for you" and Ashlee's return look of "Why would you think I'd want something more than friendship with Sol? Why would you think that?"

~

A week passed uneventfully except for the ever-present wondering about how many pages were left in Ashlee's novel. Mara finished the book she'd borrowed from Ashlee, returned it to Ashlee's reading corner, and borrowed another. A few pages in, on a rainy March afternoon, Ashlee called.

"And?" Mara answered.

"No 'Hello there. How's it going, Ashlee?'"

"This is no time for small talk. What did the report say?"

"How do you know I wasn't calling to ask for your recipe for—"

"Ashlee Maureen Eldridge . . ."

"You do enjoy making up imaginary middle names, don't you? Okay. You've been very patient."

On the outside.

"The doctor said it's mostly good news," Ashlee reported.

"What does that mean? Mostly?" Mara set the open book upside down beside her.

"It means the lesion they've been watching for a couple of years is stable. It hasn't changed. No bigger, no smaller. And it doesn't appear to be leaning against anything that would explain the migraines."

Mara didn't try to stifle her sigh. "Big relief. What's the not-so-good news?"

"Same thing. They can't explain the migraines from what they saw in the MRI. He's changing my medication to something new that has been effective for a lot of people."

"Good. That's great. Hope."

"Yes." Ashlee paused a long stretch of forevers. "However, while I'm on the medicine, I can't have . . ."

"What? Coffee? Don't say coffee. Nachos? No, that would be crazy-talk. What?"

"Sugar."

"We're toast."

"Right. No real point in living anymore, Mara."

"Ashlee, that's not funny."

"Honestly, it's okay. I was a day or two from suggesting we

make a pact to avoid sugar until after Dylan's 5K. Not the one coming up. The one in the year 2043. More later. I have to make a couple of phone calls and then get to the pharmacy. He said I could start on the new med right away."

Mara breathed deeply for the first time in a while. Not about the sugar. That would hurt. She wasn't going to lie to herself. But Ashlee had hope. And it was contagious. Barring the unknown, Mara wasn't going to have to add another grief to her list.

"Hey, Mom." Dylan was working harder than ever but rarely dragged himself into the house anymore. He bounded in this time. Full of drug-free energy. This next Thanksgiving, she'd ask for extra time at the celebration table to report all for which she was thankful.

"I'm glad you're home, Dylan. Ashlee's MRI turned out very well."

"Great. Brought the mail in. Both of us have letters here from Deep Wells, Inc."

"You and Chelsea?"

"You and me. Here you go. I assume I can just put the obvious bills in the stack?"

Mara's stack had shrunk considerably. And she still had a little time before she had to dive into taxes. How did that work? Would she owe taxes on Liam's earnings? She'd need help this year, for sure.

How easily that had rolled through her mind. She'd need help and wasn't hesitant to ask for it.

"What's your letter about, Dylan? More 5K correspondence?"

"You go first," he said, joining her on the sectional, his letter in hand.

She slid a fingernail under the flap. "Chelsea working after school today?"

"Last I heard."

Mara skimmed the cover letter on Deep Wells letterhead. It was folded around a small envelope addressed to her.

Mrs. Jacobs, enclosed is a letter . . . one of the villagers
. . . long time to get to us . . . any response you'd like sent
back to the woman, we're happy to facilitate it for you.

No more skimming. She read every word from the beginning. And fingered the small envelope that gave no hint whether it was precious or poisonous.

"That's cool, Mom, isn't it?" Dylan's expression looked as tentative as she felt.

"Might be. I'm going to save it for later. What's your letter say?"

Dylan opened his, read silently for a few moments, then folded it and tucked it in his pants pocket.

"Dylan . . . ?"

"Okay, so this needs a little setup."

Mara grabbed one of the Ashlee-ized throw pillows and hugged it to her chest. "What do you mean?"

"I can undo this if you make me. I haven't signed anything yet. But hear me out first."

"I'm listening." She didn't need to be told to give her full attention to whatever it was he was about to say.

Dylan pushed his hair back away from his face. He needed a haircut. Mara reined in her stray thoughts.

"I kind of applied . . . Well, I did apply for one of the Deep Wells summer internship programs."

"What?" Mara worked hard to neutralize the expression she must be exhibiting.

"I've been thinking about tech school, and maybe that's the route I'll go eventually. But I really want to do some good somewhere, you know?"

Like father, like son. "That's admirable."

"But . . ."

"But what?"

"No, I was waiting for your 'That's admirable, but . . .'"

Mara stared into the cold fireplace. "What I said stands. I admire your courage and your desire to make a difference. If it's Deep Wells, and you get accepted into the program, then—"

"I was, Mom. That's the letter. Here." He dug it out of his pocket and smoothed the folds before handing it to her. "Acceptance letter. I'm in. I leave for the US headquarters in Atlanta a week after graduation, and then on to Uganda at the end of June."

"Uganda?"

"I specifically requested that. I think they figured I'd pester on that point until they said yes, so . . . they said yes. I made a case for the PR it could net them. The father-son connection."

The father-son connection.

She could delay her trip to Uganda until Dylan was there. No. If anything, that would have to be a second visit. Both of them needed to work through their reasons for being in that country, on that continent, on their own.

Mara made sure her supportive mom smile was in place. "What can I do to help? Or not help? Whichever . . . helps you . . . the most."

"You okay, Mom? That was kind of convoluted."

Mara looked into her son's eyes. Clear and true, after having been glazed and bloodshot for so long. He wasn't trying to be a hero. He was a kid wanting to make a difference. A man wanting to make a difference. And he would. She was sure of it.

"I'll be okay."

"It's freaky that this letter came today," he said. "Last night before I fell asleep, I got the munchies, and don't worry, Mom. The normal kind. I saw your Bible open on the island. You'd put an asterisk in the margin by this one verse. Well, two. I hope it was okay that I kinda read over your shoulder when you weren't there."

Mara chuckled. "Dylan, I love you."

"I know."

Good.

"It was Psalm 121. The last couple of verses. 'The Lord will keep you from all harm—he will watch over your life; The Lord will watch over your coming and going both now and forevermore.'"

"You memorized it?" She should start memorizing Bible verses. She should stop "shoulding" and just do it.

"I took a picture of it on my phone so I could check back with it while I was waiting to find out if I was accepted into the program."

"You're leaving the week after graduation, huh?" *God, the pages of my story are turning so fast. A little help here?*

Maybe she should cancel her trip. Dylan could do the ashes ceremony if she asked him to. *Is that what this is about, Lord? You just wanted to see if I was willing to go, but I won't have to?*

"I know it's quick. Logan said I still have to get the court's permission, since it would mean cutting my probation time short, which I doubt they ever do. But I've gotten this far."

"Yes, son. You have. I'll call your lawyer. He might enjoy arguing for a project like this."

"Thanks." He bounded off the couch and headed for the refrigerator. "Oh, and I'm glad about Ashlee's news."

Me too. Now more than ever.

~

Mara waited until Dylan and Chelsea were both in bed, which meant staying up past her own bedtime. She needed a quiet place and a quiet mind when she opened the envelope from the village woman.

Her Bible was still open on the island, the spot her kids

called Grand Central Station. She brewed herself herbal tea—not her favorite, but no caffeine to keep her awake later—and laid the note beside her Bible. Where had Dylan been reading? Ah. There. Her eyes backed up to the beginning of the eight-verse chapter and noted highlighted phrases from years past and a few more recently.

"Where does my help come from?" Fitting question. She knew the answer.

"He will not let your foot slip." Also fitting for a woman training for a 5K. What was she thinking?

"The Lord watches over you—the Lord is your shade at your right hand; the sun will not harm you by day, nor the moon by night."

He's my shade. And my light. What else could claim to be both? No one else.

She picked up her phone to search other versions of the verses Dylan had stumbled on and memorized. "You will be guarded by God himself. You will be safe when you leave your home and safely you will return."

Guarded by God himself. *Guard the dawn, Mara, the place where the sun rises before it rises here. The sun that won't harm you.* Is that part of what God wanted her to get out of this?

The small envelope smelled like her ginger tea. She opened it slowly, half-expecting ashes to fall out. It was simply a letter, written in a child's hand on lined notebook paper.

"Mrs. Liam Jacobs," it began. "My daughter is in school because of your husband's generosity. She learns English. So I ask her to write this for me. I know English words, but not enough to tell you this."

Halfway around the world, a small hand had written these precise letters to form the words the mother was unable to write. The mental image was so vivid, she could almost imagine the mother's pride and the daughter's sense of accomplishment. Could almost hear the village sounds in the background.

"Your husband was my daughter's father . . ."

What? This was not the penmanship of a three-year-old minus nine months, not that Liam would ever—Mara read the words again. "Your husband was my daughter's father when she had no one else to pay for her uniform for school, and when she and I both needed to know that a man can be kind. He taught many of us in the village that God has many good men with kind hearts. Some of our sisters and daughters have seen none before. They work hard but their men have no hope. They do not allow thought beyond today. Or the woman's men died young in the wars that buzz around us like flies."

Mara tilted the letter to better catch the light. "Ah. The women's men."

"We pray for you as the sun rises on another day. Sometimes we walk to the river to sing the songs he taught us or the ones we taught him. Our children are healthy. We have water that is safe and flows so strong, it still makes us jump. We have heard how he died in the fire, but it started at the river."

Mara stifled the sobs that wanted out.

"May you be comforted in your sorrow. He had the comfort of another woman as he lay dying. Wasuze caught his last words and cradled him against her chest as his fever raged. That is love. She loved him well."

It was signed in what must have been the woman's own hand. Illegible, but deliberate strokes.

A woman who somehow thought Mara would be comforted to know her husband had been "well loved" by another woman.

thirty

This was not information her kids needed to know. Not now. She would not wake them, although the compulsion was strong to have someone else's eyes read the child script and see if Mara had missed something, had misread the clear words.

Dylan and Chelsea would hear their noisy garage door grinding open if she drove to Ashlee's. Unseasonably warm March weather and clear sidewalks made her decision easier.

She texted Ashlee, who said Mara should come over immediately, since she was an any-time-of-the-day-or-night kind of friend and apparently tonight her insomnia was working in Mara's favor.

It was a well-lit and well-protected neighborhood. She had a flashlight and a piercing whistle if necessary. But in a roundabout way, hadn't God just showed her that she would be "safe when you leave your home and safe when you return"? He couldn't have meant this.

Ashlee would likely give her a lecture about taking verses out of context, but nonetheless, there it was.

Almost midnight. But waiting until morning would mean staring at the clock until dawn. So, she left a note for Chelsea and Dylan on Grand Central Station, slid into her coat and gloves, and slipped out into the moonless night.

She'd been taught that if she ever had to walk alone at night, she should do so confidently, as if she had a specific destination in mind and a wicked left hook. She threw her shoulders back and lengthened her stride. It wasn't all that far. And few cars were out at this hour anyway.

One block. Two.

Midway to Ashlee's house, a truck approached and slowed as it neared her. She dug into her coat pockets and felt for her whistle with one hand and a travel-sized hairspray in the other. The hairspray wouldn't do any damage to a perpetrator's eyesight, but it might buy her enough time to escape, if necessary.

"Mara? Is that you?"

"Sol? What are you doing out at this hour?"

"I could ask you the same," he said, leaning from the driver's seat toward the open passenger window of Logan's truck.

"I'm on a mission . . . to Ashlee's house," she said semi-confidently.

"At midnight?"

"We're training for a 5K. Did we tell you that?" Mara put a faux lilt in her response.

"Again, at midnight?"

"Boundaries, Sol." She hadn't lied. They were in training. Although the statement was unrelated to his question, so some repentance might be in order. Not tonight, though.

He sighed. "Okay. None of my business."

"What are you doing out this late, Sol?"

"Boundaries, Mara."

"You're right." She let off her wrestler's grip on the can of hairspray. "None of my business."

"I was finishing up at the jobsite, if it's any comfort. Logan hopes to have an open house for it this weekend, but not if I can't get the touch-up paint done on the trim work. Always lots of that after the cabinets and furniture are moved in, and why am I telling you all this?"

"It's the best story you could think up on the spot to explain why you're driving around in Logan's truck at this hour."

He looked at the steering wheel, then back at her. "Do you need a ride? Hop in."

Mara shook her head. "Sol, it's three more blocks. I'm almost there. And no. I don't need a ride." Might have wanted one but wouldn't take it. Oh dear. Had she learned nothing?

He murmured under his breath.

"What was that?"

"I was just thinking about Independence, Missouri," he said as if it were midday and not midnight.

"Oh, you were?"

"They have a Miss Independence Contest every year, or they should if they don't. You might want to consider entering."

"Good night, Sol."

"Good night, Mara."

⁓

"Well, you know what they say," Ashlee began after finishing the letter for the second time. "When God squeezes you this hard, you don't need a laxative."

"Ashlee!"

"Mara, you don't know what this letter means. The language barrier alone—"

"Most people speak at least a little English, and school-aged children are taught to speak nothing but English," Mara said. "I don't believe this is the result of a language barrier. Cultural barrier, maybe. In their world, is it okay for a man to have a wife in Wisconsin and a—a something else in Uganda?"

"Don't jump to conclusions. There's a high risk of falling. It's dangerous to your health. From what I've read, family is very important in Ugandan culture."

Mara took the water Ashlee handed her, but changed her

mind and handed it back, suddenly thirsty for anything but water. "You've been reading up on Uganda?"

"Haven't you?"

"Yes, but earlier today I thought I might not be going after all. Dylan applied for and was accepted to a summer internship program in guess where."

Ashlee turned on one more lamp in the living room. "Really? Well, that's terribly wonderful for you."

"There's the proper use for that phrase. Terribly wonderful. I'm proud of him, scared for him, wish I'd known sooner, but then I might have tried talking him out of it, which he knew."

"But you're going to let him go, aren't you?" Ashlee leaned forward at the neck, expectantly.

"He wants to honor his dad this way. And he wants to make a difference where he can. How could I fault that?"

"You're encouraging Dylan to go." Eyebrows raised this time.

"Yes," Mara said.

"You might have to let this go too," Ashlee said, waving the small envelope. "Assume the best. And if it turns out to be the worst, you'll get through that somehow too."

Mara swallowed. Her throat was dry from walking. But she wasn't about to renege on her refusal of the water. "What now?"

"Ah, the question of the year."

"It was last year's question."

Ashlee stared at the floor for a moment, then looked up. "I think you still need to go to Uganda and find yourself some peace."

Mara waited for her heart to catch up to her head. "Yeah. That's what I was thinking too."

Ashlee prayed for her, then said, "Oh. I almost forgot to tell you. Sol called while you were on your way here. He's waiting on the front porch for whenever you're ready to go home."

—

"Solomon Edgar Coppernall!"

"It's Edwin, but that was a close guess."

Mara's ears were no longer cold. They burned. "What are you doing here?"

He stepped off the porch onto the sidewalk, arms spread. "Lovely night. I'm out for a stroll."

"That is so not true."

Solomon kicked at a clump of unmelted snow. "I thought you might need someone to walk you home."

"Which I don't." Mara raised her mini-flashlight to prove it. She had a small envelope stuffed into her pocket with all her self-protection equipment, and she did not need to fall apart in front of this guy. She bypassed Sol and headed left.

"Bars close at two," he said behind her. "There will be more traffic."

"I'll look both ways at the crosswalks. Thanks."

"And more ne'er-do-wells."

Six blocks seemed a lot farther in the middle of the night. She stopped, turned his direction, and asked, "Well, are you coming?"

He caught up quickly.

"Do you want to talk?" he asked.

"No." He'd walked all the way to Ashlee's to prove how stubborn he was? No, to show what a good friend he was. "I do want to talk. But not now. Still too many unknowns," she said, switching from power walking to strolling, from holding tight to resentment to letting a little gratitude seep in.

"Is it okay if I give you a quick little side-hug?" Sol asked. "Very brotherly like?"

"Nope." She instantly knew she should have said yes. But it was too late to change her mind.

"Okay then."

A block later, Mara asked, "What time do you have to be at the jobsite tomorrow?"

"There and ready to roll by six a.m."

The man had a lot of Ashlee in him.

Another block closer to home, she said, "Okay, so here's the deal. Dylan got accepted to a summer intern program with Deep Wells and he's headed to Africa."

Sol pulled a fist toward his waist with a "Yes!"

He probably knew because as Dylan's peer counselor, Logan would have known. That's it.

A few steps later, Sol said, "So, here's the deal. Logan wants to ask Chelsea to marry him and because she's eighteen he probably could but I told him he'd have to ask you and suggested that he wait until her birthday when she's officially nineteen and that's not a terrible age to get married because my mom and dad did and lived very happily for a lot of years."

She couldn't look at him. "I'm going to pretend I didn't just hear that. And we will remain silent for the rest of this journey."

Her self-talk, however, was flapping its jaws plenty.

That's utterly ridiculous. They've only been dating a few months. But on the other hand, it's obvious their love for one another isn't infatuation. Eighteen, okay nineteen, is entirely too young to get married. I mean seriously, plus she has a small scholarship and needs to go to college now that she's figured out how to submit assignments. But Logan does have four years on her and is more mature than that and has a stable job and a decent income and by the time she got done with the credits she could get at the community college, she'd be twenty or twenty-one. Or have three kids and no time to study. This is without doubt the dumbest idea and out of the question. But on the other hand, Chelsea would have a man who cherishes her and they share so much in common with their faith and both of them are great problem solvers and she does know how to make lovely chicken wild rice soup and a nice cup of tea. But that's no reason to get married. How about a six-year-long engagement? No, that's the most ridiculous idea of all. I may never sleep again.

"Mara?"

"Yeah?"

"We're . . . at Logan's house."

"What?"

"We kinda skipped right on past your house, but you seemed so determined, I didn't want to interrupt you."

Huh. So we did.

She glanced at her wrist. "I . . . hadn't gotten my steps in for the day. There. Done. Good. Good."

"Your house is back that way," he said, pointing.

"Yes. I'm well aware."

"Do you need me to walk you home?"

~

"When life falls apart, God's plan hasn't. It's still active but adds a soul-healing component."

Ashlee's text message greeted her when she finally admitted defeat and crawled out of bed at seven. Sol would have been at work for an hour already. She couldn't confront Chelsea. Logan hadn't asked her because he wanted to talk to Mara first, and oh good grief what was she going to tell him?

Mara got the kids off to school, then collapsed facedown on the sectional. "Alexa, solve this," she said before remembering she didn't own a voice assistant.

She rolled onto her back and spoke in the general direction of the ceiling, hoping God had a few extra minutes to spare. "Let's talk about this rationally. My biggest problem with all this is . . ."

Ahk. She didn't want to have to say the word aloud. *Fear.*

Tongue in cheek, literally, she texted Ashlee.

> What's the anti-venom for fear?

Three little dots told her Ashlee hadn't had to think before she started typing.

> Love.

> I mean it. What's the antidote?

> I mean it too. Love.

> Can you come over?

> No.

> You can't? Why?

> Because I love you. Love doesn't mean never wrestling with doing the right thing, but choosing the right thing in the end. Every time. And finding grace hidden in the choice. You and God have to work this out together. I'm not your answer. He is.

Boom. Only a forever friend could say that and get away with it.

thirty-one

Mara had left the penmanship accent wall in Jeremy's old room but wasn't sure what to do with it. What she knew today, though, was that she needed something monumental to distract her in hopes that her answers would show up while she wasn't looking. She'd figure out the room today. The rest of her life, and her kids' lives, tomorrow.

She actually liked the room without the heavy window coverings. Sunlit, and with fresh paint, it leaned toward . . . Aha! A reading room like Ashlee's sweet little corner with the two chairs, the end table and lamp, and the tears brushstroke painting. Maybe it was time for the artwork to come home.

Where had Sol and her kids found the little leather loveseat? Maybe from one of Logan's construction project leftovers. Comfy. It could stay. Liam's desk in the basement wasn't anything special, but she could paint it to fit the color scheme. Then she'd have a place to write or do art projects. Or explore reentering the world of graphic design. But she'd need . . . help. Maybe the two Coppernall men and Dylan could wrangle it up the narrow basement stairs for her.

She could picture the tears portrait on the wall opposite the windows. She couldn't risk having it fade. The wallpapered wall needed a little something. A raw wood shelf with succulents?

Maybe one on each side of the double windows. It took her a while, but she found Liam's—her—tape measure in the junk drawer. She'd install one shelf a little higher than the other. That sounded stylish. She confirmed that the windows were directly centered on the wall and measured for how much wood she would need.

Where she held the tape measure's end—or beginning, she supposed—to the wall at eye level, a word drew her attention. *Guard.* Liam's handwriting. The sentence looked like something from a journal. She traced back to the beginning. "I pray every day that you will guard my children and Mara while I'm gone, Lord. And guard my Mara's heart."

How had she missed that before? What else had she not seen?

A snatch of a Bible verse. First John 4:18: "There is no fear in love. But perfect love drives out fear."

The anti-venom.

Handwriting on the wall.

—

It was time for the sacred to win out over scared. How curious that those two words were so different but shared the same vowels and consonants with only two of them reversed. *Scared* could, theoretically, be converted into *sacred* with very little effort.

Phone in hand, she asked for courage to key in the numbers.

Answered on the first ring.

"Levi, this is Mara Jacobs."

"Mara, good to hear from you."

"How's Atlanta?"

"Starting to get warm and humid. How's Wisconsin?"

"Spring-like one day. Back to blizzards the next. Typical mid-March."

"Are you and the family doing well?"

With greater confidence than she would have imagined a

few months earlier, she answered, "Yes. We're doing well." She paused to take delight in the Deep Wells, Inc., representative asking if they were doing "well." But it was time for the hard question. One of them.

"Did you have anything to do with Dylan's acceptance into the summer internship program, Mr. Williams?"

It was his turn to pause. "I gave my strong recommendation, if that's what you're asking. Is that a problem, Mara? I know all this with Liam has been difficult on all fronts, not just his death, but the red tape and misdirection . . ."

Mara fingered the small envelope to her left. He couldn't possibly know all the difficulties. Could he? "No. I'm calling in part to thank you."

"Oh? I thought it might be challenging to imagine your son following in his father's footsteps. Not all of them," he quickly added.

"Following his father's passion."

"Right. You're so right. He's turning into a fine young man. Liam would be proud of him."

"Yes, he would."

"And of you too, Mara."

She breathed deep. "I wouldn't have believed it before now, but yes. I think he would."

"He always was. I'm sure you know that."

Mara wondered what those two men might have said to each other over the years of their friendship and working for the same cause. What had Liam told Levi about her? What would make Levi assume Mara knew Liam was proud of her? Not a question she could ask him right now. "I have a feeling you'll keep a good eye on Dylan for me?"

"You can count on it."

Unexpected friends. "I have an additional favor to ask."

"What is it? If there's any way that I or Deep Wells can be of assistance, please let us know."

Mara laid her non-phone palm over her passport to her right. The small, flat, textured booklet—empty of all but her information for now—felt like obedience, courage, a very life-rich symbol. "I'm planning a trip to Uganda to . . . to complete this leg of my grief journey."

"Oh. Oh, Mara."

"I can't explain how my passport got here so quickly. I've heard it can be a long wait for some. But it's here. That part's ready." *More ready than the rest of me.* "But I could use some professional help wading through what else I'll need for a three-day trip. From what I've read online, I think I need a visa, but there's conflicting info about that. And I'm not sure which immunizations. And I could use a recommendation for how I can travel to the village once the plane lands."

"You're not traveling alone."

"Yes." *Here it comes.* "I need to do this."

Silence.

Lord, help him see how much I need to do this. Because I'm right about that, aren't I?

"Mara, I can't advise you to travel alone. In fact, I must strongly advise against it. Uganda is beautiful and fascinating, but it's also a volatile place in some areas. Our Deep Wells people are trained for—"

"I know. Dylan will be in Atlanta in a couple of months. I do know your teams are trained. And for his sake, I don't really need to be reminded of the dangers."

"So, you're planning to wait until he's in Uganda to—"

"No." *Don't make me second-guess my second-guessing, Levi.* "My son doesn't need to babysit his mom while I'm there, or to think that I'm there to babysit him. He has his reasons for joining Deep Wells and I have my reasons for needing to go to Uganda. Both of us are making our pilgrimages supporting one another from a distance so nothing distracts us from what we're called to do."

"Mara, it's not as simple as booking a plane ticket."

"Which is why I'm coming to you for help. I need your help." *Wow. Long road to this moment.*

"Let me bring one of the Deep Wells executives in on this. Get his opinion."

In the back of her mind, she'd expected pushback. She couldn't let up now. "Levi, I came to you, personally, because you worked directly with and knew my husband. And because of your kindness when it got so messy after his death. I want to see what the country is like, yes, and get a taste of what Liam fell in love with" — *or who* — "but to me the most important part will be reclaiming his ashes, the few there were, and taking them to the river that took him."

He'd understand without her having to mention that she wasn't going searching for a charred truck in the middle of nowhere. That didn't need saying, did it? "I'm talking about the ashes the villagers saved."

"We can send one of our people to retrieve them for you."

"Not the same."

At length, he said, "You can fly to Uganda. We can help with that. And our Deep Wells people will take you to our home base, which would be much more comfortable for you. Then we could have a ceremony in the offices there."

She'd learned to hold her breath underwater so she could take a shower in the early days of her sorrow. How long could she hold her breath under silence?

"Mara?"

Whoosh of air. "Yes?"

"My idea sounded, pardon the expression, cheesier than what you have in mind, didn't it?" She could hear the strain in his voice.

"Definitely."

"Would you let me think about this?" Levi asked. "I don't have any good answers for you right now."

"But you do know whether I'll need a visa, right? And you know what shots I'm required to receive?"

For a man his age, he could hold his breath a long time too. Whoosh of air. "I'll send you an email with information," he said.

"Thank you."

After they ended the call, Mara stared at her passport. "Are you and I doing this? I half-expected Mr. Williams to say, 'Just don't come cryin' to me when the rebels attack you in your sleep.' They wouldn't."

She opened the blank booklet and thumbed through the pages waiting to be stamped at least once in her life.

⁓

Mara's closet glared at her. Drabness times ten. And interestingly, her Wisconsin winter wardrobe had little in it of value for traveling overseas and navigating in a country where many of the women dressed in bright colors. And skirts. And saw more sun in a day than she did the whole month of March.

Her research online popped with shocking vibrancy. As if solar-powered. That brick-red dirt. Clothing patterns and colors that were works of art. She could envision a fabric display at the little cottage art gallery downtown.

She'd called Ashlee immediately when her online search unearthed a fabric designer's words: "The ever-present African sun fades virtually all colors; it shines 12 hours a day on every surface, including clothing. We had to develop new colors that could withstand the African sun. The new colors required a high concentration of dyestuff; as a result the colors are highly saturated. Consumers say that even when this fabric is totally worn out, the color is still intact—alive."

"This tidbit of info makes me so happy," Ashlee had said. "The color is still alive. I may have mentioned that a time or two."

Mara added to her list of must-do's for her trip: While in the country, find a swatch of Ugandan cloth Ashlee would appreciate.

The month of May of a high school senior's year is full of activities leading to graduation. She'd watched it happen with her kids' older friends, and with their parents running hard to keep up. If she couldn't get her visitor's visa and other details ironed out before late April, she'd have to postpone her trip until June, and hope to be out of there long before Dylan's assignment to the country.

She and Logan had come to terms about Chelsea. He'd promised to wait to propose until Christmas, which would allow Chelsea a full year's distance from her dad's and brother's deaths, plus her first term of college. And it would allow them time to make sure this wasn't just cute. It was real. Chelsea would be nineteen on her way to twenty by then. And if they wanted a spring wedding . . .

Mara couldn't think much beyond that right now. The point was that nothing of a proposing nature was going to happen while she was in Uganda for what amounted to a long weekend. Although three days had been optimistic. According to Levi, the trip from the airport to the village and back would chew up most of a day.

The joy-killer would be if she couldn't coordinate the visa stamp of approval and a flight.

Or if Levi stood in her way. She could bypass Deep Wells, Inc. But that wasn't the kind of relationship she wanted Dylan to walk into. "Oh, is he the one whose mom is a troublemaker?"

Thinking about that now, sitting on her bed, staring into her closet, she found it amusing that, after his history, Dylan's *mom* might be the one to carry the troublemaker mantle.

Don't look now, Dylan, but your mama's about to order a couple of wildly patterned, color-saturated skirts.

She recanted her internal thought. Dylan might not mind. Ashlee was the one who would throw a party.

Mara walked over to the suitcase and carry-on that Ashlee had loaned her for the trip. Liam's luggage had been returned, but she and Dylan agreed he would take it on his inaugural journey in his father's honor. And she wouldn't risk its getting lost in baggage claim before that moment.

thirty-two

Ashlee's migraines were more manageable. That only served to make her more insistent that Mara needed a travel companion and she would be the perfect choice, wouldn't she? She wanted to help. But Mara's normal resistance to receive assistance wasn't the issue in this case. It was a private, sacred, Jesus-and-me trip.

In the end, Ashlee compromised by insisting Mara could not sit in the economy section for a flight that long. She personally paid for the upgrade to first class and told Mara it would be worth it to know the flight attendants would be showing her as much attention as the God of heaven for her flights.

Mara's resistance bowed to Ashlee's insistence.

At the moment, nine hours and two airport layovers into the more than twenty-hour flight, all her resistance was gone. She needed the privacy first class afforded her more than the meals, and the hot towels, and the seat that unfolded into a bed, and the exceptional thoughtfulness of the attendants. Tempted to use the word *spoiled*, she replaced it with *refreshed*, per her conversation with Ashlee in Florida, and calculated how much more water she was going to have to drink to keep from the dreaded long-flight dehydration.

Levi's advice had been invaluable regarding surviving the

flight. He'd suggested an app that helped her figure out how she could minimize jet lag by adjusting her wake and sleep patterns even before the trip. She checked the app now. She had three hours of wakefulness ahead of her.

Was she ready to read what she'd tucked in her carry-on? The pages from Liam's "Someday" folder?

Maybe during her next forced wakefulness. She'd felt compelled to bring the pages with her, unread. But her mind still swam with disjointed thoughts.

Levi Williams had handpicked someone to meet her at the airport and escort her to the village. A trusted young man who could also serve as her interpreter if needed. Deep Wells enlisted and paid for his services ahead of time on her behalf.

They'd suggested she take a day in a hotel in Kampala, not far from the Entebbe airport, for her body and brain to acclimate before she and the driver headed out to the remote village. She had a specific mission. This was no tourist trip, but she acquiesced. Admitting she was inexperienced and unknowledgeable about almost every single detail of this journey wasn't easy for her, but the men and women from Deep Wells were doing everything in their power to accommodate her pilgrimage.

Pilgrimage sounded so much holier than "crazy woman's outrageous idea."

She'd cleared the trip with her grief counselor, who also needed a little convincing. And Levi Williams's phone call reassurance.

The plane held in excess of three hundred passengers and crew. In her section, two flight attendants were assigned to the needs of only a dozen people. How is it she could feel so utterly alone?

Before the flight took off, for Ashlee's sake, she'd taken a picture of the real pillow and real comforter waiting for her in her pod-like seat. Of the ice water waiting for her in a goblet, of all things. Of the surround sound and fresh-brewed coffee—

Ugandan coffee—in a ceramic cup. She had a feeling the Ugandan countryside leg of her trip would be a stark contrast to this scene.

Supposed to stay awake three more hours. It would help, the app said.

So would leaning into that pillow, right?

⁓

Another meal? The clank of real silverware in the pod next to her woke her. She sat up and stretched her arms. The aisle was clogged. She'd have to wait until the meal service ended before she could use the lavatory and stretch her legs.

Pilgrimage remorse was in full bloom. She'd spent so much money on this idea she was so sure was what God wanted. Then Ashlee's upgrade on top of that. Seven months ago, she worked at a cheese factory and made toxic birthday treats for her kids to take to school. What was she doing here?

Silently, the flight attendant laid a linen napkin in her lap and with silver tongs offered her a burrito-like hot, steamed hand towel to freshen up. The meal was set before her as if she were the queen of an African nation rather than a woman whose baggage wasn't leather but woven from grief.

Silver clanked against china plates, among the only sounds in first class, other than the incessant roar of jet engines she was happy to hear were still roaring. She didn't want to know exactly where or how high above the Atlantic they were right now. She did know, though, they were headed east, racing to meet the sun.

After the meal—was it lunch or dinner?—she freshened, not like the cow-meaning of that word, and stood in the aisle, walking in place to keep her blood flowing. A young woman in the comfort section behind first class was doing a handstand in the aisle. Seemed impossible on terra firma, much less at this altitude, but that woman would not have puffy ankles when she deplaned. She was making sure of it.

The endlessly long flight, with a layover yet in Brussels before they turned south, seemed fitting. Most monumental moments are preceded by an endless wait. Why should this be any different?

She pulled out Liam's "Someday" file. Rather than relating a man's quest to find personal happiness, it was bullet points of ideas, most of which included her and the kids. All three of them.

"Take Mara to Arizona to reconnect with her forever friend, Ashlee."

She pressed her fist against her mouth to stifle the sob that had likely been waiting a while for expression. *Liam. I didn't know you realized how much she meant to me. You had to die before we could reconnect.* Her sob turned into a line Liam would have understood: *Not that you* had *to die. You just did. It's complicated.*

"Save for a trip to Hawaii for our twentieth anniversary."

How long ago had he started this list? How many of his plans did he have to surrender when he felt God calling him to provide water for the thirsty? Did he wrestle with the decision? He'd talked about his remorse over missing so much of such critical years in the lives of his kids. She'd worked—maybe a little too hard—to convince him they'd be fine without him. Was his exuberance about Deep Wells a front for his own debate between sacred and scared? What was he thinking about on his first flight to Africa? Certainly not real silver and linen napkins. Could he have wondered if he was headed for the biggest adventure or the biggest mistake of his life? Like she was?

Someday plans. "Take Mara and the kids on a weeklong houseboat trip on Rainy River in Canada."

Except for the word rainy *in that sentence, Liam, that would have been nice.*

"Take Chelsea to a Broadway play."
"Find a way to make a difference."
Oh, Liam. You did. You did.

—

She woke once in the flight from Brussels to Entebbe. Already tomorrow, fast approaching the day after that. No one knew she'd tucked a small sealed envelope of ashes in her carry-on. It contained the ashes of a letter from a grateful mother in Uganda. And the ashes of a letter from Jeremy that his father, and she, would never read.

—

"Beginning our final descent" was announced in three languages. She made her bed. Ashlee would be proud, although the flight attendant insisted it wasn't necessary and would be replaced with clean linens anyway after they landed.

Mara told the attendant it was important for her to do that. And Ashlee would applaud if she knew.

It didn't bother Mara that the attendant's raised eyebrows never did lower.

Levi Williams and others from the Deep Wells team had informed her what to expect at customs, how to conduct herself, how to answer the questions she'd be asked. She knew better than to mention the word *ashes* and hoped her "hermetically sealed" envelope would keep them not only safe, but safe from prying eyes and hands and TSA scanners, as it had so far.

She stepped off the plane, unprepared for how dizzy she felt. How long would it take for her to get her land legs back? She followed the queue of other travelers making their way through the snaking customs lines.

Before she got farther than the airport, it was apparent that she was on foreign soil, with unfamiliar traditions and a stew of languages and smells. Odors. And grateful, oh so grateful, to see enough English wording on signs to help her navigate.

Mara's Someday List: *Learn a foreign language or two. Find out if Ashlee's medicine really did require a sugar fast or if that was Ashlee's clever way of controlling Mara's donut consumption. Love her kids and whoever her kids loved with all her heart. Support their dreams. Allow herself to dream.*

It was her turn. She stepped up to the waiting customs agent.

"Reason for your travel to Uganda?"

The long flight had messed with her brain. She almost spat out, "To discover why my husband left me." But that wasn't correct. He hadn't left her. He'd been obedient to do a hard thing for the sake of people in need. And it had cost him his life.

"I came to heal." No, that wouldn't work either. It was true but would take way too long to explain.

"I'm here to take a drink of living water." Not going to cut it with this guy staring at her, waiting for her answer.

She settled on, "Tourist."

thirty-three

*T*he hotel provided both rest and restlessness. Mara needed her land legs back. Her body needed to adjust. But her soul craved the opportunity to do what she'd come to this continent to do.

She ate in the hotel restaurant, not wanting to venture farther than the protected space. She was served a vegetable stew seasoned so carefully that she could taste each layer. Ugandan coffee accompanied her meal. The hype was real. It might have been the most flavorful and richest coffee she'd tasted. She reserved the Ugandan ginger tea as her dessert, and mentally apologized to Ashlee for breaking their sugar fast for that divine cup.

The drive to the village was said to take seven hours, depending on traffic. She carefully calculated the time changes so she wouldn't miss connecting with her driver. And, as she'd promised, she checked in with both her praying American friends and with the Deep Wells, Inc., Ugandan team.

Deep Wells said they would connect with Levi Williams, who had become her personal advocate for the journey. Levi had been holding his breath on her behalf.

She remembered how well he could do that from their first conversation about her coming to Uganda.

Night or day, it didn't matter. Her eyes could stay open no

longer. She set her alarm and hoped she could ignore her racing heart and catch a few hours of rest.

~

"Excuse me? Sir?"

"Yes?"

"Haven't we been driving the wrong direction for a long time now?"

"I get you to your destination."

Flat statement. Matter of fact. As close to emotionless as a person can get in conversation. Mara recalled a few months ago when that could have described her, everything about her. *Shut down emotions to survive. They're too much of a drain on what little energy you have. At least try to pretend you don't care. It'll be less painful.* Instead, it had the effect of intensifying the pain and turning off the oxygen on her life support. She'd nearly suffocated.

Mara checked her itinerary. "Jebale village?"

"Yes?"

"I understood it was north of the airport."

"Yes?"

"But we've been driving west for—" Time meant nothing anymore. She wasn't even sure what day it was. All she knew was that she was in a jeep-like truck, bouncing over dirt roads with indescribable beauty on either side. They'd survived the wild ride from the hotel near the airport through the city without incident. How was that possible? Such chaos of activity and people, and such a contrast to what she imagined Liam had been living in, what she'd soon see.

The roads distant from the city had little vehicle traffic, other than bicycles, but constant foot traffic. People—usually women, she noticed—clogged the edges of the roadways carrying heavy bundles of bananas, sticks, water.

They passed a matatu (minibus). Locals rushed the bus to

sell its passengers mystery meat on sticks, mangoes, plantains, avocados. The air was filled with sounds and smells unlike any she'd witnessed. Brightly colored birds flashed through tree branches. Tea plantations stretched for miles. Children laughed, apparently uncaring that the ball with which they played had long ago lost its air. Such a mix of abundance and poverty.

"West. Yes?" The young man was deliberate, but not harsh with her. And he'd been Deep Wells's top choice for her driver, if she was going to insist on heading straight for Jebale, a point on which she would not budge.

She'd been warned. A woman traveling alone in a region with a history of random uprisings and long-standing skirmishes—not a good idea. She should have listened to those who'd counseled her to take a companion with her. Mara's suddenly wise daughter had suggested it. Her perpetually wise forever friend had volunteered, insisted, but eventually caved to Mara's solo travel. Or she could have asked wise Solomon. Not surprising she should consider a man named Solomon and the concept of wisdom in the same sentence.

She'd give anything to have Sol with her now.

As the year had ticked by—seven months now, soon to be eight—it was getting harder to think of Sol's presence in her life as an affront to her grief. Who else but Sol would have been so patient with her? So thoughtful about her grief seizures that struck randomly and often without warning?

He'd been what she needed. A listening ear. A steady presence. In some ways a male version of Ashlee. In some ways, completely different.

Maybe when she crossed the one-year mark of Liam's loss, she'd allow herself to look some man in the eyes like Chelsea looked into Logan's. What a sweet love they shared.

Her daughter. Solomon's son. Who would have thought?

"West. Yes?" Her driver's lilting voice pressed her again for a response.

"I don't have much time." She left out the part about how much the flight had exhausted her. "Isn't there a more direct route to the village?"

"I get you there. Two routes. I choose the safe one." His smile competed with sunlight glinting off the few spots on the truck's hood that still boasted paint.

She tightened the seat belt across her lap. Her cotton blouse and skirt—a change from her trans-Atlantic flight outfit and the southern leg that flew her thirty thousand feet above most of a continent that had swallowed Liam—couldn't get more wrinkled. As she and her driver bounced and jostled their way with Africa's dust so near, even seeping into the cab of the small truck, she kicked at a quarter-sized clod of red earth on the floorboards. It disintegrated, as if reminding her how desperate had been the need for water. Clumps of trees that dotted the far landscape on either side could survive on muddy water unsafe for human consumption.

Jeremy could have recited the varieties of foliage that lined their journey, if he'd chosen to stay alive. *Oh, Jeremy! You hollowed me! Did you not know you can't come back from an act like that?*

Of course, he'd known.

He'd worked so hard to please her. He'd been her bright light. Until his unmanageable loss crippled his ability to think clearly. That part, she understood. "Rest in peace" never meant as much as it did now. Was Liam taking care of his son? Or was it the other way around?

Billows of dust now flooded the cab. Her driver had rolled down his window and indicated she should do the same. They were traveling north now. The sun had switched positions. No, they had. She didn't miss the deeper connection.

Mara glanced at the worn dashboard. A small button with a snowflake sign—air-conditioning. How many decades had it been since it had run out of coolant? She turned the window crank one rotation. The window dropped like a magician's curtain would to reveal the stunt he'd pulled. The handle fell into her hand. Her driver kept his eyes on the dirt road ahead of them but reached to take the handle from her and tossed it into the doorless glove box.

What seemed like an hour later, he pointed past her to a spot beyond her door. A flash of bright blue. He then indicated his similarly colored cap that sported once-white letters: Deep Wells, Inc. His wide smile returned.

One of Liam's wells? Evidence he'd been here, in this place. Evidence he'd made a difference. As if she needed more than the television appearances, the humanitarian awards he'd earned, the letters from grateful—

She fingered the envelope of ashes now in her skirt pocket. *He did not suffer alone. Wasuze held him to her chest. Do not fear.*

Such a strange message. Its comfort instilled nothing but fear, a fear she'd already suspected in her most cynical, self-pitying moments. It had been more than these people and their need and maybe even media hunger that chained Liam to this place. A woman held his heart captive. And in a culture that apparently thought Mara would consider it a comfort that if he didn't have his wife nearby, he could have a pretty fine substitute to observe his final breaths.

Ashlee would not tolerate Mara letting her mind get caught in that toxic whirlpool again. But Ashlee slept eight time zones away at the moment, awaiting the dawn of the day Mara had already been living.

"Your husband. Good man," the driver said.

"You met him?" The minute this line of conversation deteriorated further, Mara intended to feign motion sickness and ask to be let out so she could heave in private.

"Yes. Many times. I was his . . . Dylan."

What? What could he mean by that?

"He rescued me from the path his Dylan traveled. Yes? Rescued?"

Mara knew nothing of the local language. Lugandan. Or the Swahili that many in Uganda spoke. Any communication between her driver and her—she should probably ask his unpronounceable name again—depended on his bilingual skills. Or multilingual.

She'd only recently begun to understand her own thoughts in her native tongue. "My husband rescued you?"

"Yes? Rescued."

Liam had talked about his family with these people. The Jacobs family's personal business. She had no reserves of anger left. Had spent it all. If she could have mustered any, now might be a good time.

"Your Dylan, he make . . . make trouble."

What could she do but agree? *Dylan, he make trouble. Yes?* She nodded. That's all Liam would have known. He hadn't seen his son changed.

Her driver must have caught the movement in his peripheral vision and thought it a green light to keep talking.

"Mr. Jacobs sheltered me until my mind was right again. He say I his Africa son, and if he help me when he could not help his Dylan, it make his heart strong."

This wasn't why she'd come. She didn't need more stories of the impact Liam had made, especially not for his *Africa son* and however many other children he claimed instead of the ones he'd already fathered, the ones he'd left up to her. The ones she'd kept distant from him because she needed him to know she was capable. The word tasted bitter in her mind.

"I lost one," she said, overcome with the truth that edged out the lies she'd once believed.

"Pardon me, Mrs. Jacobs. Lost one?"

"One of Liam's America sons."

"Jeremy?" Over the roar and clank of the rattling truck, his question rang soft but unmistakably clear. "The quiet one with the tender heart?"

How did this young driver know? It might have been nice if Liam had told her he thought about their children that much.

"The quiet one. Lost him." She choked on Ugandan dust.

"My mother lost sons too. And daughters," he said.

Against all conventional wisdom, she reached across the space between them and laid her hand on the dusty shoulder of her husband's African son.

~

A flock of brightly colored "birds"—young children—greeted her when they reached the village. They danced around her like fearless pigeons hoping for a scrap of bread. But it appeared they were not hungry for food. They sought her gaze.

Jesus, how long did I think I needed some scrap when my true need was your gaze?

When she smiled at each child, they greeted her by name in English, giggled, and darted away to find a friend to drag into the circle of color. The vibrancy of the traditional garments they wore startled her. She could hardly move for the press of children. A young, fair-skinned woman emerged from a cement block building. She wore a Ugandan skirt with her marine blue polo shirt and cap. Deep Wells.

The young woman parted the sea of children so she could shake Mara's hand. "Mrs. Jacobs, I'm Ella Garmond. We've corresponded."

"Yes. Ella. Nice to finally meet you in person."

"I've only been stationed here for six weeks, so I was unaware of all that had transpired surrounding the time of your husband's death. I wish we at Deep Wells could have made that easier on you. Not that losing someone you love is ever easy. I mean, the paperwork. And the governmental red tape.

And . . . all that sounds petty compared to your heart's loss. I don't have the words."

"None of us do, Ella. But I appreciate your kindness."

"I . . . I wasn't sure if you'd want to stay in your husband's quarters. So the director and I prepared both that room and our guest house, which is practically a duplicate. Not as fancy as it sounds. But it is quieter and more private. And it has—"

"I'll take the guest house, please. I'd like to see Liam's quarters, but I can't . . . I can't stay there."

"Understood. The educational arm of Deep Wells—that's my area—intends to convert his room into another classroom, but the villagers asked us to wait."

"Wait for what?"

Ella's head tilted slightly, as if in deference to the awkwardness that had marked Mara's life far too long. "For you."

"I never intended to come."

Those soft, clear blue eyes spoke before she did. "They somehow knew you would. Especially Wasuze, from what I hear."

God had altered—or altared—her heart in so many ways. The name had once sickened her. Now, it flowed off Ella's tongue as a gift. How could that be?

"Miss Garmond?"

"Ella, please."

"Would you tell me what the name Wasuze means in Luganda? Lugandan?"

Ella's widening smile sent an odd thought through Mara's soul. She'd make a great daughter-in-law, a great wife for Dylan, now that he was looking in the right places. Must be the jet lag kicking in again. She was on this soil for a completely different reason.

"Wasuze. Yes. It means *morning*."

"Mourning. As in, grieving?"

"No. Like the dawn. And here she is."

The woman approaching strode toward Mara with confi-

300

dence, rare and elegant beauty, clothed in deeply hued sunset orange and black kintu cloth, and her eighty-year-old arms spread wide. She could have been Liam's grandmother. Or Mara's Grandma Lou.

"Ah, my child!" Wasuze said, her honeyed voice low and rich. "You have come. It is time."

She hadn't said, "It's about time, young lady!" Simply, "It is time." And it was.

Mara's throat tightened, but she managed, "Wasuze, what an honor to meet you."

"Oh, so formal, young one. This is how I greet you, the woman who sacrificed so much so we could find living water."

The term "squeeze your brains out" came to mind, but despite the crushing hug from the woman who appeared to be the village's matriarch, Mara's synapses all fired at once. Living water? They considered what she'd done a sacrifice for their sake?

Wasuze released the embrace and held Mara's shoulders in her wide hands. "I have made tea. We will take it together, yes? But first, a gift."

She took a garment from a lanky teen boy standing near and laid it across Mara's outstretched arms. A stunning turquoise, black, and bright gold dress, its color so vibrant, it seemed alive.

"A garment of praise in place of mourning," she said. No further explanation followed, but Wasuze leaned close and said, "If you accept. And if you—as I suspect—would like to wash some of our beloved soil from your face and hands before we take our tea together. Yes?"

Much needed. What were the odds the guest house had indoor plumbing? And what did she care? "How will I find your . . ." She trolled for the right word. *House? Room?* "Home?"

"He will wait for you."

Jesus? He sure had. Far too long, by Mara's standards.

Oh. The young boy. Someone had been provided to walk

her to Wasuze's home. Her driver stayed close, chatting with some of the older boys.

"The children have a gift for you too," Wasuze said. She signaled "Come" to the little ones. They gathered into a circle around the women. "A song your husband taught them."

Their faces more than glowing, eyes alight with joy, the children looked to Ella, who simply hummed one note and nodded for them to begin. The young voices started softly, in unison:

> Let us break bread together on our knees.
> Let us break bread together on our knees.
> When I fall on my knees with my face to the rising sun,
> O, Lord, have mercy on me.

The second and third verses grew in volume and intensity, each word enunciated perfectly with an accent that melted Mara's heart and a passion to match. By the third verse—*Let us praise God together on our knees*—they sang in sweet harmony and raised their beautiful arms in worship for the final line. *O, Lord, have mercy on me.*

Through her tears, Mara looked to Ella for a clue if applause were appropriate. Wasuze answered for her by starting the swell.

If she didn't need a moment alone before, she did now.

The guest room welcomed her with its promise of sleep and a clean pillow on her horizon. She freshened up and changed quickly, not wanting to keep the tea or "Morning" waiting longer than necessary.

Wasuze's thatched cottage and hospitality seemed rooted in British culture with Ugandan warmth. The older woman explained how local agriculture had changed since the Deep Wells project—and Liam—had provided clean and abundant water. She nudged small biscuits across the table toward Mara. "Try these. Liam helped me start my herb garden and the irritation sys—" Her laughter erupted as if the first spurts of wetness from a well project. "The irrigation system. We are able to grow so many fine vegetables and fruit near or in the village now."

They talked like friends reunited. Not the image Mara had entertained the entirety of her flight. Eventually, Wasuze ventured into sober territory.

"The night the river took your husband, or tried to, I cradled him in my arms as if I'd given birth to him, so deep was my pain. And so great was my joy as I watched the lines of his face soften and his spirit reach out toward the hand of the Jesus he served. We would still try to save him. But it was a holy moment, I assure you, Mara."

As if she'd given birth to him. Jeremy. The umbilical cord had felt somehow virtually still attached, so Mara internalized all the pain that drove him to end it all. She'd been cradling her missing son ever since.

"And now." Wasuze stood and retrieved a bright blue and green fabric bag from a board serving as a counter. "It is time for your arms and mine to let him go."

Mara hesitated briefly, then took the small bag from her. It was heavier than she imagined. "Liam's ashes?"

"Let's say yes," Wasuze said.

"Excuse me?"

"They represent Liam's ashes. Dust to dust. Dust is dust. We collected what we could after his remains were burned. This"— she nodded toward the bag—"will do?"

Ashes to ashes. "Yes. This will do. Thank you."

"When you visit the river tomorrow on your way back to the airport, could it be with the promise that you will someday return?"

"I intend to visit my Dylan after he's gotten established here. He has two months of school and the training with Deep Wells before he's assigned overseas. But the company knows his intentions to carry on his father's work."

Wasuze leaned back in her chair, satisfaction washing over

her face. "And another prayer is answered." She drifted into thought for a moment before adding, "Have you met the young intern, Ella Garmond?"

Mara chuckled softly. How strange, this earth life. She held her husband's ashes in a blue-green bag, felt a breeze of space where she'd been clutching Jeremy too tight, and was captured by the wonder of new beginnings. Logan and Chelsea. Dylan and someone. Maybe Ella. Sol and . . .

Unfinished business remained.

Unfinished *remains* business.

Gravity had lessened its grip on her. Sleep, however, pressed in hard. Her eyes popped open when Wasuze took back the small, deeply colored bag from Mara's hands.

"This will be waiting for you in your husband's quarters when you need it tomorrow. Right now, rest is more important than conversation," she said.

"You sound like my friend Ashlee."

"She is wise?"

"Yes. Very."

"Then I like her."

Mara laughed again. "I still have questions."

"Questions that cannot be postponed without expiring?"

Mara shrugged but asked, "How do you get such depth of color in these beautiful fabrics?"

"Ah yes. A treasure, to be sure. The sun's rays can fade here."

At home too.

"What once was bright can be washed of all color. Pale. Lifeless," Wasuze said. "So we must choose only the best dyes, and we drive them deep into the threads of the cloth, to stand up against a sun that fades."

Mara's faith hadn't been driven deep enough into the threads, until recently. That explained a lot.

"But that same sun provides power." Wasuze drained the last of her tea. "You will have a light for your room tonight because of it. Solar panels on the roof. Our people can create items to sell much faster now because God gave us Liam who brought us water and power, so we can feed our children and provide medicine when needed. We can support ourselves. Yes, the sun fades. But it brings the dawn, lights the day, and powers the darkest of nights."

The light Mara had left on in Jeremy's room after his death. It hadn't changed anything. Hadn't brought him back. But it had kept her from stumbling over the threshold.

"Sleep well, Mara Jacobs. And may your journey to the river tomorrow be flooded with light."

thirty-four

*I*t shouldn't have surprised her that the sun at dawn was as hot as it ever was in Wisconsin at midday. She'd asked her driver, whom she'd taken to calling Buddy, to allow her to make her way from the village to the river on her own.

Wasuze had intervened for her and instructed Buddy to follow Mara's directions. "She will be safe," Wasuze said, her confidence unwavering.

Had she read the same passages Mara and Dylan found so comforting? Or did God speak directly to that woman in a way Mara might never understand?

They'd said their goodbyes privately in Wasuze's cottage, then publicly in a raucous display of unbridled joy and color and chaos with the village women's voices subdued and the children's voices exuberant, dancing.

Mara promised she'd be back, and added, "Lord willing."

She couldn't wait for Dylan to meet these people. He would fall in love instantly. And she wasn't even thinking about Ella at the time. Ah, but she was.

Evidence of Liam's handiwork was everywhere in the village, maybe most prominently in the health of the children and the abundance of their produce. One family approached Mara, eager to gift her with their goat, whom they led not by a rope around its neck, but around its ankle.

Wasuze explained it was their only livestock possession, and explained to the family that Mara would not be allowed to take it home with her on the plane across the ocean. For a moment, Mara thought she might provide some competition for women who do handstands in the aisles of trans-Atlantic jets. The family seemed satisfied when they heard Liam's son would soon live among them.

The river waited. It would continue waiting until the dry season shriveled it, temporarily. But Mara could not wait. With final hugs all around, she set her bags in Buddy's truck and, dressed in Wasuze's turquoise and black and sun-gold garment, took the blue-green bag with her to the path that led to the river.

The children's song followed her until the distance was too great to hear it anymore. She stood along the shore at the spot that had been marked with a bright blue plastic jug with Liam's name on it and prepared her heart to surrender the last of her regrets.

The dress she wore did not make her feel African. But it made her feel free. She lifted its hem just above her knees as she knelt in the grasses along the river and opened first the crumpled envelope she'd been holding on to for too long, then the small cloth bag. The varied sources of ashes mingled in the river's current and disappeared under its churning surface.

It was finished.

"How did you get here?" Mara stood less than four feet away from him, the Ugandan sun and the sight of him making her squint.

"Airplane," he said. Sol lifted his arms like wings, then let them drop against his sides. "Kind of the only option. There's no land bridge across the Atlantic."

Good one, Sol. "You hate flying." The sight of him stole what little breath she had remaining.

"A tunnel would have been nice. But with the kind of gas mileage Logan's truck has been getting lately, that wouldn't have been a viable option anyway."

He was here. On the same continent. Looking as out of place as she felt. "Sol! The shots! You didn't get the shots. How did they even let you into the country?"

He rubbed a spot on his left shoulder. "I got them. Weeks ago. Hepatitis A, hepatitis B, typhoid, cholera, yellow fever, meningitis . . . I'm forgetting something."

Weeks? He'd been planning this? Why hadn't he told her?

She knew why. Because she would have objected, would have insisted she didn't need his help, thank you very much. Because he somehow knew she had to make the journey to this place on her own. He hadn't told her because in his own way, he was respecting her boundaries and her need to finish the final round of her wrestling match with God.

He didn't have to say it. It's who he was. Who he'd always been.

Some heroes speak at global conferences. Some get a passport expedited so they can make sure you're okay. Some dig wells. Some bring an extra bottle of water.

Mara took the one Sol offered her. Opening the twist cap would take both hands, which meant she'd need to do something with the ashes cloth, the vibrant sack Wasuze sewed with her lovely long fingers and with devotion Mara prayed she could emulate. The fadeless fabric was still a little damp from its unintentional baptism in the river. But she tucked it under her arm, near her heart, remembering.

Some heroes cross oceans to make a difference in the lives of a nation. Some cross an ocean to quench the thirst of one parched woman.

A breeze tickled the grasses along the river's edge. They rustled their gratitude in a distinctly African song. The surface of the water shivered as if mirroring the shudder that ran through Mara's frame. Waves and wind that still knew the name of their Creator. River water that had tried to steal Liam's last breath and now claimed whatever it was Wasuze had found to represent his body's ashes.

And the ashes of her regrets. And a little boy's pain. And a Ugandan mother's gratitude.

"You have a little color on your cheeks," Solomon said. "It looks . . ."

"What?" All she could manage was a half whisper.

"Looks good on you." He took a step toward her, then stopped. Slid his hands into the pockets of his khakis.

He'd bought khakis. And braved the vaccinations. And flown all the way to—

"Why did you come? I told you I could handle this myself." Seven months ago, the words would have been spoken with a snarky edge. Or anger. Or both. *I know you're powerful and all, Jesus, but what have you done to me? You don't have to answer that. I like it.*

"I knew you could." Sol wiped a bead—several beads—of sweat from his forehead. "And you *did* handle it. Beautifully. That"—he pointed to the spot twenty yards down the shoreline where she'd stood minutes ago—"was a moving ceremony. Not gonna lie. I cried."

He'd been watching her? She was torn between resentment and gratitude that someone else had been witness to the holy moment. "How long have you been here?"

"I booked myself on the flight right after yours. Landed the next day, technically. You know. Time zones. That jet lag thing? It's real."

"I meant, here at the river. Have you been spying on me?" The thought made her shiver. A bodyguard, she wouldn't have minded. But a spy? A stalker?

Wait. This man had flown to Africa to watch her dump her soul on soil the color of dried blood? He'd been staying out of sight, hiding for three days?

No, not hiding. He'd been there. She'd sensed it, even if she hadn't seen him. With her. For her.

And on the night Dylan was arrested. And when Chelsea told him and her possibly future husband about her miscarriage. And when Mara told him that Jeremy believed Liam's death was all his fault.

He'd been there. This man.

Peace had washed over her like a tidal wave when she'd surrender-knelt by the water. Now, peace settled like honey flowing over buttered toast. Hard doesn't mean unsurvivable. Mistakes don't automatically dictate a future. And regrets have an antidote. God's love and peace.

The sun can fade the fabric of life. But it can also make art. Some of it hung on the walls of her home. Invisible art now decorated the once bare walls of her heart. The cracks in her emotional plaster weren't so noticeable, so unsightly anymore. Ashlee had played a role in that. And this man standing in front of her.

"Why did you come?"

Sol caught her gaze and held it so tenderly she no longer felt the sting of the sun's heat but reveled in the embrace of its warmth. He opened his mouth but pressed his lips together without speaking.

At long last, he drew a breath, his chest expanding with the air she'd been breathing, and said, "Our flight leaves in eight hours. It's getting late. I thought you might want a friend to walk you home."

author's note

*I*nspiration for this story came from so many sources—a typical (for me) mix of personal life experiences, observing the joys and pain of others close to me, and imagination. A novel steeps and brews until it seeps into my very soul and changes me. I emerged from writing *Facing the Dawn* with a greater understanding of the winding path of grief, the inexpressible power of friendship, and God's relentless love. Your experience with the story may yield other outcomes, reader. Please know I was "there," reading over your shoulder, in a way, thinking of how you would react as you watched it all unfold. Thank you for taking the journey.

Special thanks are due to my ever-faithful agent, Wendy Lawton from Books & Such Literary Management, who encourages me every day, who worked hard to make sure this story had a chance to be told, and who found creative ways to get it in front of the right editor for the project.

Thank you, Lonnie Hull DuPont, for championing this book and for believing it has a place on readers' bookshelves and in their hearts. Your editorial thoughts held my feet to the flames in the best of ways. It's been pure joy to work with you. Thank you, too, for sending the link for "We Are Not Alone." I played it in the background on repeat for days.

Rachel McRae, Kristin Kornoelje, and the rest of the team at Revell have made this pursuit a dream come true. So many have worked behind the scenes to help this novel face its own dawn. I considered many of you dear friends before we had an opportunity to work together in this way. I could not be more grateful.

Reconnecting with a childhood forever friend, Sheryl, inspired the presence of Ashlee in the story. Thank you for not abandoning me, Sheryl, and remaining a true friend despite time and distance. Another forever friend, Becky Melby, helped shape the Ashlee in this book, helps shape me daily, and graciously read each chapter as it emerged from my laptop. Among other people who prayed for me as I wrote, I owe a never-ending debt of gratitude to another forever friend, Jackie, for almost around-the-clock prayer for me that started more than four decades ago and will live on beyond her last breath, which she exhaled mere days after this manuscript was completed.

I drew from the wisdom and firsthand knowledge of long-time friend Gari Meacham (president and founder of The Vine Uganda, a community center in the heart of Kamuli, Uganda, that empowers the local community by providing education, life skills, medical treatment, and spiritual discipleship) and friend Kit Tosello (Ugandan tea and coffee), who put me in touch with Kathleen Keranen (Africa Area Administrator, Free Methodist Church USA) and with Karen Williams, who often travels with Kathleen, for more essential details about Ugandan culture. Thank you for your time and support, Gari, Kit, Kathleen, and Karen.

Many of the thoughts expressed during "Anna's" talk for the novel's Christmas Tea scene were inspired by author and speaker Emily E. Ryan's moving Christmas message. Thank you, Emily, for sharing your passion and allowing me to draw from it. The table decor, ambiance, music, and wonder of the

Christmas Tea are a tribute to the elegant way my church serves its people and the community.

Although we didn't fly first class, I'm grateful for the opportunity to use my passport when my daughter Amy and I flew on a seemingly endless transcontinental flight across the Atlantic in 2019, which eventually enabled me to know details about people doing handstands in the aisle, the necessity of staying hydrated (which we found out the hard way), and the wonder of a burrito-roll steamy towel to clean up before meals. Also, any snarkiness in the novel, I learned from my daughter.

My husband, children, and grandchildren make it possible for me to tell stories and are my favorite brainstormers. Their patience when I'm on deadline is exceptional and much appreciated. They're a constant source of inspiration and have taught me so much about the depths of genuine love and the lengths to which it will go.

Extended family, church friends, and author friends, you may see yourself in these pages, in the integrity and faithfulness of the characters. Thank you for living out your faith in a way that others long to emulate.

I'll close these thoughts with gratitude to the One who perfectly defines Light, Life, and Love, with intentional capital letters. *And yes, Lord, I will keep guarding the dawn.*

discussion questions

1. What dynamics were at work—both from Mara's side and Liam's side—that created the emotional distance between them?

2. Have you ever experienced a season of time when you were in essence single parenting? Deployment, spouse's extended business travel, spouse's long-term illness? If so, what did you find in common with Mara Jacobs? If not, what do you imagine you would find most challenging?

3. Some say that grief thrusts us into emotional upheaval that keeps us from seeing a clearly defined line between sanity and insanity some days. How was that exhibited in the character actions or reactions (or inaction) in the novel? For Mara? For Ashlee? For the children?

4. *Facing the Dawn* pulls back a curtain on grief and friendship and the connection between the two. Where do you think Mara would be today without Ashlee's friendship? Without Sol's? Who were the people who walked Dylan and Chelsea through their grief, and how? What do your answers tell you about your relationships?

5. A novelist strives above all to tell a good story. Interesting but believable characters on a challenging but believable journey. With which character did you most closely identify?

6. List the characters in the story who were given a second chance. Does it surprise you to note how many you named? Do you have your own second-chance story to tell?

7. Mara discovered an uncommon link between sacred and scared—that they're made from the same letters rearranged. How did that play out in her grief journey?

8. What did you consider the most poignant symbolism in the story (Jeremy's faded comforter, the portrait from the art gallery, the gas fireplace, the wallpaper, cyanotype, the riverside ceremony . . .)? Why did you choose that symbolic item or moment?

9. Why do you believe the author chose not to write one more chapter?

10. What single lines, phrases, or scenes most strongly resonated with you? The author would love to hear what they were. You can connect with her at hemmedinhope.com or cynthiaruchti.com.

Cynthia Ruchti tells stories hemmed-in-Hope through her novels, nonfiction, devotionals, and through speaking events, drawing from thirty-three years as writer/producer and on-air voice of the fifteen-minute scripted Christian radio broadcast *The Heartbeat of the Home*. Cynthia is a frequent speaker for women's groups, women's retreats, and writers' groups and conferences. Her books have garnered industry recognition from reader, reviewer, retailer, and other awards. She is a literary agent with Books & Such Literary Management and serves as the professional relations liaison for American Christian Fiction Writers (ACFW), connecting with retailers, libraries, book clubs, authors, and readers. Cynthia and her grade school sweetheart husband live in the heart of Wisconsin, not far from their three children and six grandchildren. Her tagline is: "I can't unravel. I'm hemmed in Hope."

Find Cynthia online at

CynthiaRuchti.com

to sign up for her newsletter, subscribe to her blog posts, and learn more about her stories hemmed in hope.

• • • • • • • • • • • • • • • • • • •

Follow Cynthia on social media!

- CynthiaRuchtiReaderPage
- cynthiaruchti
- cynthiaruchti1994